TWISTED

She'd waited at the front door for what seemed like forever. Finally, Ed had followed her inside and up toward the master bedroom.

"I'm sorry, Georgette."

She'd almost gagged on the thick emotion in his voice. He was always big on apologies in those minutes before he passed out.

They had just reached the top step. "I'm sorry, too," she'd said, and then spun quickly, giving his chest an almighty push as she watched him tumble down, praying the crack that she heard was his neck.

Georgette had stared at the lifeless body, intoxicated by the glorious animal rage she possessed. Her heart had started beating like mad. Oh, God, she'd loved it. Killing him had felt so amazingly good, almost orgasmic. And it had been executed so perfectly. There'd been actual witnesses to his heavy drinking and clumsiness. How could it have been anything other than an accident. . .

THE PERFECT MOTHER

Jon Salem

Pinnacle Books
Kensington Publishing Corp.
http://www.pinnaclebooks.com

PINNACLE BOOKS are published by

Kensington Publishing Corp.
850 Third Avenue
New York, NY 10022

First Printing: July, 2000
10 9 8 7 6 5 4 3 2 1

Printed in the United States of America

For my sister, Betsy, her husband, Kenny, and their twin miracles

Prologue

Stockton, California, 1986

"You'll forget about the baby and get on with your life. This will be over soon. Trust me."

Georgette Herring stared coldly at Peyton Drake as a vision of that fateful advertisement on the side of a bus flashed in her mind. . . .

PREGNANT? SCARED?
ARE YOU READY TO BE A SINGLE PARENT?
CALL 1-800-55-ADOPT

She remembered dialing the number from a downtown pay phone outside Nehme's Clothier. Five minutes into the conversation, Peyton Drake had promised her twenty thousand dollars for a healthy white baby. Ten minutes after that a car had arrived to pilot her to his law office in Sacramento.

Everything had happened so fast. Before realizing the

enormity of the situation, she'd agreed to sell the life growing inside her, to surrender forty percent of the windfall to Peyton's firm, and to allow him to choose the adoptive parents and amend the birth certificate. "It's better this way," he'd said.

Georgette felt her chest tighten and turned away from him. She wasn't sure anymore, and a sense of panic possessed her. Here she lay, eighteen years old and alone in the delivery room of St. Joseph's Medical Center, fighting off second thoughts.

Her baby was two days late. Dr. Ridgeway had induced labor, but the stubborn little thing still wasn't coming. Could this be a sign? Was God trying to tell her something? The child didn't want to leave the safety of her womb. Maybe she was meant to keep it after all.

Dr. Ridgeway stepped back into the room, offered Georgette a quick nod, and consulted briefly with the labor nurse while starting up a discussion with Peyton about golf scores.

Georgette heard the nurse mention something about a deceleration in the baby's heartbeat during the last contraction. Her heart lurched with fear.

Dr. Ridgeway studied a printout and shrugged. "I don't see anything wrong."

But the uneasy feeling wouldn't go away. Dr. Ridgeway gave her the creeps. Peyton had insisted that he was the finest obstetrician in the area, but Georgette knew better. Even the nurse seemed to dislike him.

Throughout Georgette's pregnancy, he'd displayed an unusual interest in her sexuality, always pressing her for details about the baby's conception. Hoping that confiding in him would secure the emotional support she craved, Georgette had told him everything.

About gaining entry into the San Francisco bar that night with a fake ID. About the handsome college guy who'd taken her to a cheap motel, made love to her quickly, and passed out in a drunken slumber. About how she'd shown up at the fraternity house to tell him she'd missed her period, only to have him shove a few hundred dollars in her face and tell her to "get rid of it." About her crack fiend mother calling her a stupid slut and refusing to feed another mouth.

Yes, Georgette had told Dr. Ridgeway the truth that was her fucked up life. But instead of offering words of comfort or advice, he'd made the odd announcement that it was safe for her to use a vibrator throughout her pregnancy.

Now she was watching him scan the printout of her baby's heartbeat a second time, still with the same casual regard. Never had she felt so isolated, so unloved, so disrespected. The only thing that could offer solace was her baby, and once Dr. Ridgeway placed it in her arms, Georgette would never let go. Peyton would try to persuade her otherwise, but her mind was made up now. The deal was off. She was keeping her baby.

"I'm concerned, Doctor," the nurse said forcefully.

Dr. Ridgeway shot the woman a disapproving glance and moved closer to Georgette.

"Is . . . my baby . . . okay?" she stammered, her voice cracking.

"I promised the couple waiting outside a beautiful, healthy baby," Dr. Ridgeway said. "Now you just think about how you're going to spend all that money."

Georgette shut her eyes to block the tears. She didn't give a damn about the money. For the past few weeks she'd prayed that her pregnancy would never end because as long as the baby was still inside, it belonged to her. Only her. In fact, she'd been carrying on long conversations with her swollen belly, creating a romantic fantasy about the little one's father. He was a dashing, daredevil naval aviator, just like Tom Cruise in *Top Gun.*

Georgette experienced a sinking feeling, then a flush

of alarm. Dr. Ridgeway was muttering something about going ahead and rupturing her membrane.

She opened her eyes. The perverted doctor was right there, the disapproving nurse dutifully at his side.

"Look at this!" Dr. Ridgeway demanded crossly. "The amniotic fluid is clear. We're fine here, and the head is applied to the cervix just as it should be." He gave the nurse a triumphant look and turned to Peyton. "What do you say we grab a bite to eat? This baby's not coming for a few hours."

Soon after they left, Georgette settled back and attempted to ride out a sudden and excruciating wave of nausea. Unable to endure another moment, she sat up and weakly announced, "I think I'm going to vomit."

The nurse reached for a basin.

Georgette felt a heady dizziness. The room dipped and swayed. She slumped back against the pillows.

The nurse was turning her over on her side, asking, "Where are you?"

Weakly, Georgette fluttered her eyes. "The hospital."

"What's your name?" the nurse demanded.

Georgette opened her mouth to answer but couldn't find the strength to form the words. She felt her arms and legs jerk slightly before going limp. And then she stopped breathing.

"She's turning blue! Page Dr. Ridgeway!"

Georgette was dimly aware of more nurses, frenzied activity, and then Dr. Ridgeway's frantic voice.

"The uterus isn't torn . . . there's no placental distress . . . her vascular system's shutting down. . . . Jesus Christ, we've got an amniotic fluid embolism on our hands!"

"She looks dead!" one of the nurses shouted.

Georgette awoke in ICU, feeling groggy, bloated, not realizing that more than a day had passed. Gingerly, she groped her abdomen, desperate to feel the mound of the baby growing inside her. But all she felt were stitches. Even in her heavily sedated state, the sense of emptiness and loss was overwhelming.

Suddenly Dr. Ridgeway appeared and touched her forehead. "You're lucky to be alive. We almost lost you."

"Where's my baby?" she asked.

He hesitated.

A terrible fear registered.

"There were a few complications. But we saved her."

Her. She had a little girl. A daughter. Georgette decided to call her Savannah. She'd always loved that name.

"The good news is that you and the baby are healthy."

Something in the man's voice indicated there was more. She searched his eyes for what remained. "And the bad?"

"You'll never carry another child to full term. In fact, I seriously doubt that you'll even conceive again, but I performed a full hysterectomy just to be safe."

"I want to see my little girl," Georgette managed through choked sobs.

"I'm afraid that's not possible. Peyton explained that to you over and over again." His voice was tight, his eyes hard and unyielding.

In spite of the drugs and the pain and the trauma, Georgette experienced a moment of total clarity. She had failed the life that she created, abandoned an innocent baby, neglected to love no matter what. The forces that had propelled her into Peyton Drake's office four months ago now seemed trivial and selfish.

So what if she was poor? There was welfare. At least she'd have her baby. Even now, after the big payday, she was still poor. Peyton had kept eight thousand, which left her only twelve. Almost a quarter of that would go to pay off credit card bills. The rest could maybe get her a cheap Japanese car. And to drive where? All over the San Joaquin

Valley to seek out babies and wonder which one was hers? Oh, God! What had she done?

"Please, Dr. Ridgeway, I'm begging you. Let me see her. Let me hold her."

He shook his head.

Her eyes were pleading with him to deliver the salvation. *"Just once."*

"It's too late. The baby's new parents took her home yesterday. Follow Peyton's advice. He's been through this with over a hundred girls just like you. Forget about the baby and get on with your life."

I'll never forget, Georgette thought. *Never.*

Chapter One

Atlanta, Georgia, 2000

Sharon Driver shot a surreptitious glance to her husband the moment he sauntered into the kitchen for his morning coffee. The sight of the thick Rolex gleaming on his wrist provided the answer she was waiting for: Yes, he'd found her surprise—the little erotic note that she twisted around the watchband after he'd fallen asleep last night.

Heath grumbled a greeting, sloshed some java into his mug, and sat down to bury his face in the newspaper. "I can't hang around," he said without preamble. "I'm doing Kit Jamison's radio show."

Sharon stood frozen at the sink, waiting for more, but hearing only the rustle of pages being turned.

Suddenly two-year-old Liam bounded into the room, dragging along his Tinky Winky and a tattered security blanket. "Mommy, I want milk."

She was grateful for his entrance. It took the edge off her humiliation. "Coming right up," she remarked sunnily, busying herself with Liam's request, while Heath kissed him good morning and inquired about the Teletubbies.

I can't hang around. The words pierced her heart. *Cosmopolitan* had assured her that this trick would drive a man wild, so in a moment of weakness and wanting, she'd scribbled a tantalizing promise to send Heath to work with a smile if he waited long enough for the children to leave for school.

The weeks since they'd made love had turned into months—two, in fact. And Sharon couldn't even remember the last time they'd done it in the morning. She closed off the thoughts of self-loathing that stood ready to flood her brain. No. Wait a minute. Not just no. *Fuck no.*

Sharon wasn't twenty-two and implanted; she was forty-four and fighting gravity. But she still felt smarter, sexier, and more beautiful than ever. If Heath didn't want to ravage her, then it was because he was ravaging someone else. *Again.* No doubt another woman young enough to have an alluring body but not the mind to go with it.

She knew he felt entitled to stray now and then. The Successful Man Syndrome. What bullshit it was. As coach of the Atlanta Infernos, the city's NFL franchise, eager women were part of Heath's benefits package. There was little that pro sports groupies wouldn't do to get near their favorite players. In the Infernos' case, that included men like corn-fed Oklahoma hunk Doug Conover, the quarterback, and Adonis Waters, a hot wide receiver who lived up to his name. So in the mind of an NFL whore, Heath Driver at forty-eight wasn't an object of desire—he was just a window of opportunity. One day soon she would break that bit of news to the stupid asshole.

Until then, Sharon would do just what she'd always done. Go on loving him as a companion, great provider, and father to their kids. Continue believing that their twenty-two year union could survive the occasional tramp. Keep remembering that rapturous us-against-the-world phase of their first few years together. Granted, theirs wasn't an ideal marriage, but it was better than most.

"Here you go, boo bear," she cooed to Liam, tousling his hair as she offered him more milk.

He accepted the Crayola spill-proof cup with a giggle, all blond hair, blue eyes, and bronzed skin, a mirror image of his father.

Sharon sniffed the air. "It's time to change that diaper."

"I'm okay," Liam said, but the sag in his pants told a different story as he tottered back toward the television in the next room.

Alone with Heath again, she played along with her husband's game, ignoring him with impudent nonchalance. The scene was conspicuously silent.

Until Katie slapdashed into the kitchen. Fifteen years old, bright, and provocatively sarcastic, she wore brown jeans that endangered her circulation and a powder-blue baby tee with YUMMY emblazoned across the front in big pink letters. The thin cotton clung to her jutting breasts, pulling the bottom hem of the shirt up and beyond her belly button.

Sharon took a deep breath to compose herself, to select her words carefully. But did it really matter? These days something as innocuous as "Good morning" could start an argument with Katie. She decided to get right to the point. "Honey, you're not wearing that to school. Please go upstairs and change right now."

Katie flipped her black, marvelously thick hair, then leveled a poisonous stare with her Midnight Disco eyes. "Just because I like to dress sexy doesn't mean I'm some slut."

"No one said—"

"But that's what you were thinking," Katie cut in. "This is state of the trend, *Mommy*. We can't all dress like those time warp bitches who shop at Bliss."

Sharon was instantly ablaze with heat and anger. The

dig at her fashion boutique really stung. By most accounts, Bliss was one of the most fashion forward shops in town. Suddenly she turned to Heath, who hadn't even bothered to look up from his goddamn newspaper.

More anger. This time it threatened to recircuit her whole central nervous system. "Do you approve of our daughter showing up at school like this?" she asked hotly.

Heath continued scanning the sports section. "Don't put me in the middle of this," he remarked absently.

"Look at her." Sharon's voice was pure venom.

Heath glared at his wife first, then got an eyeful of his daughter. He was visibly taken aback. "Not a chance, Katie. Your mother's absolutely right. Go change. And if I ever see you in that kind of getup again, I'll personally start picking out your clothes for school each morning."

Katie scowled. "No thanks," she snarled, turning to go upstairs.

"Not so fast," Sharon halted her, still seething. "I don't know what's going on to make you so hostile and disrespectful this early in the morning, but you better find a quick way to fix it. As for your hair and nail appointment this weekend, I'm canceling it. Same goes for your driving lesson."

"Mom!" Katie wailed.

"If you're as tough as you talk, young lady, you'll manage just fine."

Katie stomped upstairs, teen fury in every step.

Sharon sensed Heath reaching for her hand, and she snatched it away, as if avoiding a dangerously hot surface.

"Jesus Christ, Sharon."

The move startled even her. Only a few hours ago she was craving his touch. Now she recoiled from it. "I'm sorry. I didn't mean that." Her throat felt constricted.

Heath stood up, trapping her against the stove with his rock solid muscular body, his hands cupping her elbows. "What is it?" he whispered.

She avoided his gaze, unable to answer that or other questions of comparable gravity.

"Meet me here for lunch," he suggested, his voice thick. "That is if the offer to put a smile on my face still stands."

Sharon could sense the heat of his stare. Even without looking up, she knew his lips were curled into that careless grin, the one that broke down her defenses no matter how mad she was. She waited several portentous heart beats before saying, "I can't. I'm meeting a sales rep from Prada for lunch."

"I'm sorry about that scene with Katie. I should've stepped in right away."

She was aware of him easing away from her, and she wanted to make a move, to say the proper words, to keep him there . . . but the moment passed without any action on her part.

"I have to go," Heath said. He scooped up his keys from the counter and left.

Sharon's mind spun, not with emotion, but with wave after wave of guilt. She thrust her hands into the deep pockets of her luxurious terry-cloth robe, the one with the silly looking cows all over it, her favorite. In the right pocket she fingered the letter that could possibly destroy their lives. It had arrived weeks ago, and she'd read it hundreds of times. The attempt to repair her sex life had been an act of sheer desperation. It seemed like a good idea to fix *something*, especially when so much else was in danger of falling apart.

Katie was back, dressed sensibly in an Old Navy T-shirt, silently searching for something. She went from the dining room to the living room and back to the kitchen, finally murmuring, "I can't find my planner."

"I think it's in the study," Sharon said quietly, wishing they weren't at war with each other.

Katie returned a few moments later with it clutched in her hand.

A car horn beeped.

Sharon peered out the window.

"It's Angel," Katie explained. "She and Mamiko are picking me up today."

Sharon preferred that Katie take the bus but didn't argue. There'd been enough of that for one day. "You haven't had any breakfast."

Katie grabbed a banana and walked out the door.

Liam shuffled into the room and hugged Sharon's leg. "Katie's mad, Mommy."

Sharon brushed the hair away from his eyes. Liam was so young and sweet and innocent. He didn't know how complicated the world could be. She didn't want him to find out.

Chapter Two

Before Angel Fisher's all-silver Audi TT backed out of the driveway, Katie had divested her peacemaking shirt and tossed it to the floorboard. "My parents expect me to dress like a nun."

Mamiko Kim twisted around in the front seat to face her. *"Yummy!"* she exclaimed. "More like *yuck.* That is so Hooters waitress."

Katie glared at the Japanese-American wild child. With her shocking pink Betsey Johnson garb and her head full of piercings—ears, nose, and one eyebrow—she looked like a one girl punk movement.

Sometimes Mamiko could be such a bitch. Her life just seemed to fall into place, like some perfectly choreographed ballet. She already had a scholarship to Smith College, and even her dorm room had been picked out. All this when two years of high school still remained.

"At least I've got tits," Katie fired back. "You're built like a little boy."

"Enough!" Angel shouted. "Next stop is the vet if you two hellcats don't detract your claws."

With that, all three girls howled with laughter, racing toward Riverside Central High, blaring the blistering rock-rap of Limp Bizkit, the fight over as soon as it began.

It was strange, Katie mused, but sometimes she felt most at ease with Angel and Mamiko. At Riverside, they were a formidable triumvirate: she the beautiful, daring one with a quick and devastating tongue; Angel the smart one with mountains of cash; and Mamiko the style chameleon with ambition to burn.

Katie felt grounded with her friends, like she had a voice of her own. Most important, they made her feel *real.* At home, she often felt cut off, almost invisible. That sense had heightened over the last two years, since Liam was born. She loved her brother, but sometimes one look at him made her feel like a boarder in her own family.

Liam looked like Mom and Dad. The same blond hair, the same almond-shaped eyes, the same skin that the sun kissed bronze with the slightest exposure. And here she was, like a freak of nature, a black-eyed gypsy with dark hair that went on forever. How could she not doubt that she was really theirs? But she was. It said so on her birth certificate.

That didn't stop her from fantasizing, though, about another set of parents who resembled her, understood her, and treated her differently. They would let her wear whatever she wanted, never ground her or set forth punishment, and always make her feel like she was being told everything. In Katie's dream family, there were no secrets.

Angel maneuvered the Audi like a bumper car. Killer speed and death turns were the order of the day, but somehow they managed to arrive at the gas station near the school in one piece.

"Girl, when I get my driver's license I am never riding

with you again. If I wanted a Six Flags thrill, I'd go there!" Mamiko said good-naturedly.

"I've never had a wreck," Angel announced proudly.

Katie shared a secret smile with Mamiko. "Tell that to the ten car pileup back there."

Angel waved a dismissive, bejeweled hand. "Whatever."

They tumbled out, ready to stalk the aisles of the mini-mart for candy, snacks, and drinks.

"What's up, Katie?"

She was trailing the girls and heard the cool, thick voice in that split second before her Skechers went from concrete to linoleum. It stopped her cold.

He stood at the pump, fueling up a cheap Chevrolet that had seen better days. Derek Johnson reminded her of Will Smith with his handsome face, neatly trimmed facial hair, and ears that stuck out like small wings. Derek was on the football team, a wide receiver who moved like a bullet, just like Adonis Waters on her father's team. The key difference—Derek played high school ball and was poor. Dirt poor. Tongues wagged that he really came from a south-end housing project but put down a rich cousin's address in order to attend Riverside.

Katie smiled saucily. He looked really cute this morning in his washed-out Gap gear. She headed over and noticed that he'd stopped the pump at three dollars.

Derek gave her chest a carnivorous glance. "Yummy," he read, then locked his eyes on her. "I agree. You look good enough to eat."

Katie was speechless, her lips parted. She just stood there, a familiar stirring taking over her loins.

He almost smiled. "Pay for my gas and get me a Snickers and a Sprite."

"Okay," she agreed instantly, turning to dart inside. He was a seventeen-year-old senior. She would've bought him anything he wanted.

Mamiko stood idly at the magazines, thumbing through

the latest *Teen People.* She slung it back on the rack when she caught Katie coming inside. "Have I mentioned lately that I hate Britney Spears?"

Katie smiled and sought out Derek's candy and soda request as if it were an order from a high commander. She opted for king sizes, then made a beeline for the counter and asked the clerk to ring up the gas, too.

"Which pump?" the surly woman snarled.

"I don't know, but it was three dollars," Katie said quietly, not wanting Mamiko or Angel to hear.

"I gotta know which pump," the clerk said testily, her voice up at least two octaves.

Angel looked up from hovering over the doughnut bin. "We didn't get gas. My tank's full."

Curious, Mamiko peered outside and, quick on the draw, sized up the situation. "Tell me you're not paying for that scrub's gas."

"I ain't got all day. Which car?" the clerk demanded, all patience gone.

"The red piece of shit," Mamiko said.

"Hey, why not ante up for *my* gas? I pick you up and take you home all the time!" Angel argued, her mouth full of a glazed, jelly-filled concoction.

Katie regarded her size fourteen friend. She needed help with gas money like she needed another doughnut. Angel's father was some kind of computer software genius and worth megamillions. The Fishers lived in a mammoth estate overlooking the Chattahoochee that was equal parts Versailles, Fountainebleau, and Hearst Castle.

No matter her size, Angel insisted on dressing like a video vamp. Today she was stuffed into leather pants that wouldn't zip all the way up and a sheer top with visible bra. Girls would snicker and guys would hoot, but Angel didn't care. She liked the attention and notoriety it gave her.

They'd only known each other for a year, and for Katie,

the first twelve months of Angel Fisher had been like a crash course in how to be a nutritionist, therapist, fellow sanatorium inmate, and friend. In other words, theirs was a relationship that would withstand the erosion of time. She couldn't say the same about Mamiko. Something told her that once they graduated, Mamiko would take off for New England and never look back.

Katie paid the damage, sneering at the ugly clerk whose nails were bitten to the quick.

"You're, like, the only girl at Riverview with her own broker, but I'll slide some gas money your way if it'll make you feel better." She grabbed the white plastic bag filled with Derek's goodies and spun around to face Angel, whose gaze was now oscillating between chocolate-covered and cinnamon twist.

Mamiko pulled on Angel's arm. "Come on. You're gonna be diabetic before you're old enough to drink."

"Ya'll, wait for me in the car," Katie whined, following them outside.

Mamiko cut a disapproving glance to Derek like he was a mess on the side of the road. "He's poor."

"So?" Katie challenged.

Mamiko shrugged. "Poor guys are a pain in the ass. I like a level playing field."

Angel leaned in to whisper, "I've heard that he's trouble. He beat up a girl once because she wouldn't do it. Hit her in the face, pushed her out of the car, and just left her!"

"I heard it was because she wouldn't give him a blow job," Mamiko said.

Katie waved them off. "That's nothing but an urban legend. There's a story like that about almost every hot senior guy."

"Yeah, but what if it's true about him?" Angel asked.

Katie widened her eyes like a slasher movie victim. "I'll take my chances. See you in a minute." She strutted over to Derek's car and leaned into the driver's side window.

Without so much as a nod, he twisted down the volume on the bass-heavy Jay-Z rap and tore into the Snickers right away. "You should come home with me one day. We could hang out."

"You mean, like, a date?"

"No, I mean *hang out.* If you're a good girl, then maybe I'll take you on a date." Derek was all eyes, staring boldly into her chest. He moistened his lips with his tongue.

Katie's heart was thrumming, her armpits feeling the heat. A senior guy. A sophomore girl. She couldn't believe it was happening to her. "What does a good girl do in your book?"

Derek turned the key over, and the engine coughed to life. "She makes me feel just right." And then he drove away, music pumping at top volume.

He hadn't even bothered to thank her for the gas and the snacks, Katie realized. But that didn't matter because her nervous system had sunk below the threshold of logic. There was a new power of invention at work now—desire.

Angel had called it right. Derek Johnson was trouble. In fact, he was the kind of trouble that her parents worried about.

Which made him exactly the kind of trouble that she was looking for.

Chapter Three

Kit Jamison sucked in a tiny breath the moment Heath Driver entered the modest studio of WTOK-FM. Here she sat, a lesbian, mildly distracted by a motor-mouth caller, yet still aware enough to swoon over the coach who gave off strong Robert Redford vibrations.

She let the caller ramble on, something about perks the fat cats in the sky boxes get while real fans go broke on bad seats, parking fees, and concession prices.

Heath wore a blue blazer, a crisp white dress shirt, pressed khakis, and shined black lace-up shoes. She never noticed a man's clothes, but she always noticed his. He raised an eyebrow in mischief and sat down, methodically peeling a Granny Smith apple into bite-size pieces with a knife.

His scent filled the room, and it wasn't an ambisexual fragrance like most men romping the earth wore today. Heath Driver smelled masculine, an original graduate from the guy school. Hints of rich saddle leather and spice itched at her nostrils.

Suddenly a scene from *The Way We Were* crashed into Kit's brain. A drunk Robert Redford makes love to Barbra Streisand, not really knowing who she is. Kit reminded herself that she and Heath were regular drinking buddies, that they got looped enough to do something stupid like fall into bed together. But if they did, would he know who she was? And after the bourbon haze lifted, would he even remember the act?

Heath slipped on his headphones and immediately smiled at the irate caller. The squinting, laughing lines around his eyes created a starburst effect, and his face was so sun blasted that Kit knew instinctively he never bothered with something so sissy as sunscreen.

The caller thundered on, seguing into a diatribe about players who make too much money. Apparently Adonis Waters's new contract had really rubbed this fanatic the wrong way.

Heath jiggled his hand in the male semaphore that means "Jerk off."

For Kit, the crude gesture broke the spell. Now she remembered what an asshole Heath could be and that men like him were part of the reason she was glad that she preferred women.

"You've given us a lot to think about, Barnett," Kit interjected, retrieving the yack's name from the scrawl on her yellow legal pad. "After this break, we'll be back with Coach Heath Driver of the Atlanta Infernos. What are his thoughts on the controversial movie *Score* that starts shooting in the area this week? We'll find out. I'm Kit Jamison. Stay with us for more *Adrenaline.*"

She peeled off her headphones and helped herself to one of Heath's apple slices. "We've got three minutes."

He gave her a dirty wink. "I only need two."

"Oh, can't wait to get *you* in the sack." Kit rolled her eyes. She considered lewd comments like that harmless. Her late father had been a Georgia Tech football coach, and she'd grown up on the sidelines, never missing a practice or a game. By her eighteenth birthday she could outdrink and outcuss any man stupid enough to take her on.

That's why she hated political correctness and all this shit about sexual harassment. As long as a woman had a knee, she didn't need a lawyer. Bam! Right into the balls of any dumb-ass who crossed the line.

"You don't know what you're missing," Heath trilled.

"That's where you're wrong," Kit said dryly. "I *do* know what I'm missing, and it suits me just fine to keep on missing it."

Playfully, he punched her shoulder. "There's a lot of talk about you," he said earnestly.

Anxiousness spread across her abdominals. "So tell me."

"I was shooting the shit with a guy from New York yesterday. He likes *Adrenaline,* thinks it has national syndication possibilities."

Kit fought hard to filter the news. The castles in the air would have to wait. She still had a show to do. "Hey," she began easily, "if it happens, it happens. I'm cool either way."

Heath tilted his head. "You'll get rich."

My lawyers will get rich, Kit wanted to correct him. Or rather, *richer.* Like a brand-new morning, Cameron's sweet face rose up in her mind. And then the pain of loss, the agony of separation . . . crashed down. She hadn't seen her son in months.

Fuck you, Leslie, Kit thought. *Fuck you for your betrayal and selfishness and cruelty.* When their relationship hit the skids, Kit never imagined that Leslie would take off with Cameron, never to be heard from again. And the worst part of all—Kit had no recourse. There were no laws to protect nonbiological mothers in lesbian families. Kit had already paid thousands to hear that from one hotshot lawyer after another.

Each time she answered the phone, opened the mailbox,

received a fax, or checked her e-mail, her heart stopped for one breathless moment, hoping, praying, that it would be Leslie getting in touch, telling her how Cameron was, agreeing to allow her visitation. How long could Leslie continue this inhuman punishment?

"It's going to happen, Kit," Heath was saying. "You're too good to stay local. Everybody realizes that."

She stared into Heath's eyes. They were blue, but today they looked mossy green. Smiling, she stole another apple slice, thankful that he'd steered her away from her personal drama. "You can be such a sweet guy."

"Do you have a special place in your bed for sweet guys?"

It was funny how men considered lesbians a sexual challenge. To straighten out a dyke was the ultimate in stud status. Yet women never thought that way about gay guys.

"Come on, tell me that I'm in with a chance."

Kit wondered how serious his passes really were. One day, she feared, if she was just lonely enough, just drunk enough, she might try to find out. "Don't hold your breath, coach. The team needs you." She returned the bulky headphones to her ears, bracing herself for the saxophone-heavy intro music. "Let's hit it.

"Welcome back to *Adrenaline.* I'm Kit Jamison and joining me in the studio this morning is Atlanta Infernos Coach Heath Driver. Thanks for stopping by."

"It's great to be here."

"The Infernos suffered an embarrassing preseason. Care to explain that?"

Heath laughed. "So much for the soft approach."

"No one's ever confused me with Leeza Gibbons."

"Then I'll give it to you straight—our defense sucks. But we've got a new coach in that department who has earned respect in every corner of the locker room. You'll see a revamped defense and a new attitude in our first regular season game against Philadelphia."

"Adonis Waters looks good."

"He's a machine of speed, muscle, and precision."

"You sound like a proud father."

"Worse—I'm a man in love."

Kit cackled. "I'm not going near that one. Let's talk about *Score*—"

"Let's not," Heath cut in.

"It's getting too much media attention not to. Your former assistant coach, Reid Sanderson, wrote the screenplay."

"The key word there is *former.*"

"Reportedly the movie's not kind to the NFL, not to mention a fictional team that closely resembles the Infernos and a fictional coach who closely resembles you."

"What's the old saying? Those who can't coach . . . write bad movies?"

"I haven't heard that one."

"Seriously, I've read the screenplay, and it's not sour grapes—it's fantasy. The real talent on this film is the hype behind it. *Score* has nothing to do with the Infernos and nothing to do with me."

Kit decided to move on, even though her bullshit alarm was screaming. Heath didn't fool her for so much as a nanosecond. This story had only just begun.

Chapter Four

Kit wants to fuck me, Heath thought. He was sure of that like he was sure of the best cigars, Montecristo, and the best cognac, B&B. That she was twenty-nine years old and a confirmed lesbian sent his ego into hyperdrive. Not only could he still get them young, he could even pull them from the other side of the sexual fence.

But he didn't dare with Kit Jamison. She wasn't some NFL groupie who traded her body for a spot on the sidelines. Kit was a friend, a *real* friend, the first woman, in fact, who'd held that distinction in his adult life. No way was he jeopardizing that. It meant too much.

Just considering the possibility of nailing Kit had him all wound up. For a moment, he cursed the fact that Sharon had a lunch appointment. The erotic promise of her note had hit him like a bolt from the blue. She didn't pursue sex outside their marriage like he did, but she had needs, too. Feeling a tinge of guilt, he made a solemn promise to be more attentive in the bedroom.

I'll never be husband of the year, Heath thought wryly, turning into Stone Mountain Ranch, the team's training facility. A fiery red Miata was speeding out as his white Dodge Durango was charging in. He honked the horn and waved.

It was Dawn, the blond cheerleader he'd been screwing for the last six months. But the fling was over now—her boyfriend back home had proposed. The little minx still thought she had been the one to break it off. Technically, that was true, but she'd only beaten him to the punch by a day, if that much.

Heath knew that his exploits were unfair to Sharon, but he couldn't help it. He possessed an appetite for sex matched only by his appetite for winning football games. But he was faithful in one regard—he spread himself thinly among several women, leaving no room for emotional involvement. *That,* Heath reasoned, was the dividing line. What he did was harmless cheating, a purely physical rogue urge that meant nothing. When *feelings* got involved, that was adultery.

"Good morning, Coach Driver."

His secretary's eager greeting hit the air as he rounded the corner to the reception area of his office. Before heading in to study several hours worth of computer printouts, he exchanged a few pleasantries with Patsy, no pinup beauty but efficient and reliable.

The moment he stepped inside his sanctuary, he noticed the photograph of Liam atop his credenza. Picking up the frame, he traced the outline of his son's mouth with an index finger, still, even after two years, not quite believing it.

Sharon had shockingly, inexplicably, turned up pregnant at forty-two, the first time she had ever conceived. *Miracles do happen,* Heath admitted, returning the frame to its special place.

Next to Liam, a portrait of his beautiful Katie smiled back. *Another miracle,* Heath thought, recalling the seven years of disheartening tests and failed infertility treatments that had led up to her adoption. Gazing at her gypsy eyes, he frowned. Part of their daughter was so fiercely unreachable. But that was as it should be. Part of her parents was unreachable, too. *We should've told you baby,* he admitted silently. *It was wrong not to.*

He stood there for one long, melancholy moment, wishing he could put family first. But he couldn't. Winning football games was number one. It always had been. It always would be.

His telephone buzzed. It was Patsy. "What is it?" he asked irritably.

"You have a visitor, a young woman. She doesn't have an appointment."

Heath scanned his brain. He always used condoms. No bimbo would be knocked up at his expense. Curious, he instructed Patsy to send her in.

There was one impertinent knock before the door opened and a fragile, doe-eyed, porcelain-doll beauty stepped inside. She possessed a certain slacker chic, barely covered in a futuristic metallic tank top and micro wraparound skirt of indestructible nylon that gave a view of one leg all the way up to the hollow over her hip joint.

Heath was all eyes. This girl's lush lips could only do him good, and her blue-black hair—morning-after-a-great-lay messy—begged for a man's fingers to run through it.

"I heard you talking about the movie on the radio," she said in a low, husky voice that carried a thick Australian accent. "I almost didn't come here."

He smiled with protective reassurance, liking the way she used her hands when she spoke. "What can I do for you?"

"I don't how to ask you this. . . ." She trailed off for a moment, pressing her luscious mouth into a painful pout, a vision of elusive loveliness.

He paused, searching for the right encouraging words. "Why don't you start by telling me your name."

"Holly . . . Holly Ryan."

"From the land Down Under."

She grinned, bright eyes brightening.

After five or six seconds the silence seemed to sizzle. Heath wondered what would happen between them as he watched her, drinking in every detail of the beautiful stranger.

"I'm an actress. I have a role in *Score.*" With great charm, she covered her mouth in a big-eyed look of mock terror.

"Back to my original question then—what can I do for you?" He meant it to sound intimidating, but it had an open, overly solicitous quality to it.

"This movie could make or break my career. Except for a daytime drama in Australia, this is my first big part."

Her big insinuating eyes compelled him to ask, "What part is that?"

She paused. More silence stalked the room. "The coach's mistress."

Chapter Five

"I want my Infernos shirt," Liam insisted, standing naked in the middle of his room with a gleam in his eyes that held no compromise.

Sharon knew it was downstairs in the laundry room and began to protest in the interest of time, then thought better of it. "Okay, kiddo. I'll be right back."

Liam pounced onto his bed and flailed about, his pink, little choir boy's butt high in the air.

She laughed and started out.

"I love you, Mommy."

Sharon hesitated in the doorway. "I love you, too."

"I want you to smile."

His simple request brought an immediate lump to her throat, and she could already feel the tears forming in her eyes. "Mommy's okay. She just has something on her mind, that's all. But you make me smile. You're my little man, right?"

Liam stopped rolling about and stared intently, thinking hard. "Yeah, I want Daddy to smile. And Katie."

She eyed him adoringly but said nothing. Her lips parted, but the words didn't come out. It amazed her how much he noticed, how aware he was of the relationship dynamics under this roof. How much were these private wars affecting him? And how would that impact his development?

"Can I watch my Batman story later?"

Sharon smiled, relieved that he was back to considering issues appropriate for a two-year-old. "Of course you can. I'll be right back with your shirt. Stay here and play."

Halfway down the staircase, she gripped the banister and sank to one of the steps, tormented by the secret she carried. She massaged her shoulders, alarmed at the tightness there. Her stress level was way off the mark. *You have to take a walk later,* she told herself. *It's been days since you've had any exercise.*

She reached into her pocket and pulled out the letter. It felt radioactive in her hands. A stab of self-loathing overwhelmed her. If she could turn back time, do it all over again, she would tell Katie as soon as she was old enough to understand.

The fear had started the day Dr. Ridgeway placed Katherine Michele Driver into her arms. Sharon responded by burying the fright, refusing to face the reality. And Dr. Ridgeway and Peyton Drake had only encouraged her denial. They'd turned over an amended birth certificate, as if Katie had actually been born to her and Heath, and when they'd counseled her to love Katie as her very own, the glue to never tell was firmly set.

"This is a onetime legal event," Peyton had said.

No, Sharon argued silently today, *this is a lifelong process that impacts all involved in so many different ways.* She concentrated on the signature at the bottom of the letter.

Georgette Tucker. The name worked like a trigger of terror. This anxiety, that one day Katie's biological mother would make contact and plead for a reunion, had always lurked within Sharon's nervous system.

She thought of Heath, who'd disagreed from the beginning with her decision to keep the adoption a secret. On almost every birthday, he advocated telling Katie the truth about her past. But Heath gave up so quickly, never quite pushing hard enough. He'd rather go out and fuck cheerleaders than stay home and fight for what he believed was right for his family. Sometimes she hated him for not giving one hundred percent to the people who mattered most.

Sharon took a deep breath to steady herself. Her heart was pounding. She was churning with fear, anger, and guilt. Trying to pretend that Katie's birth mother didn't exist had been futile. All she'd done was create a hereditary ghost. The truth was, Georgette Tucker was a powerful force in the family dynamic; she had been all along. What once was a nameless, faceless skeleton in the closet was now a physical presence asking to be seen and heard.

"Go away," Sharon whispered, crumpling the letter into her fist. "Leave us alone."

The years of anxiety seemed so wasted now. Keeping the secret had created distance with Katie, not closeness. Ironically, Sharon's efforts to protect her daughter had only endangered her more. But for Katie to find out about the adoption at fifteen, amidst the painful angst of adolescence, when issues of confidence and identity and safety were so mercurial . . . it was unthinkable!

It frightened Sharon that Georgette knew who they were and where they lived. How did she find out? What else did she know? Would she try to contact Katie on her own?

The fear of the unknown was so draining. It was barely nine o'clock in the morning and already she felt fatigued. She forced herself to think optimistically. Perhaps nothing more would come of it. There had been, after all, a timid, shameful quality to Georgette's letter. Sharon's reply, delivered to the return address in the Hamptons by Federal

Express, had left nothing to interpretation. Her answer had been an emphatic no.

To pictures, report cards, or any other artifacts of Katie's youth.

To phone calls.

To a reunion.

Sharon's desire for family preservation outweighed her guilt, even when she had lied and told Georgette that Katie knew of her adoptive status and harbored no interest in developing a relationship with her biological mother. She prayed the rebuke was strong enough to kill Georgette's longing for a reunion.

She prayed hard.

Chapter Six

East Hampton, New York, 2000

Georgette Tucker never tired of the breathtaking view in her West End Road home. She paused, allowing the peaceful image to sink in. With one glorious, sweeping gaze she could take in Georgica Pond, a tidal estuary separated from the Atlantic Ocean by a wide stretch of East Hampton beach.

Long ago she had billed this oasis Landing Bay. The home was a symbol of how far life had taken her from those humble beginnings in California with her addict mother. The bitch had gotten exactly what she deserved in that crack house twelve years ago—a knife to the gut by a teenage dealer looking to earn a ruthless reputation.

She pushed away the unpleasant thought. There was pressing personal business to consider, business that, regretfully, would take her away from this gated, high-hedge-rowed refuge. But she would be back soon enough, armed with precious love.

The purr of an expensive European motor car captured her attention. Georgette peered out. The crunch of tires rolling on the gravel top signaled an imminent intruder. Shit! It was Tiffany Shamblin, that second tier model who managed to fellate her way into a Bridgehampton residency every summer. Men on the fast track seemed to pass her around like a salt shaker.

Georgette headed outside to meet her in the driveway. Anything to avoid inviting this social fucker into the privacy of her home.

Tiffany alighted from a gleaming Mercedes, her hands clutching an acrylic cake pan. "I decided to bake something and stop over to check on you," she announced with calculated sweetness.

Lying cunt, Georgette wanted to hiss. *You've never baked anything in your life. You bought that frozen at the market and thawed it out.*

"I hope you like carrot cake."

Georgette grimaced politely. "Actually, I'm allergic." *To brainless bimbos,* she dreamed of adding.

Tiffany looked crestfallen. "I almost got . . . made German chocolate."

Georgette tilted her head, feigning misery. "Oh, I wish you had. That's my favorite." She made no motion to accept the dessert.

Tiffany struggled with the awkward moment. Models weren't highly skilled in social situations that didn't happen in bars. "I'll take it home to Rick. He'll eat it."

Rick Haley was a Wall Street wanna-be who worked on Fridays in the summer and had to be back in the office on Monday mornings. Translation: not successful enough to live in the Hamptons but determined enough to live on tuna and keep up rent on a lousy cottage. Poor Tiffany was too stupid to realize that there were better men to get down on her knees for.

"I'm sure he'll make it last a week or more. Rick really knows how to stretch a dollar. For instance, take that rental you're driving. Doesn't his brother-in-law own a dealership in New Jersey?"

"Yeah," Tiffany said absently, obviously learning for the first time that her sugar daddy was made of artificial sweetener. "How are you, Georgette? Is there anything I can do?"

Get back in the car and drive straight into the ocean. "I'm taking one day at a time, but thank you."

"I hope you're not burdened with all of Ed's business affairs."

Georgette narrowed her gaze. She knew where this was going. "They're being handled by the right people."

Tiffany's bright eyes glistened. "So the movie's still on?"

She nodded and turned to go inside.

"He promised me a part in it," Tiffany blurted.

Georgette laughed. "Ed was so careless about building up hopes, especially when he drank. Most people knew better than to pay attention. Oh, and, Tiffany, if you decide to visit again, I prefer that you call first." And then she shut the door on the dazed beauty, praying she was the last of the mourners.

Throng after throng had come to pay respects to Ed Tucker's widow. They'd weaved in and out of her life from the obituary to the funeral, trickling down to out of the blue visits like this one.

Widow. The sound of it, even in her own head, serenaded her, like Mozart. Ed Tucker, veteran producer of hip, edgy, and controversial movies. Ed Tucker, miserable bastard who lived at the bottom of a bottle. Marriage to him had been like a seven-year sentence in a prison of emotional cruelty. Until that glorious night when she'd set herself free. . . .

* * *

The decision to kill him had arrived like an internal thunderbolt. They were at a dinner party being hosted by Steven Spielberg and his gorgeous wife, Kate Capshaw. Sometime between the peri-peri chicken with Portuguese savory rice and the lemon-coconut cake with mango sorbet, Georgette had dreamed up a plan to murder the son of a bitch.

As was his custom, Ed had too many drinks too soon. Before the second course had been served, he was drunk and loud. Talk had turned to children, and except for Georgette and Ed, everyone at the table had a large family.

"I'd love to have children," Georgette had said.

"God made you sterile for a good reason," Ed had said sharply. "You're not mother material. Why don't you get one of those baby turtles?" Then he'd laughed uproariously at his own remark.

There'd been a few uncomfortable titters, but for the most part, a silent tension had thickened the room.

Georgette had called forth all her strength to ignore him, his words vibrating in her bones and resonating in her solar plexus, steam rushing inside her skull. That had been unusually cruel, even for a mean shit like Ed.

She'd turned to face him, staring into his bloodshot eyes. Why had he twisted the knife like that? Early in their courtship she'd confided in him about the sleazebag lawyer who'd sold her baby like a box of detergent and the perverted doctor who'd butchered her uterus without her consent. He'd known that the anniversary of her daughter's birth brought on chronic anxiety, that Mother's Day was the darkest holiday of every year. Yet he'd made her the punch line for one of his booze-sloshed outbursts.

Then, with his hand shaking, he'd lifted his glass to down his drink. "Tell them about your doll, Georgette."

She'd eyed him balefully but said nothing. His fate had been sealed by that one unforgivable sentence.

It had been an early Friday evening, which meant Montauk Highway, the only road in or out of the Hamptons, would be bumper-to-bumper for miles. The only hospital was in Southampton. If she followed through with this early enough, it would be impossible for an ambulance to pass. So even almost dead would become definitely dead.

"Go on, tell them," he'd taunted.

"Leave her alone, Ed. This isn't funny. Your behavior is disgusting." The scolding words had been spoken by Betsy Steel, a formidable fixture of East Hampton power, a woman whose name and credentials were listed each year in the Blue Book, a privately published social register sold under the counter at Book Hampton. Add to that her status as a founding member of the Vanderbilt Club and her permanent place as a trustee of the Historical Society. A rebuke from her was industrial-strength social annihilation, the kind that could penetrate even an alcohol-soaked mind.

Ed had lurched up from his chair.

Stealthily, Georgette had seized the moment, stabbing the back of his calf with the sharp tip of her Manolo Blahnik pump.

His knee had buckled, and the rest of his reflex-slow body had followed, crashing to the floor.

She'd accepted help from a few of the men in getting Ed to his feet. Bill Frye, a character actor who appeared regularly in Ed's films, had ushered him outside for some air.

Georgette had returned to the table to fetch her handbag. "I'm so sorry," she'd apologized to the group, making a point to connect with Betsy. "His drinking is getting worse."

"Well, don't *leave,*" Betsy had exclaimed. "Ed's the asshole, not you."

Georgette had been unable to hold back a brief half smile to the spunky queen of East Hampton. "It's better this way," she'd politely insisted. "He needs to sleep it off."

Ed had offered up no protest about going home. He'd appeared ready to say yes to anything short of facing Betsy Steel again. Still, he'd belligerently resisted the idea of Georgette driving—until Bill wrestled the keys from his primary employer's pocket and put them in her hand.

The short ride home had been unbearable.

"You've got everybody thinking you're so sweet and innocent," Ed had slurred, angrily slumped in the passenger seat, his shirttail halfway out of his trousers. "They don't know you're a crazy bitch. One day I'm gonna take out that fucking doll with the morning garbage."

Georgette had scarcely heard him. A rushing sound had filled her head. All she had been able to think about was how free she would be, free to spend money without getting the third degree, free to reunite with her beautiful baby girl. Ed would never have allowed that. He had to die. There was no other way.

She'd tried to go on living, to pretend there was no part of her out there in the world. But each year the pain intensified. She looked at every young girl as if she could be her own, and her mind spun with the rites of passage her child had celebrated—first steps, first day of school, first date.

And Ed had rarely displayed a moment's sensitivity. Two years into the marriage she had figured out why. She knew his dirty secret, the reason why he'd wooed and married her. But now she was the one with an itch. The deadly seven-year kind.

When they arrived back at the house, Ed had wanted to stay in the car.

"Come on, enough of this fighting," she'd coaxed him gently. "Let's go upstairs and go to bed."

She'd waited at the front door for what seemed like forever. Finally, Ed had followed her inside and up toward the master bedroom.

"I'm sorry, Georgette."

She'd almost gagged on the thick emotion in his voice. He was always big on apologies in those minutes before he passed out.

They had just reached the top step. "I'm sorry, too," she'd said, and then spun quickly, giving his chest an almighty push as she watched him tumble down, praying the crack that she heard was his neck.

Georgette had stared at the lifeless body, intoxicated by the glorious animal rage she possessed. Her heart had started beating like mad. Oh, God, she'd loved it. Killing him had felt so amazingly good, almost orgasmic. And it had been executed so perfectly. There'd been actual witnesses to his heavy drinking and clumsiness. How could it have been anything other than an accident. . . .

Suddenly the sight of the red, white, and blue Federal Express packet on the Indian teak dining table broke Georgette's reverie of weeks gone by. She snatched it violently and raced upstairs to the guest room she'd converted into a nursery.

She tiptoed in, not wanting to disturb her baby. The little doll was bundled in a pink cashmere blanket, resting peacefully. She settled into the rocking chair beside the crib and began to move back and forth as she read Sharon Driver's letter . . . again. Each dismissive word seemed to speed up her heart a little more. The bitch had told her no.

Georgette had lost so much to the Drivers. Now it was their turn to lose.

Chapter Seven

"The front window is all wrong," Sharon said, bustling into Bliss for the second time that day, on this occasion with Liam in tow, having just picked him up from preschool.

Mary Payne Lockhart, her just-out-of-college assistant manager, sighed the sigh of the weary. "We only worked on it *all* morning. What's the matter with it?"

Sharon retraced her steps to take another look, Liam hoisted onto her hip. "It simply doesn't work."

Liam nodded. "Doesn't work," he echoed.

Mary Payne crossed her arms in defiance. "Just what I need—a two-year-old fashion critic."

Sharon laughed, stroking Liam's head. "We just need to tame it down. I want women to walk by and get a sense of adventure, but I want the more fashion timid to feel like Bliss is a place for them, too."

Mary Payne walked out to review the window display for herself. She stormed back in, head shaking. "What were we thinking?"

"It just needs a little tweaking, that's all," Sharon assured her.

Bliss was a small boutique nestled inside Phipps Plaza, an upscale shopping center anchored by Saks Fifth Avenue and home to Gucci, Versace, Tiffany and Company, Jil Sander, and other ultra-chic shops. Sharon had opened the store five years ago, after Katie was well into school and before the incredible discovery of the pregnancy that would be Liam.

Knowing that top-of-the-line fashion is a volatile business and that standing still means certain disaster, Sharon worked tirelessly to mix items from the big designers with impressive pieces from new labels. That way her customers felt at once safe and daring. They could buy clothing immediately recognizable to their peers yet still stand out by being the first to wear the newest hot name.

Juggling the shop with family life was sometimes an exhausting challenge, but she loved it. She *needed* it. Bliss provided her an outlet to lose herself in, an exercise that worked to dull the pain brought on by her marriage. *Goddamn you, Heath.* As Sharon got older, she noticed that her anger toward him grew more ferocious.

Suddenly a cluster of model-type beauties ventured into the store, moving to inspect the racks with practiced, critical eyes. Sometimes just the sight of youth exhausted her. They had thinner waists, blonder hair, firmer breasts. How could she compete? And it *was* a competition. At least it felt that way whenever Heath came to bed. If they did make love, she worried that she wasn't desirable enough, and if they didn't, she wondered about the women who satisfied him.

"I love your hair. Who does it?" The compliment came from the leader of the pack, a willowy blonde whose pallor reflected a champagne-and-cigarettes diet. Her disciples nodded in affirmation as they waited for the answer.

Sharon fingered her cropped do and smiled guiltily. "I

cut it myself," she admitted. "My master bath has a three-way mirror, so I just grab the scissors and go for it."

"No!" the girl exclaimed with genuine shock. "Well, it looks great!"

Sharon nodded her thanks, adjusting the shy Liam on her hip. She gestured toward him. "It saves me an hour, which is more precious than diamonds these days."

"Hey, cute thing," the girl chirped, moving her hand in to tickle Liam as he buried his head into Sharon's shoulder. "You are so lucky." And then she led her crew to the sportswear section, where they fussed over the latest arrivals from Paul & Joe, a French line designed by Sophie Albou.

The last statement stunned Sharon into a brief silence. Sometimes she took her blessings for granted. The truth—she *was* lucky. Her family was safe, healthy, and financially okay. Granted, things with Heath were a mess, but they were still together, and probably always would be. She'd listened to relationship experts on talk shows maintain that it's lonelier to live in an unhappy marriage than it is to live by yourself. But she didn't buy that.

"Mommy, I want down," Liam whined.

"Okay, but don't leave the store. We'll go into the mall for a cookie in just a bit."

"Have you seen the guy who leased the space next door?" Mary Payne asked.

Sharon shook her head, watching Liam zigzag through the racks, his arms outstretched like an airplane.

"He's a hottie," Mary Payne went on. "The place is called java.com. It's like a coffee and cyber cafe. Really cool. You've got to check him out. This man is *so* good-looking. I don't even drink coffee, but starting today I'm making it a daily habit." She fanned herself.

Sharon laughed. "Let's fix this display."

They worked fast, substituting Mary Payne's wild accessory choices for more classic pieces from the new Prada collection. A color-splashed blouse was deep-sixed for a safer solid white number, and then they stepped back to inspect their work.

Sharon nodded, thrilled with the transformation. "Now that's Bliss."

"Totally Bliss," Mary Payne agreed.

She'd been keeping a close eye on Liam while they worked. But suddenly he was no longer in sight. "Liam!" she called, getting no response. "I hope he's not in the office," she murmured, moving briskly toward the back in search of her son.

The office was undisturbed.

Her heart tripped a little bit faster. She flung open the door to the storage room and called out, "Liam, it's time to go get a cookie!"

Nothing.

She speed-walked back to the sales floor and made a beeline for the fitting rooms. Sometimes he liked to play hide-and-seek there. Crouching down, she checked for feet. One of the three dressing areas was occupied. But Liam was nowhere.

"Have you seen my son?" Sharon demanded.

The curtain opened. The sweet blonde girl stood there in bra and panties. "No," she said. "He was out—"

Sharon didn't wait for the rest. Her eyes were pure panic now as she searched for him, kneeling down, calling his name, scolding herself for being so preoccupied.

Mary Payne joined the hunt. Five minutes turned into ten. But the store wasn't that big. Sharon didn't want to believe that Liam could have ventured out. She ran to the only store entrance, the one that fed into the mall, aware of her own heart drumming away, staring lasers at the shoppers going this way and that.

"I'm calling security," Mary Payne said.

"Liam!" Sharon cried, surprised by the hoarseness in her voice. To her sense of alarm was now added an overwhelming terror.

Chapter Eight

Katie took one glance at the scrawled D in red marker on the bottom of her book report and shoved it into her canvas messenger bag. One run-on sentence and she barely passes. What's up with that? Fuck it. She had more important things to do than worry about English class. Besides, that stupid bitch Mrs. Boozer hated her. She could write like William Faulkner and still get a bad grade.

She checked her watch. It was almost time.

Someone tapped her shoulder and passed her a note, nodding to the back of the room. Katie twisted around in her seat.

Thomas Prewitt smiled back at her. He was white, the son of one of Atlanta's top cardiologists, and in serious need of racial identity counseling. Thomas was so deeply immersed in hip-hop culture that he talked and dressed like a rap star.

She unfolded the ragged sheet of spiral notebook paper. The message read: It sure looks yummy, baby. Can I have a taste? Peace, TP.

Maybe in a wet dream, loser. Who needed sophomore *boys* when senior *men* were available? Katie slung her bag onto her shoulder and approached Mrs. Boozer's desk, stopping to drop Thomas's note into the wastepaper basket. Her movement created a ministir—catcalls, whistles, whispers, the whole high school bit.

Mrs. Boozer hushed the class and glared disapprovingly at Katie. "Anyone who dresses like that must be desperate for attention," she hissed.

Katie answered with a ho-hum shrug. "Maybe so, but right now I'm desperate for a ladies room. May I have a hall pass please?"

Mrs. Boozer was serious about the butch look—no makeup, bluntly cut hair, and men's dress shirts. Her mouth was set in a tight, angry line. "You should've made time for that before class. Go sit down."

"It's, like, a *female* problem," Katie lied. "I wouldn't expect you to understand, but, I don't know, try hard."

Seething, Mrs. Boozer scratched out a hall pass. "When you find the trouble you're heading for, Katie, don't come crying to me."

Katie snatched the freedom paper from her teacher's manly fingers. "I'll make a note to cross you off my list of potential rescuers." She curled her lips into a quick, insolent smile and hit the door, feeling triumphant.

"You're late." Angel was waiting for her, like always, in the second-floor ladies room next door to the computer lab.

"I'm lucky to be here. That dyke Mrs. Boozer had Melissa Etheridge's guitar up her ass."

Angel cackled. "She's not gay. I heard that she's a widow."

Katie rolled her eyes. "Maybe she's just a woman in touch with her masculine side."

"Let's do it," Angel said. "The last thing I need is another in-school suspension."

Katie reached into her bag and pulled out a thick packet of screaming pink paper. She cut the deck, giving half to Angel, keeping the other stack for herself. "I'll take the right side, you take the left."

They hit the trail like political campaign slaves one week before the vote, slipping the four-page zine *Grrl Talk* inside lockers as they watched for assistant principals stalking the halls.

Katie felt flushed with excitement. She loved circulating the zine almost as much as creating it. *Grrl Talk* was her secret baby. She wrote, designed, and printed the underground monthly all by herself. Angel enjoyed the controversy that always followed, so she helped with distribution.

Grrl Talk had become a powerful mode of self-expression, giving Katie the chance to anonymously rant on teachers, student cliques, sex, violence, and other stuff. She'd read about the zine phenomenon in *Seventeen,* then decided to cobble together one of her own. It was like being editor and publisher of her own magazine!

At Angel's suggestion, she only printed a limited number of copies. "The more exclusive, the better," her friend had said. About one hundred went out to Riverside students, the rest to Tower Records and movie theaters throughout Atlanta. The big thrill had been getting a rave review from *Factsheet Five,* a national zine about zines based in San Francisco. Since then, she'd received e-mails from all over the country—and the world—begging for a copy of *Grrl Talk.*

Katie didn't make a dime off the project. In fact, printing the damn thing usually ran about two hundred bucks. Luckily, she knew her father's PIN number and slipped away with his ATM card to get cash whenever she needed it. He fucked around so much that he didn't know where his money went, so he never suspected a thing.

They'd just inserted the last zine into a locker when Katie heard Angel mutter the fateful words, "Oh, shit."

Mr. Santoyo, the assistant principal who no student wanted to deal with, was heading straight for them.

Katie and Angel started a fast walk in the opposite direction.

"Stop right there, ladies," Mr. Santoyo's voiced boomed, bouncing off the metal lockers and boomeranging around their heads. "Let me see your hall passes."

They turned over the evidence and watched him inspect it like a border patrol guard. He leveled a suspicious gaze on Katie. "Mrs. Boozer's room is on the west wing. What are you doing over here?"

"The janitor must be out sick today. That bathroom is so nasty I couldn't even use it."

"Mr. Taylor happens to be very healthy, and that restroom was cleaned before the school doors opened," Mr. Santoyo replied, folding his arms.

"A lot can happen in a few hours," Katie said, unwilling to abandon her lie. It was always better to push it all the way.

Mr. Santoyo made no move for the walkie-talkie hooked onto his belt. He could've easily made a call and busted her right there. "If I didn't have to report to the cafeteria right now, I'd check that out. Get back to class."

Katie and Angel took off, breathing heavy sighs of relief.

"Great save," Angel praised. "I'll see you at lunch." And then she darted inside crazy Mrs. Larson's Spanish class.

Katie felt restless. She couldn't wait until fourth period. That's when she, Angel, and Mamiko shared first-shift lunch together. They could sit back and watch as the pink pages of *Grrl Talk* got passed from table to table. By the time the last bell rang, the mystery zine would be the talk of the school.

Especially this issue, which marked the debut of "Her Fantasy," an erotic short story about a girl who hooks up with a guy she's been admiring from afar. In this case, the guy was hot jock Derek Johnson.

Katie knew he'd be dying to know who wrote it. She decided that she would let him in on the secret this afternoon. After all, there was no time like the present to take him up on his offer to hang out at his place.

Chapter Nine

The situation was too serious for panic. Her son had been missing for fifteen minutes. Despite the gelatinous feeling in her legs, Sharon began searching the mall area in front of the store. "Liam!"

Strangers regarded her with embarrassed pity but offered no assistance. The world was full of such selfish pigs . . . and sickos. Fear of the possible swept over her in a scalding wave. It only took one unguarded moment to eviscerate a perfectly good life.

Please, God, let him be safe, Sharon prayed. She tried to ward off the morose thoughts, but they pounded into her mind with no mercy.

Kidnapping.

Molestation.

Torture.

Murder.

Every mother who watched the news knew the horror stories. If anything happened to Liam, Sharon knew that she wouldn't be able to go on living, not for Heath, not even for Katie. She thought of the gun that her husband insisted upon keeping in the house. For so many years she'd asked him to get rid of it. Now she was thankful he'd been so stubborn because a way out was there if she needed one.

Her concentration was so intense that she could almost feel her eyebrows wrapping around her nose. *Oh, Liam, where are you?*

"Mommy!"

At first she thought it was her mind playing tricks, but then she heard his beautiful voice again.

"Mommy!"

Sharon opened up her heart, the pores of her skin, the very marrow of her bones to the incredible sight of Liam Christopher Driver. He charged toward her, chocolate chip cookie all over his face, hands, and Atlanta Infernos shirt.

Her every synapse, from head to toe, transmitted the relief. She threw her arms around him and held him too tightly, massaging his back, telling herself it was safe to stop worrying, allowing the tears to finally come.

"I found him on the first level. He'd taken the escalator down all by himself."

Sharon looked up to see a pretty brunette in a smart navy tank dress smiling down at them. Suddenly the impact of the stranger's words hit her. *"Downstairs?"*

"They move like lightning at his age. He claimed to be on a mission to get a cookie, so I treated him to one. Then I started asking around, and a woman on break from one of the cosmetics counters recognized him. By the way, Carmen says hello."

Sharon still couldn't fathom the notion that Liam had managed to get so far away so quickly. She wanted to spank him and kiss him at the same time. "You gave Mommy a big scare. Don't you *ever* run off like that again. Do you hear me?"

Liam drooped his chocolate smeared lips into a pout. "I'm sorry, Mommy."

Sharon wiped away her tears and rose to greet the woman who had saved her life. She extended her hand and said, "Sharon Driver, emotionally frazzled mother of this cookie monster."

The woman laughed and shook firmly. "I'm Linda Moore."

Sharon placed her hands over her ears, still aware of her racing heart. "God, I feel so ashamed. How could I have taken my eyes off him like that?"

"Don't beat yourself up. It happens to the best of us," Linda said.

"How old is yours?"

"I don't have any of my own. Until recently I was a nanny to two-year-old twins. Talk about double trouble!"

"I can't imagine."

"They were so much fun, but the family moved to the East Coast, so here I am," Linda said, making a face, "job hunting."

"Here at Phipps Plaza?"

Linda nodded.

"I know there's a nanny placement service in Atlanta. Why take the retail route?"

"That situation was unique. They were old family friends. I don't think I could work in the home for complete strangers."

Sharon liked Linda Moore instantly, and not just because she'd rescued Liam. She was sweet, sophisticated, and stylish. "I have a small boutique here called Bliss. I wish I had an opening. I'd hire you in a minute."

Linda shrugged. "There's an opening at Saks's Chanel counter. Maybe something will happen there."

"Come back to the store with us," Sharon said. "Pick out something to wear—my treat. It's the least I could do."

Linda begged away the offer. "I found a child, not a piece of expensive jewelry. I don't expect anything in return for that."

"It's not reward money," Sharon said, understanding and appreciating Linda's reluctance. "Sending you home with something from Bliss would be just as much fun for me. What do you say?"

Linda mulled the thought and finally acquiesced.

Mary Payne stormed the Bliss entrance as they approached. "Oh, thank God! I'm *still* waiting for mall security. What morons! Where did you find him?"

"Downstairs if you can believe it," Sharon said.

"Stop lying!" Mary Payne exclaimed.

As Sharon made the necessary introductions, Liam offered the last of his cookie to Linda. "Want some?" he asked.

"I'd love it," Linda said, gobbling up the piece right away. "That was yummy."

Liam beamed.

Sharon stood transfixed for a moment. "I've never known him to share a cookie with anyone."

Linda dusted the top of Liam's head and smiled. "What can I say? He's my new boyfriend."

"I'm serious about you picking out something to wear. Take a look around," Sharon encouraged.

Before Linda could respond, Mary Payne, ever the hyper-kinetic wardrobe consultant, pounced on the opportunity. "You would look *great* in the new cashmere twin sets we just got in. By the way, I hate you for having a perfect body. Come with me." And off they went.

Sharon swooped down to scoop up Liam and kiss his chubby cheek with a loud smack. "Do you remember what you wished for when we were getting dressed this morning?"

"A light saber!" Liam said enthusiastically.

She pinched his nose. "No, silly, you wished that Mommy would smile more. Remember?"

"Yeah."

"Well, I promise to smile more if you promise never to go off on your own like that again. Do we have a deal?"

He placed a comforting hand on her shoulder. "Okay."

"That's my boy," she murmured, temporarily dazed by an incredible surge of love. She wondered if Georgette Tucker ever felt that way about Katie. If the answer was yes, then she knew without a flicker of doubt that a letter wouldn't be enough to keep her away.

Chapter Ten

"You must be Sharon."

She spun around to greet the thickly accented baritone voice, which belonged to a man who looked so sexy he was practically liquid. He had a great smoldering stare, dark eyes, and a tasteful sprinkling of chest hair.

An aloof smile found its way to her lips. "I must be."

"I'm Antonio Miguel, your new neighbor." He crooked his neck to the left. "Java.com opens in a few days."

Now Sharon knew why Mary Payne had made such a fuss, though the advance hype didn't even begin to do this man justice.

He stepped closer and stroked the back of Liam's head with a neatly manicured hand. "Who's this little man?"

"Liam." Sharon felt like her eyes were lit up with a thousand watts. Normally, good-looking men didn't capture her attention so sharply. But this one had—like the explosive uncorking of a champagne bottle.

He grinned something electric. Perfect smile. Perfect

teeth. "I just made a banana smoothie. Can he have some?"

"I'm sure he'd love it."

Antonio dashed away to make good on his offer, exiting with the grace of a bullfighter. On his feet were the kind of European boots that looked ridiculous on most men. He, of course, carried them off with ferocious dignity. Before so much as a minute passed, he was back.

Liam accepted the treat with an attention span close to awe and sipped greedily.

"Are you ready for the big opening?" Sharon asked.

"I will be. Impossible deadlines inspire me."

"Really? They scare the hell out of me."

"Come on," Antonio said doubtfully.

"It's true."

"You work; you're a mother. I bet you *live* on impossible deadlines."

Sharon laughed. "Oh, so it's my *life* that has me so frightened all the time. Thanks for clearing that up."

He leaned in to address Liam. "Is that good?"

Her little boy removed his lips from the straw just long enough to murmur, "Yeah," then went right back to slurping.

"He's beautiful. And I mean that. To just say he's cute is selling him short."

"Do you have kids?"

Antonio shook his head regretfully. "I will one day, though. I just went through a divorce."

"I'm sorry," Sharon said. She meant it, yes, but part of her was oddly delighted to hear that he wasn't married. "How long were you together?"

He ran his finger across the toe of Liam's sneaker. "Four years."

Sharon was touched by the attention he paid to Liam, and she couldn't take her eyes off his beautiful hands.

"I want to be a daddy," Antonio said, more to himself than to her.

She was moved by his openness. In fact, his naked need for a child reminded her of herself once, amidst all the infertility tests and procedures, before Katie, when the sight of every baby, every child, rose up in her a deep and lasting envy that could easily ruin a day, sometimes a week.

"You have to plan it," Sharon instructed, always an advocate for plotting out goals and going after them with a vengeance. "Find the right woman, then have your baby."

"Will you help me find her?"

He had a quality that intrigued and captivated. The intensity of his gaze forced her to redirect her focus to Liam, whose own eyes remained fixed on the gorgeous Spaniard. "Besides my daughter and her friends, who are only fifteen years old but would happily marry you, I'm sure, the only young single woman I know is Mary Payne."

He glanced to the back of the store where Mary Payne and Linda were browsing the new fall arrivals. Then he zeroed in on her. "I like older women. They're sexier."

"I wish I could record you saying that. I'd play it back for my husband."

"American men are stupid that way."

"Yes, they are," she replied slowly, savoring her answer, experiencing a rush of pleasure at the sharpened and animated energy of flirtation.

Sharon remembered reading something by Helen Gurley Brown once that said marriage was the bran muffin of sex, that a little fear and risk had to be in the mix in order for the act to be as delicious as it could be. She felt nervous, almost sick to her stomach, the same way that Heath had made her feel twenty-two years ago.

It was strange, but the idea of a dalliance had never entered her mind until now. How wonderful it would be to have a planned rendezvous to look forward to during the week. After all, sex didn't arrive by UPS. If she wanted some and Heath was too busy with his slut-of-the-month to provide it, then maybe she should get in the game, too.

"I feel like we're friends now," Antonio said.

"I think you're right," Sharon replied.

Chapter Eleven

"This is *too* cool," Angel said.

"You have to find a way to make money on this," Mamiko chimed in.

Katie threw her greedy friend a look. Didn't she understand that Katie did this for *herself,* not for cash, controversy, or any such crap?

They were standing in a tight huddle, watching the scene unfold in the parking lot. *Grrl Talk* had officially eclipsed *The Riverside Flyer,* the student newspaper, as the hottest school read.

After the body crush to read over shoulders during lunch, a student office assistant had xeroxed reams of the steamy zine on the sly. Then some band geeks ducked out of practice early enough to slap a copy under the wiper blade of every windshield.

As Derek Johnson loped to his car, he fielded back slaps and high fives from other jocks. And it wasn't for acing the impossible *Macbeth* test that had most seniors heading for a minor breakdown. No, Derek Johnson was getting macho congratulations for being the stud of "Her Fantasy"—a well-hung one who makes all the right moves.

"He's really hot," Katie said, checking out his ass.

"The poor shit could probably go for an after-school snack. Want to buy him one?" Mamiko teased.

Katie glared. "You know, that's really mean. So he's not rich—big deal. Look at Bobby Canizaro over there—loaded, yeah, but he's a prick."

"Hey, *Grrl Talk* just tapped a new market," Angel announced. She pointed across the parking lot to the school.

In the doorway, Mr. Santoyo stood stone-faced, reading one of the crudely copied bootleg versions as Mrs. Boozer looked on disapprovingly. They talked back and forth for a moment, then marched inside the building.

Katie's stomach took a fast trip down. "What do you think they were saying?"

"Maybe they got hot reading it, and they're going inside to do it on top of her desk," Angel cracked.

"You are *so* gross," Mamiko said. "Besides, everybody knows that Boozer has it bad for Angela Glover."

"The cheerleader, the judge's daughter," Katie sang derisively.

"Anyway, tomorrow morning's announcements should be *very* interesting," Mamiko went on. "I know the office assistant and the band geeks will at least get Saturday morning yard detail. Keep it low profile, girls, if you know what's good for you."

In a show of solidarity, Katie and Angel clasped hands.

"I know nothing," Katie said, putting a robot spin on her voice.

"I know less than you do," Angel mimicked.

Together, they burst into laughter and piled into the car.

Mamiko made a move for the front seat.

"Hey," Katie objected, "I got stuffed in the backseat this morning. It's your turn."

Mamiko pulled a face. "Calm down. Listen to Yanni or something." And then she folded herself into the rear of the Audi.

Angel reached inside the glove compartment, pulled out a candy bar, and started munching. "I'm hungry," she said. "Let's go to Lenox Mall."

"Whatever," Mamiko said.

"Fine," Katie murmured, tracking Derek Johnson's movements in the passenger-side mirror.

He was directly behind them, pumping Kid Rock to the maximum, bobbing his head to the aggressive beat. Suddenly he jerked the wheel and coasted his vehicle side by side with Angel's.

"Oh, what a surprise," Mamiko remarked in her snappish little way. "He must be out of gas."

Derek turned and gazed straight at Katie. Their eyes locked, a truly electric moment. It lasted for several seconds. He looked at her as if he owned her, giving just the slightest nod to the empty passenger seat beside him. An invitation? A dare?

Gridlock in the exit lanes kept the cars in parallel position. The question rocked Katie. To stay with her girls or to steal away with this older, dangerously sexy guy? She could feel her heart speeding up, taking off.

"I'll call you later," Katie blurted, jumping out of the car.

"Are you crazy?" Angel called out.

But by then she was in the front seat of Derek's Chevrolet. He bulldozed his way to the front of the line with obscene gestures, menacing looks, and verbal threats. The thrill was incredible. Derek Johnson personified cool—a true, hard-core bad boy.

Katie thought of her parents. They would freak if they knew she'd just hopped in the car with this almost thug to go God knows where. The volume of the music was so loud that she feared permanent damage to her hearing. She twisted the knob down a bit.

"Don't fuck with the stereo!" Derek shouted, then turned it up even louder.

Katie shrugged diffidently and settled back to accept the sonic assault. She caught him stealing glances at her chest as they drove into a small cul-de-sac not far from her Columns Drive home.

He parked on the street in front of a corner lot and swung out, taking her hand and leading her up to the door.

She started to speak but thought better of it. Derek Johnson was a man of few words. If she wanted to be with him, she better get used to it.

Derek retrieved a key from underneath a planter and let himself inside.

MTV blared from the big-screen television. A twenty-something man lay sprawled across the couch drinking beer.

"What's up, Ty!" Derek called.

Ty didn't bother to rise. He just raked Katie up and down with a crude gaze.

"I need a little private time," Derek said.

"Looks like jailbait to me," Ty replied, his attention back to music videos. "Hit it in Mama's bedroom. She's away at a conference all week."

Derek led her down a short hallway and into a master bedroom that had shades of older woman all over it—floral bedding, frilly window treatments, antique furniture.

Katie felt herself plunging helplessly into the icy lake of second thoughts. Could she turn back now? They were *alone* in some strange person's bedroom. The bum on the couch had told him to *hit it.* How had things moved so fast? She'd wanted to flirt with the idea, not dive into it without any planning!

"Do you live here?" she asked.

He approached her slowly, hooked his thumbs through the belt loops of her jeans, and kissed her on the lips. "This is my cousin's house. It's like a second home."

"Did you read what that girl wrote?" Katie asked silkily, testing him, trying to decide if she should confess.

He ignored her, his hands skating up her torso, taking her shirt with them.

"Wait," she protested.

Faster than she knew was possible, he pushed up her shirt, unhooked her bra, and roughly pawed at her exposed breasts with both hands. "Take off those jeans," he said thickly.

"Slow down!" Katie insisted, surprised at the forcefulness in her voice. She tried to twist away from him, but he held firm, biting down on her nipples.

"Stop!"

"Shit," Derek muttered. He ripped off his shirt and flung it into the corner. "The last thing I need is some tease. I thought you were my girl."

"I am . . . I'd like to be . . . it's just that—"

"You got in my car because you want me. Right?"

She merely stared.

"Am I right?"

"I want to hook up with you, yeah. But there's such a thing as moderation. I'm not some road whore."

"You write stories like one."

Katie felt exposed like never before and wished she could depart the room via astral projection. "How did you know it was me?" Her voice barely registered.

His lips puckered triumphantly. "I didn't. You just told me."

A rage to flee surged through Katie's nervous system, but before she could act on it, Derek locked the door.

Chapter Twelve

It was five o'clock and Katie still hadn't returned home from school. More pissed off than worried, Sharon dialed the Fishers. Rebecca, the family's live-in housekeeper, answered on the second ring. Sharon knew the help better than Mr. and Mrs. Fisher. In fact, she'd never spoken to Angel's father, and only once to the girl's mother.

"Hi, Rebecca, it's Sharon Driver. I'm calling to check on Katie. Is she there?"

"No, the girls aren't here. Angel called from the car. They were going to Lenox Mall."

Sharon released a defeated sigh. "Okay, thanks." She banged the phone into the cradle. Angel's *housekeeper* knew more about Katie's whereabouts!

The rumble of the garage door startled her. Moments later Heath strode inside through the kitchen door. "Hey," he said, kissing her on the lips before grabbing a beer. "You look upset."

"There's a problem with Katie."

"When isn't there a problem with Katie?"

His question was more of a shot to her than to their daughter, but Sharon resisted the urge to return fire. Instead, she calmly explained the situation.

"So Katie went to the mall," Heath reasoned, as if she were some maternal ogre. "Teenagers live at the mall. Cut her some slack."

Sharon stared at her husband. There he stood, leaning against the counter, one hand on his thigh, the other clutching a cold Corona. What a clueless bastard.

"Cut her some slack? It was just this morning that our fifteen-year-old daughter tried to walk out of here looking old enough and willing enough to jump in the sack with one of your fuck 'em and run players!"

Heath winced. She'd painted a powerful visual image that was no doubt tattooing itself on his brain.

"I want to know in advance what her plans are, and you should want to know, too, goddammit. All it takes is a simple, 'Mom, the girls and I are going to Lenox Mall after school.' Is that so much to ask?"

Now he nodded in solemn agreement. "I'll talk to her."

Suddenly Sharon felt guilty for attacking him with such ruthless fervor. Hell, he'd walked in the door less than five minutes ago. No wonder their marriage was such a toxic wreck. She stroked his chest, still amazed at how firm it was as he approached fifty. "Thanks." Allowing a beat to pass, she added, "You sounded great on Kit's show this morning."

"You listened?"

The genuine surprise in his voice stung. What were they to each other? Why did they share so little as husband and wife, both physically and emotionally? Even now, in the glow of this momentary truce, she could never dream of telling him about the letter from Georgette Tucker that was burning up her brain stem. Yet they continued to go on together. "Yeah, I listened," she whispered sadly.

"Kit's great. She's going to be big. I just know it," Heath said, his voice brimming with pride and admiration.

Sharon tried not to dwell on the fact that he'd never uttered a single word about her success with Bliss. The clock ticked past five. She needed to start moving. "Listen, I have to get ready. Liam's dinner is in the microwave. Just heat it up. Maybe you and Katie can order a pizza or something."

He gave her a strange look. "Where are you going?"

The question conjured up a familiar storm of anger. How many times had she told him about tonight's meeting? *At least fifty.* If it wasn't happening to *him,* it never seemed to register.

"I'm chairing the AIDS fund-raiser at the Swissotel next month," she said patiently. "I still need Doug and Adonis to serve as celebrity blackjack dealers for the casino theme. And put me in touch with *them,* not their asshole agents."

Sharon left him to finish his beer, then checked on Liam before heading upstairs to change. She was seminude and touching up her makeup at her dressing table when Heath entered the bedroom.

His warm hands massaged her neck. "Be late for the meeting," he said, slipping her camisole off her shoulders to expose her breasts.

How typical, Sharon thought. When she had no time for his amorous attention, he was suddenly Mr. Romance. "I can't, Heath. I'm the chairman. How would that look?"

"Like you were a busy woman." He caressed her breasts with an instinctively languid cadence, playing with her delicately arrogant nipples until the little pink tips swelled and hardened. "Mmmm," she breathed involuntarily. God, his hands felt good.

"Blow it off."

She placed her hands over his to freeze their delicious movement, determined to keep her commitment. Too many people were counting on her. "Liam is—"

"Liam is halfway into *The Lion King* and won't move until it's over. You know that." His head swooped down to her neck, covering it with ardent, thirsty mouth kisses.

"Heath, I wish I didn't have to go . . . but I do. Can't you save up all this passion and meet me here for lunch tomorrow?"

He groaned like a horny high school boy who'd just been turned down at make out point.

Sharon eyed him through the mirror with a vampish gaze. "And don't lock yourself in the bathroom with my Victoria's Secret catalog. Stay all wound up."

"It's a date," he said, butterfly kissing her shoulder.

And then she felt it with her pinky finger, near the surface of her right breast, on the outside, something about the size and softness of a raisin. The discovery produced an instant of pure panic. "Let me get dressed," she said quickly. "You should check on Liam. He'll need to eat dinner right after the movie."

As soon as she was certain that Heath was downstairs, Sharon probed her breast again, more closely this time. Yes, it was indeed a lump. She raised her arm, noticing a bit of a dent in the suspicious area.

She stood stock-still, her lips parted, her eyes wide, motionless, as if holding her breath. There was no denying the enormity of what it might mean. Her mother had died from it. So had her grandmother.

Oh, God, she had so much love to give, so many things to accomplish. Please don't let it be cancer.

Chapter Thirteen

The moment Liam disappeared inside, Sharon waved to his teacher and dashed toward the car. So anxious to finally have the opportunity to make a phone call in private, she couldn't get there fast enough.

Thankfully, Keri Ward answered on the second ring.

She took a deep breath. "Keri, it's Sharon Driver from Bliss. I'm sorry to call you at home, but your office told me you were booked, and I really need to see you. This morning, if possible." She swallowed hard. "I found a lump on my right breast."

"How soon can you be there?" Keri asked evenly.

Already Sharon felt slightly more at ease. Not only was Keri Ward one of Bliss's most loyal customers, she was one of the top breast surgeons in the country. "Now."

"Good. I'm on my way in. I'll phone the office and clear you as my first appointment. When was your last mammogram?"

Sharon scanned her brain. "It hasn't been long . . . maybe six months." Her voiced cracked.

"Relax, Sharon. We'll get a read on this right away."

The cancer deaths of her mother and grandmother flashing in her mind, she experienced a pronounced shiver. "Thanks, Keri. I'll see you soon."

Thirty minutes later Sharon was scared to death, sitting in the cold examining room with her arms above her head as Keri Ryan's probing hands went to work.

"Okay, you can slip your robe back on."

Sharon covered herself, searching the woman's eyes for a sign of what was to come.

"You were smart to call me so soon. It looks suspicious. There's a radiology clinic next door. I want another mammogram and a chest X ray. Then you'll come back for some blood work. I can do a biopsy here in the office. We're backed up in the lab, so pathology reports will take a few days."

"What are the odds that it's . . ." She couldn't bring herself to say the word.

"Most women have a one in nine chance of developing breast cancer." Keri paused a beat. "But given your family medical history, your chances are fifty-fifty."

Sharon closed her eyes and thought of her mother, who, after being diagnosed with advanced breast cancer at thirty-two, had endured unspeakable misery yet still clung to life. Watching the sun set. Petting her beloved cat. The most simple things had brought her pleasure until she died, her courageous spirit unbroken to the end.

The rest of the morning passed in a daze. She filled out endless insurance forms. A rough nurse flattened, squashed, and zapped her breasts for the mammogram. Another one jabbed a needle into her arm to draw blood. Then Dr. Ward administered a local anesthetic, performed the biopsy, and sent her home to wait for the results.

All Sharon could think about was the inscrutable sadness in her mother's eyes when she had realized that in the queue of life and death, she would exchange places with her daughter, just as her own mother had with her.

She tried to take a nap but couldn't quiet her racing heart long enough to drift away. A distinct chill came over her, and she clutched a cashmere blanket around her body. Sharon lay there, almost catatonic, waiting for Heath to come home for what he thought would be a lovemaking session.

Liam and Katie weighed heavily on her mind, too. If she died, who would mother them? Suddenly her gaze zeroed in on the dressing table across the room, the contents inside the top drawer calling out to her like a siren.

Georgette Tucker's letter. *She won't stop at just writing,* Sharon thought. Deep down she was sure of that, and it scared her as much as the threat of cancer did.

Chapter Fourteen

It was one o'clock and Heath still hadn't come home. Their marital tryst had been set for noon. A tiny part of her knew that he wouldn't show. Sharon couldn't explain the feeling. It was just there, buried in her gut.

She tried to keep the pain of rejection at bay. There was no way she could deal with it, not now. Heath's rebuke was directed at the healthy Sharon, not the cancer-stricken one she might actually be. And he was such a breast man, the son of a bitch.

Against her better judgment, she reached for the cordless on the nightstand and punched in his office number.

Patsy answered with a perky, "Coach Driver's office."

"Hi, Patsy, it's Sharon. Is Heath around?"

A pregnant pause. "No . . . he's out to lunch."

She gripped the phone so tightly that she thought the plastic casing might actually crack. *Poor stupid Sharon. How long will she be the last to know?* That's what Patsy was thinking. She was sure of it. "What time did he leave?"

"About eleven."

"I'll try his cellular. Thanks." She hung up and fondled the place on her breast where Dr. Ward had performed the biopsy. Fear of the possible ransacked her mind until she was breathing in rapid, shallow gasps. Her heart felt like a tightly closed little clamshell.

Suddenly her craving for Heath knew no bounds. Her husband was good in times of crisis, so stoic, strong, and competent. She should've made time for his horny advances last night. The charity ball meeting had turned out to be a waste of time with several no-shows and incomplete committee reports.

She wandered through the house, stopping in Liam's room to just sit on his little bed and take in the innocent surroundings. He was the most handsome, natural, and honest male she had ever known. But then again, he was only two years old. Sharon laughed at the notion until she cried. Burying her tear dampened face in Liam's pillow, she drank in his sweet smell.

The telephone jangled.

She raced into Katie's room to answer, praying that it was Heath. He could be trapped in a meeting or stuck in a traffic jam. But it was a fucking telemarketer. She was tempted to take the call, if only for the connection. That's how lonely she felt right now.

Absently, she began to pick up and fold Katie's clothes. Her things were strewn this way and that in typical teenage disorder. It suddenly dawned on Sharon how sullen and withdrawn Katie had been this morning. She made a mental note to find out where her daughter had gone yesterday and what time she'd come home.

The idea of moping around the house all day made her sick. Cancer or no cancer, she had to survive—for Katie, for Liam. This setback wasn't going to crush her in two. No way. Because the minute she surrendered, her life would be over.

Feeling a surge of energy, Sharon touched up her

makeup, donned a pair of great fitting jeans, and slipped into one of Heath's white dress shirts taken straight from the dryer, wrinkles and all.

Then she jumped in the car and drove with purpose. Heath could do whatever the hell he wanted to. There was only one man she wanted to see right now, a man who made her feel desirable, a man who really talked to her, a man who really listened.

Antonio Miguel.

Chapter Fifteen

"You've got such a beautiful cock." Holly Ryan murmured the rave review as she licked her way up its sternly distended shaft.

Heath wrapped his hands around her thighs and pulled her body toward his mouth, straining up to plunge his desperately eager tongue between her magical lips.

"It's so long and thick," she praised, taking the head between her lips for some excruciatingly good attention. "You should have it dipped in gold."

"I'm going to fuck you so hard," Heath promised, loving her dirty talk, feeling a deliciously hot burn where it mattered. He was forty-eight years old; he felt eighteen.

His tongue stabbed at her fragrant softness, parting the hairs, exploring her slick heat for a moment before bathing her clitoris with his tongue and sucking deeply, listening with delight at the sigh that escaped her.

"Oh, yes," Holly half whispered, half moaned, releasing his penis from her mouth, hovering over it with a look of agonized, wanton desire.

Heath marveled at the engorged state of her living flesh as the wetness between her legs practically dribbled down his chin. "Suck it, baby. Finish me off."

Teasingly, Holly moved her head away. "Look how excited you are. You don't need me." And then she pushed her body hard into his face.

Heath rose to the challenge, using his tongue, his lips, the insides of his cheeks, knowing that with each advancing gasp she was closer to the essential prize. "Come on," he begged. "Let me inside."

"No," Holly insisted. "It's too soon. I have my principles." She reached out and started rubbing the hairless patch of skin between his testicles and his anus.

"Oh, God!" Heath cried. He used his pelvic muscles to grind his hips up and down, to drive home the peak of excitement as she massaged the magic area. When he climaxed, the sensation was so long, so intense, so ferocious, that the beauty of it was matched only by the sight of his semen bursting forth into the air. He felt instantly weak and totally drained.

Holly climbed off his exhausted body and slipped inside her bathroom. She returned with a damp washcloth and proceeded to clean him up. "That was hot," she said, wiping some evidence off his chest.

Heath closed his eyes and grinned. "It was almost perfect."

"*Almost?*" She leaned back, hand on naked hip, striking a seriously insulted pose.

He opened his eyes and rose up on his elbows, admiring her youth and flawless tits. "I wanted to come in your mouth."

Holly smiled smugly, fluttering her eyes. "I'm an old-fashioned girl. I never swallow on the first date."

He laughed and tweaked one of her rosy nipples. "You got any lunch around here?"

She laid back and gazed invitingly at him. "You just ate the only meal I know how to make."

Heath couldn't believe how exciting and nasty this girl was. They hadn't even fucked yet and already she was the best lay of his life.

The big numbers on her bedside alarm clock captured his attention. It was one-thirty. And then it hit him. He'd forgotten his appointment with Sharon at home. *Shit.*

Holly reached over and started playing with his dick.

Heath felt it stiffen slightly and gently pushed her hand away. "Don't tempt me. I've got a team to get back to." He rose and started to get dressed.

"You're supposed to be helping me with my part in the movie."

"I am." He gave her an obvious look. "Let's review. Lesson number one—swallow the coach's come. Lesson number two—accept the fact that his next game is always top priority."

Holly giggled. "Fuck you," she snarled, turning over to show him her ass.

"Next time, baby." He really wanted to stay and give this bed devil another tumble, but there was an afternoon practice to get to. Plus, he should probably save some energy for Sharon. Missing their date was a bad move, but he'd give her a thrill in the sack tonight. Everything would be fine after that.

Chapter Sixteen

Katie kept her head cast downward as she speed walked into Mrs. Boozer's classroom and slid into her desk. She wore bulky sweats from head to toe, successfully concealing the body that only yesterday had attracted a torrent of attention.

A burst of laughter erupted from a group of guys sitting in the back.

Katie tensed, her knees began to shake, and a burning heat flushed her face and neck. They were laughing at her. They knew. A sick feeling swept over her.

Someone tapped her shoulder.

She took a deep breath and turned to face her tormentors. There were three of them, all jocks, making crude sucking noises with their thumbs in their mouths.

Everyone was laughing now. Knowing looks and gossipy whispers bounced around the room.

Katie wanted to run away and never come back. Desperately, she turned to Mrs. Boozer, silently imploring her to hush the class, to get on with the subject of English. But the look on Mrs. Boozer's pinched face was odd, almost triumphant, as if she knew of Katie's humiliation and took secret pleasure in it.

"Is this a new look, Katie?" the teacher asked. "I've never seen you with so many clothes on."

"That's because she likes to take them off!" It was one of the jocks.

The class roared. Even Mrs. Boozer surrendered a brief chuckle before her lame attempt to quiet them down.

Katie merely sat there, stunned by the horror of it all, watching the scene as if outside of herself, feeling more alone than ever before. She hated the jocks. She hated Mrs. Boozer. But most of all, she hated Derek Johnson.

When the bell rang for the first lunch shift, it triggered none of the usual excitement. Today she dreaded it.

The moment she entered the cafeteria, the gawking looks and vicious whispers started again. Katie did her best to ignore it, making a beeline for the table she shared with Angel and Mamiko. Not feeling hungry, she sat hunched over, sipping slowly on a can of Coke.

Angel plopped down with pizza, chips, and ice cream.

Katie looked at the feast, then to Angel.

"My parents put me on a new diet," she explained. "I get, like, almost nothing at home."

Mamiko swooped down with a small salad and bottled water, turning up her nose at Angel's junk food. "Oh, that's healthy."

Angel waved a dismissive hand. "Whatever."

Mamiko focused a ray gun gaze on Katie. "What exactly happened with Derek Johnson yesterday? There are rumors."

Katie felt her throat constrict. "I hate that son of a bitch."

"What did you expect?" Mamiko countered. "You jumped into his car half dressed like some hot little whore. Of course he's going to treat you like one."

Katie felt the fire of rapidly rising blood. "Thanks a lot," she began bitterly. "It means so much to have the support of my friends."

"I *am* your friend, Katie. Everyone else in school is calling you a slut behind your back. At least I'm saying it to your face. By the way, your *Grrl Talk* cover is blown. Everybody knows about that, too. I guess you opened your mouth and your legs. Must have been a busy afternoon."

Mamiko had gone too far, but Katie didn't have the strength to fight back. The tears came without warning, and she just sat there, covering her face with her hands.

"What's up, Katie?" Immediately she recognized Thomas Prewitt's put-on urban-dweller voice and uncovered her eyes.

"This is from all the guys." He placed onto the table a long, thick wad of foil molded into the shape of a penis, then sauntered back to rejoin his friends, Derek Johnson among them. The group laughed so hard that news of the fake phallus spread like V.D.

"Show us how you suck it!" Thomas shouted, winning another rowdy chorus of laughter.

For a moment, Katie couldn't comprehend the cruelty. It didn't feel like it was happening to her but to an actor in a foggy tableau.

Angel snatched the awful thing and flung it down to the floor. "Those pencil dicks wish they were that big. Don't pay any attention to them, Katie."

But all Katie could wonder was what would be worse—yesterday, today, or tomorrow. As far as she was concerned, it didn't matter anymore.

Chapter Seventeen

"So to sum up the main points of my rambling—I haven't had sex in months, my husband's an asshole, and my teenage daughter is out of control. It sounds very ordinary, doesn't it?" Sharon said, sipping the last of her espresso.

Antonio regarded her carefully. "There's nothing ordinary about you."

She glanced down at her empty cup, feeling at once relieved, for having someone to talk to, and nervous, for the subtle way he let her know that he thought more of her than she thought of herself.

"How's Liam?"

It touched her that he asked, that he remembered his name. "He's wonderful . . . easy . . . uncomplicated." She glanced at her watch. "Speaking of Liam, I have to pick him up from school soon."

Antonio leaned back, briefly diverting his attention to the electricians finishing up the high speed connections for java.com's futuristic Internet pods. "We should have lunch together."

"I'd like that," Sharon said, basking in the weightless feeling that came over her in his presence. It suddenly occurred to her how sexy a man could be when he simply *listened.* And Antonio Miguel was a great listener. Plus, it was a welcome relief to talk to someone who wasn't on her payroll or two years old.

"You seem preoccupied," he said.

"By my problems, you mean? Yeah, well, that's the story of my life."

He gave up half a smile, as if to say that he appreciated her humor but didn't buy the explanation. "I mean on a deeper level. Something else is troubling you. It's pretty obvious."

Sharon felt an uptick in the beating of her heart. In twenty-two years of marriage, such an astute observation about her mood had never fallen from Heath's lips. "Both my mother and grandmother died of breast cancer early in their lives. Last night I found a small lump on my breast. I'm waiting to hear the results of a biopsy."

His lips parted, but no words were forthcoming. The velocity of her honesty seemed to astonish him.

"You're the first person I've told. I don't know why. Maybe it's because you're here. Maybe it's because you're interested in *me*—that's so rare these days."

Antonio reached out to trap one of her hands between both of his. Bringing it to his lips, he kissed it twice. "Do you believe in deals with God?"

"What do you mean?"

"Spiritual negotiations. I told God that I'd never gamble again if my career would start moving in the right direction, and then this business opportunity came along."

Sharon considered the concept, determining the bargaining points she could offer up for a matter as important as life and death. Instantly she thought of the secret she'd kept from Katie all these years, of the lies she'd Federal Expressed to Georgette Tucker only recently.

"Are you a religious person?" Antonio asked.

"The worst kind," Sharon said wryly. "I only show up when times are bad."

He stood up and without warning pulled her in for an embrace. "I'm sorry, Sharon. I hope you don't have to wait much longer to find out more. It must be driving you mad."

The solace she found here, in his arms, seemed to have a healing property all its own. It amazed her how comfortable he made her feel, how much she was willing to share with him so quickly. "I . . ." Suddenly her voice collapsed. She clutched him tighter, searching for the strength not to break down.

He held her firmly, his espresso breath warm in her ear. "It's okay. It's okay."

"My children need me, Antonio. I don't want to die."

Chapter Eighteen

Another day had gone by without a word from Dr. Ward. Besides Liam, who always provided her joy, the only lightness in Sharon's life was Antonio. Morning espressos together had been instantly declared an everyday ritual, no matter what. She needed the distraction, something new and exciting to look forward to outside the home.

Katie was more sullen than ever, deflecting inquiries about her welfare with increasing hostility. Even her friendship with Angel and Mamiko had suffered. She had stopped riding with them in favor of taking the bus.

And then there was Heath. Sometimes he made Sharon feel like that comic-book creature, the Incredible Hulk, because the mere sight of him often triggered in her an unspeakable internal rage. She still hadn't told him about the biopsy. But by shutting her husband out, was she punishing him or herself?

"Okay, I discovered Antonio, and you've totally stolen him away from me," Mary Payne said.

Sharon had made the mistake of returning to Bliss with

her java.com cup. There was no hiding where she'd been. "He likes to *talk,*" she said with a grin, feeling a slight blush warm her cheeks. "You won't befriend him by just standing there and salivating."

"Is it that obvious? You know, I really need to get laid. It's been seven months. A dry spell like that should requalify me for virgin status. I can't wait to get married. Regular sex must be great."

Sharon rolled her eyes. "You'd be surprised how *irregular* it can be."

Mary Payne stopped folding the new shipment of Italian sweaters and propped her elbows onto the counter. "What? Your husband is hot. He's, I don't know . . . virile."

"You're not the only twentysomething girl who thinks so." She exhaled deeply, a sign that the conversation was over.

Just then Linda Moore, the woman who had rescued Liam, stepped into the store all dolled up in Chanel cosmetics gear. "Greetings from Coco."

"You got the job!" Sharon exclaimed.

"Thanks to you."

Sharon waved off the credit. "I put in a good word with the counter manager. No big deal. When did you start?"

"Yesterday." Linda made a pained face. "I forgot what a bitch retail can be to your feet and legs. I'm not eighteen anymore."

Mary Payne grabbed a pile of sweaters and started for the back. "You'll get used to it."

Linda shrugged. "I hope I'm not sounding ungrateful, Sharon. I actually stopped by to thank you."

"For a lousy phone call when you saved my child's life? Don't be silly. It was my pleasure."

"Maybe we could get together for a meal break sometime."

"That sounds like fun."

"Well, let's make it soon. I'm hoping this Chanel business will be brief. I took your suggestion and signed with one of the nanny agencies here. Being with Liam just that hort amount of time made me realize how much I miss aking care of children."

"Any family would be lucky to have you."

"Sharon!" Mary Payne shouted. "There's a call for you."

"I have to go, too—a makeover in five minutes. See you ater," Linda said.

As Sharon scanned her brain for a family that might want the services of a gem like Linda Moore, she took the call at the front register, expecting it to be a customer or a sales representative.

"Hi, Sharon. It's Keri Ward."

Fear of what would come next seemed to suffuse every pore in her skin. Suddenly her hands turned alarmingly cold, and beneath her breastbone, her heart began to bang.

"I'd like you to come by the office as soon as possible."

Medical speak for very bad news. Sharon gripped the counter for support. "Don't make me wait, Keri. Tell me now. What's the verdict?" She shut her eyes.

"You have cancer."

Chapter Nineteen

Sharon sat in the dark, waiting for Heath to come home. Part of her wanted to shut him out completely, to turn to Antonio for support, but she couldn't. There was so much history between them—the heartbreak of infertility, the excitement of Katie's adoption, and most recently, the miracle of Liam's birth. No matter how often Heath disappointed her, she still sought him out in times of need. He was, after all, her husband.

But now it was eleven o'clock, and he hadn't bothered to call and tell her that he'd be late. Finally, he showed up, smelling of booze, cigarettes, and sex.

"Hi," he said quietly, guiltily, avoiding eye contact. He was surprised to find her awake. "I took the coaching staff out for a few drinks. Time got away from us."

"We need to talk," Sharon said tonelessly.

"Let me take a quick shower first. I smell like a barfly."

"You smell like a man who's been fucking another woman."

He halted, regarding her as if a stranger. Then he parted his lips to speak.

"Don't say anything," she said calmly, holding up a hand to underscore the words. "You'll only insult me with lies and excuses, and I can't take that right now."

"Jesus Christ, Sharon, I just went out for—"

"Stop," she whispered. "I have to tell you something that's honest and real and frightening. Please don't pollute this moment with your bullshit reasons for staying out late."

A worried look skated across Heath's face, replacing the perplexed one. "Something happened to one of the kids," he said gravely.

"Something's happening to me," Sharon countered. "I have breast cancer." She swallowed hard. It was the first time she'd uttered the words out loud.

Heath stared at her for long, silent seconds, then sank down onto the love seat in their master bedroom, looking scared and full of regret. "How long have you known?"

"Keri Ward called me with the results today. I had a biopsy done earlier this week, the same day you stood me up for our lunch date at home."

He opened his mouth to explain, then seemed to think better of it. The lie wasn't in him, at least not right now. "Didn't your mother . . ."

"Die from it? Yes. So did my grandmother. They were both younger than I am when they passed." Sharon felt emboldened by this sudden new version of herself, the one who dropped all circumlocutions and just spit out the harsh truth.

But Heath seemed weakened by her brutal honesty. She could almost hear the synapses firing in his skull with each announcement. "That was a long time ago," he said, sounding like a man on a mission to convince himself. "There's new research. Nothing's the same."

Sharon turned away, gazing through the French doors

into the dark forest of the trees. She saw movement. A tremor of fear seized her. Was someone watching them? She stepped closer to the balcony and peered down. All she could make out were Liam's brightly colored toys that dotted the yard. Instantly she relaxed, crediting the vision to a trick of the night.

"What about treatment?" Heath was saying, his voice thick.

"My tumor's small. The doctor recommended a lumpectomy followed by radiation therapy."

"That's good, right? It means you can keep your breast."

She spun angrily to face him. "Is that important to you? Because I'm considering having both of them removed."

Heath's expression was a masterpiece of incredulity. He seemed repulsed by the thought. "What are you talking about? You just said that the tumor was small."

"This time. My family history puts me in the high-risk category. The cancer could come back more aggressive, more difficult to treat."

He still looked shocked and dismayed. "But to choose to have a double mastectomy . . . it's so extreme."

"If I don't have breasts, I can't get breast cancer. Besides, what do I need them for? Our sex life? We don't have one. You go outside the marriage for that." She wasn't being fair; she knew that. But she didn't give a damn. Life wasn't fair.

Heath remained stoic, taking the attack like a man, gazing at her as if he expected such hysterics. "We're in this together."

She felt her tough stance weakening. Tears sprang to her eyes. "Since when?" Her voice quivered.

In one fluid movement he stood up and wrapped her in his arms.

Sharon soaked up the comfort, willing herself to forget his betrayal, replaying their happier moments in her mind like scripture. He felt like the savior she wanted him to be, but he smelled like the bastard she knew he was.

The perfume of the woman he'd been with tonight clung to his body like the spray of a skunk. Still, there was no letting go. She needed him, and right now, he was hers for the moment.

It was sad solace, but solace nonetheless.

Chapter Twenty

Deep in the darkness, nestled amongst the trees, Georgette Tucker watched angrily as Heath and Sharon made love. The coach handled the shop girl with such China doll care—slow caresses, gentle thrusts, attentive gazes. There appeared to be an intense connection between them. But she knew it wouldn't last. He'd be fucking Holly Ryan again by lunchtime tomorrow.

She knew their secrets, thanks to a thick and revealing report from Investigative Group International. It had cost her a small fortune but would prove to be the best money she ever spent. Georgette had insisted that the head of I.C.G. oversee the case personally. His past was impressive—Harvard Law School, a long tenure with the Justice Department, even a stint on the Senate Watergate Committee. Most important of all, he gave good dirt.

Heath Driver was a cheat. His infidelity had started the night before his wedding, when he took home a waitress from his bachelor party. He liked his women young and sexually aggressive, he drank too much when the pressure was on, and he could get violent if the right buttons were pushed. Once he'd even been arrested for taking on an obnoxious Infernos fan in an Atlanta bar.

Sharon Driver was a loner. She interacted with her staff and regular customers at Bliss, but she primarily focused on her family. Several years ago, just before becoming pregnant with the little boy, she'd seen a therapist to help her with a bout of depression. I.C.G. had secured copies of the session tapes, and they played like a window into Sharon's soul. Instead of solving her infertility problem, the adoption had become a constant reminder of it. Sharon had tearfully explained her feelings of loss—for the joy of pregnancy, the experience of birth, and the continuity of genetic offspring.

And then there was the guilt over keeping that adoptive status a secret. Sharon had confessed that sometimes she felt no sense of parental entitlement toward the girl and that she even wondered if she had the right to parent her. This had not only fostered a difficulty in setting limits for the child, but created an awkward environment in which to talk about problems openly.

Georgette felt a burning sensation inside her skull. She was breathing with rapid, shallow gasps, staring lasers at the dysfunctional couple in the throes of passion. She hated them. For robbing her of a life with her precious little girl. Savannah deserved better than this facade of a family.

Yes, Savannah. That was the name Georgette had chosen for her fifteen years ago, and when all was said and done, that would be the name she would take for their new life together. Clawing at the bark of a tree with a gloved hand, Georgette recalled the agony of walking out of that Stockton, California, hospital with no baby in her arms. . . .

* * *

Like a fool she'd gone back home to a mother who scoffed at her sadness and sense of loss. "You can't take care of a baby," the drug addict had hissed one day after being fired from yet another dead-end job. "Just like I can't take care of you. I wish I'd had the good sense to give you up for adoption, or better yet, have an abortion. That girl's better off where she is, so quit your moping."

Something had clicked inside Georgette then, the realization that she had never known the joy of being loved, the sense that God had forgotten her. But at least she knew how to love. Savannah had taught her that.

Leaving her mother's house and never looking back had been easy. She had a good used car and a few thousand in cash—everything she needed to set herself up in Los Angeles, a crazy, exciting place.

Jobs had been plentiful, and she skipped from one to the other, always chasing a bigger paycheck. She'd worked in snooty retail shops, enjoyed an extended run as a cocktail waitress, danced in clubs, and modeled for soft-core nude magazines. At every turn, men had used her, but that didn't matter. Being with them had passed the time. Plus, who was she to deserve anything better? After all, she'd allowed Peyton Drake, Dr. Ridgeway, and those nameless, faceless strangers to take Savannah away from her. Whatever disrespect came her way was good medicine.

But finally Georgette had grown tired of the abuse lowlife men threw her way, so when the chance to mingle with a better clientele presented itself—a hostess gig at an exclusive new restaurant called Destiny—she'd signed up right away. Maybe it was time for a classy guy to make her feel like shit. By now seven years had gone by, which made her twenty-five, not an old broad, but in a city obsessed with youth, not the youngest girl around either.

Georgette's gypsy-eyed brunette looks had always stood out among the legions of silicone blondes. Hot new film producer Ed Tucker had thought so as well. He asked for her phone number one night at Destiny, after she'd escorted his party to their table. One dinner date had turned to two, then three, and suddenly he started to announce her as his girlfriend, taking her to premieres and industry functions. It'd been like a fairy tale.

The strangest part of all—no sexual demands. In fact, they'd made love only once, after a studio mogul had watched a rough cut of Ed's latest movie, *Power Trip*, and advised him to prepare speeches for the Golden Globes and the Oscars. His technique had been rather technical, lacking passion and sensuality. A short time later he'd proposed, yet their tepid sex life had never entered her mind. This man was giving her his name. Georgette Herring would disappear forever. Nothing else had mattered.

But life as Georgette Tucker had not been a magic carpet ride. *Power Trip* had bombed with the film critics, failed at the box office, and even ended up on several worst-of-the-year lists. The doors to bigger things in Hollywood that had been held ajar for Ed suddenly slammed shut. He'd taken the rebuke badly, insisting on leaving California for New York. Though he'd continued to make films, he did so underneath the mainstream Hollywood radar.

His thoughts of What Might Have Been had made him increasingly hostile. He'd started to drink heavily and verbally abuse her at every turn. And where once he'd been discreet in his preference for men as lovers, he suddenly began to flaunt his affairs and blame Georgette for turning him into a faggot. . . .

A twig cracked underfoot, breaking off the past with it. The neighbor's dog barked something wild. Georgette waited for the beast to quiet down, then crept over to the other end of the house, making her way to the spot where she could see into Savannah's bedroom window.

The room was dark. Just a few hours before she had

watched her daughter sit on the bed, hug her knees, and stare morosely at the television. It was so obvious that the girl was hurting. But that bitch and bastard, those selfish fuckheads who dared to call themselves parents, had no idea.

"Be patient, Savannah," Georgette whispered into the night. "Mama's going to make it all better soon."

Chapter Twenty-one

Katie stood frozen outside the bedroom door. She'd decided to eavesdrop, worried that the school might have called her parents to inform them about the rumors. What she heard came as a shocking blow, and her mind reeled with the life-changing news.

Her mother was dying.

For the first time, Katie considered her own mortality. It would happen to her, too. Breast cancer was part of her genetic history.

She went back to her room, undressed in the dark, and crawled into bed. Usually she fell asleep watching MTV, but her head felt like a radio station not quite in tune. So much static. Nothing quite clear.

Except, of course, the afternoon at the home of Derek Johnson's cousin. That stayed in her mind with total clarity. The vengeful part of her wanted Derek and Ty arrested for what they'd done, but the fearful part of her won out.

Katie had watched the news and seen the movies. She knew how this would play. They would attack her for the way she dressed, read aloud the racier sections of *Grrl Talk,* and call attention to the fact that she had eagerly jumped into a senior guy's car. Derek and Ty wouldn't be on trial. Katie Driver would. And everyone would think that she had asked for it. No way was she putting herself through that.

She curled into a fetal position, clutching her comforter tightly under her chin. These days it felt better to wear bulky clothes that covered her from head to toe, not showing an inch of skin or a hint of her female curves. Tomorrow she'd take it one step further. If she caked on some creepy makeup to color her face corpse white and outlined her eyes in black, then she'd be like one of those Goths, the scary kids no one wanted to be around. *Yes,* she thought groggily, *that's what I'll do.*

When Katie woke up several hours later, the weight of her world crashed down immediately. Whoever said that things looked different in the morning was a stupid liar. She stood listless under a hot shower, worrying about her mother, wondering about Liam. Who would take care of him?

She stepped out and wiped the steam from the mirror with the palm of her hand, gazing at her naked reflection, trying to imagine herself as a normal teenager, one who looked forward to the future. On impulse, she began a self-examination in search of a lump. How old did you have to be to develop breast cancer?

"What are you doing, Katie?"

She was genuinely startled. Her heart took off.

With arms full of freshly laundered towels, her mother stood in the doorway, looking perplexed.

"How do you know?" Katie asked.

"Know what, honey?"

She stared at her mother for a long time, trying to determine if a dying woman looked different. Then a wave of emotion rolled over Katie as she suddenly realized how much she loved her mother. Maybe she didn't act that way all the time, but she felt it.

And finally she said, "How do you know if you have cancer?"

Sharon stared at Katie with a look of stark, transfixed bewilderment.

"I heard you and Daddy talking last night."

Passing Katie a bath sheet still warm from the dryer, Sharon loaded the towels into the cabinet and braced herself for the storm of inevitable questions. "It's true. I was planning to talk with you about it."

"Are you going to die?"

She turned to stroke Katie's damp hair and give her a solid, ray gun gaze. "No, sweetheart. I have the benefit of early detection. It's treatable."

"This means I'll get breast cancer, too, doesn't it?"

"No—"

"But you've got it, and your mother had it, and her mother had it," Katie cut in, the fear on her face total.

The realization that Katie was worried about a genetic history that didn't belong to her hit Sharon like a clap of thunder. In that moment, she decided to tell Katie the truth about her birth. There was no other way. It would be unthinkable to ignore this and allow Katie's mortal thoughts to go on plaguing her.

"Before you'll even have to begin worrying about your health, there'll be a cure. I really believe that. Don't let this upset you. I'm going to be just fine."

"I could use the Internet to do research on new treatments," Katie said. "Maybe there's something new that your doctor doesn't know about."

The offer touched Sharon deeply. Maybe this horrible turn of events would bring her closer to her daughter. If so, at least she could count one silver lining in the ordeal.

"Thanks, honey. That would be very helpful." She clapped her hands. "Now get dressed and come downstairs for breakfast. You need to fuel up for your soccer game this afternoon."

"I'm not playing anymore. I quit."

For a moment, Sharon couldn't believe it. The 1999 Women's World Cup had been a defining moment for Katie. A poster of Mia Hamm was plastered on the wall of her room. "When did this happen?"

Katie gave a diffident shrug. "A few days ago." Her face darkened with teenage scorn. "Like it's a big deal. Besides, Daddy only came to one game."

"Is that the only reason why you play? So your father will come watch you?"

The question seemed to trip Katie. "No."

"Sharon!" It was Heath, calling from the doorway, sounding rushed and annoyed. "Can you watch Liam now?"

"This is an important decision. We should talk about it." She left Katie to get ready for school and happily took possession of Liam, lifting him into her arms, loving the smell of him. There was nothing sweeter. "Did you know that Katie quit the soccer team?"

Distracted, Heath started down the stairs. "No, I didn't."

Sharon frowned, wondering if he'd even heard what she just asked. Following him into the kitchen, she said, "This is alarming."

"Babe," Heath began impatiently, "Katie's a teenager. One minute she's into something, the next minute she's not. That's what teenagers do." He snatched a Granny Smith apple from the fruit bowl.

Sharon fumed at his sexist words and patronizing tone. "If this were your teenage *son* quitting a sports team, you'd be upstairs right now wanting to know why."

"What are you trying to say?"

Briefly, she closed her eyes, as if in search of strength.

"I'm saying that Katie is disturbed about something. She needs more of our attention. She—"

"I have to go, Sharon. There's a team of professional athletes I need to worry about right now. We can take this up later." He leaned in to spark her cheek with a kiss and walked out the door.

"Bye, Daddy," Liam said sadly. But Heath was already gone.

Several minutes later Katie entered the kitchen, and the sight of her was like an assault. Her dark hair was greased down and combed to hang in her eyes, which were circled in black like a raccoon's. Pasty white makeup gave her a look of death, almost demonic, not unlike shock rocker Marilyn Manson. From head to toe, her body was covered in shapeless black garments.

It was a complete—and frightening—metamorphosis. This wasn't her daughter, Katie, but a creature from *Night of the Living Dead.* Sharon felt a moment's disbelief. "Go pick up your toys in the playroom, honey," she managed to tell Liam calmly.

"Katie looks scary," he said, running out.

Sharon struggled for the right words. "Why are you dressed like this?"

"Because I want people to leave me alone."

"What people?"

Katie didn't answer.

It pained Sharon to see Katie made up like some freak. She saw kids like this in the school parking lot, in malls, sometimes on the news. Never once did she think her own child might fall into it. Sharon treaded carefully, not wanting to push Katie further away. "Dressing like this could bring you even more attention. Have you thought about that?"

"People stay away from the Goths at school because they're afraid of getting killed."

Sharon was shocked by her fifteen-year-old's reasoning. "But you would never hurt anybody."

Katie's black-painted lips thinned into an angry line. "Never say never."

Chapter Twenty-two

Patsy was holding calls, the office door was locked, and Iolly Ryan was bent over the couch, urging him on with ıer dirty talk. She made noises like a porn star, and he oved it.

In a couple minutes it was over, though guilt diluted he pleasure of his orgasm because Heath's mind was elsewhere, thinking about how he'd rushed out of the house, lismissing Sharon, ignoring Liam. What an asshole he was.

But getting his hands on this hot little Australian import s often as possible had become an instant addiction. He opped her on the ass, slipped off the condom, and pulled ıp his pants. "I've got some calls to make. Will I see you onight?"

"Maybe, maybe not," Holly replied coyly.

"I'll come by right after practice, about seven o'clock. Be naked and ready. I won't have much time. There's some rouble at home, so I should eat with my family tonight."

Holly rolled her eyes. "Oh, how impressive. You better get started on that speech for father of the year." She

snatched a compact from her tiny purse and proceede
to check her face. "Did you read the script yet?"

He grinned, thinking back to their first meeting and th
way she'd roped him in with her wide-eyed, poor-pitifu
me stare. What a con artist. One hour and two drinks late
he saw her for the barracuda she was. But the fact tha
they were both so shamelessly honest about what the
wanted from each other turned him on. He got minc
blowing sex; she got tips on nuance for her role in a sh
movie.

Tossing a glance to the package on the corner of hi
desk, he said, "I made some notes for you."

Holly went straight for it, her eyes big, as if the on
hundred twenty pages fastened together with butterfly clip
had a chance at being the next *Citizen Kane.*

At first Heath had harbored concern about *Score,* th
ax-grinding script penned by an assistant coach he'd fire
a few years ago. An early draft had concentrated more o
bashing him and the Infernos than on telling a story. Bu
this shooting version had obviously been given the ful
Hollywood treatment.

Now *Score* read as if everyone from the studio head t
the caterer had put a hand in for the rewrite. It was banal
melodramatic, and unrealistic. Critics would savage it. H
could only find two positive elements in the whole movie—
Holly Ryan's torrid sex scene and Holly Ryan's nud
shower scene. Still, he gave her some feedback on the role
if only to make her feel like the real actress she wasn't.

Holly ignored Heath's hint to scram in favor of parkin
her sweet ass on the couch and leafing through his scrip
notes.

Heath didn't mind her hanging around. After all, sh
was easy on the eyes and might be good for a blow jo
before lunch. He frowned as he mulled over the events a
home, realizing that this business about Katie quitting th
soccer team was eating at him more than he thought i

would. On impulse, he picked up the phone and called Kit Jamison.

"How's my friend the *Adrenaline* junkie?" he teased her.

"Wondering who to put my wager on for Atlanta and Philadelphia."

"The Infernos will kick ass and win by fourteen points."

"I never trust the word of a cocky coach."

"Since when?"

"Since I was old enough to understand my own father's bullshit."

Heath laughed. He always enjoyed their tit-for-tat banter. If Kit wasn't a lesbian, she would be the perfect woman. "I'm calling to ask a favor. You've met my daughter, Katie, haven't you?"

"Yeah, she's hung out with me at the games a few times. Beautiful girl. Smart, too."

"Thanks. She just quit the soccer team at school."

"Bummer."

"Would you mind talking to her, seeing if you can find out what's going on in her head? Chances are she'll open up to any adult who's not one of her parents."

"Is it that bad?"

"She's fifteen."

"It's that bad," Kit agreed. "Sure, I'll take her out for hamburger or something."

Heath was startled by a jangling of the knob and a loud knock. "You're a great lady. Thanks, Kit," he said quickly, hanging up to go unlock the door.

The sight of Sharon on the other side stunned him into silence. She never showed up unannounced at the training camp. But this morning she had. And here Heath was, his tie still loose, his dress shirt unbuttoned to his breastbone. In the corner, Holly radiated intimate nonchalance, slung back on the couch in a skirt up to there, looking like a girl who had all the time in the world.

Oh, shit, Heath cursed silently.

* * *

Sharon cut a polar glance to the slut on the couch. " need to talk with my husband, and it looks like your wor is done here. Do you mind?"

The young woman—not a day past twenty-five—glov ered as she stood up.

Self-consciously, Sharon ran her fingers through he hair. This girl cornered the market on perfection– supermodel face, centerfold breasts, and legs that went o forever.

Suddenly it dawned on Sharon that Casting Centra would've had no trouble booking her in the role of th cheated-on housewife. Save for mascara and a quick swip of lip gloss, she wore no makeup, and the T-shirt she ha on was stained with remnants of her toddler's breakfas Add to that a pair of discount-store sweatpants so ill-fittin that even Cindy Crawford would appear bloated in them

But the way she looked this morning had never entere her mind. After seeing Katie's bizarre appearance an hearing her detached hints about violence, Sharon ha ushered Liam to school and ignored the speed limit a the way to Stone Mountain Ranch, the Infernos's trainin camp.

No one would mistake Heath for Braveheart. As his ne girlfriend made her way toward the only exit, he merel watched the floor.

"I'll see you tonight," she purred, a Parthian partin shot meant more for Heath's wife than for Heath himsel In her wake she left a trail of expensive perfume.

Sharon recognized the fragrance. It was called Envy *How appropriate.*

"It's not what you think," he started to explain. "She' an actress in a movie about pro football that's being sho here. I was just—"

"Reading lines with her? Try again, Heath. I have cance

in my breast, not my brain." She dared him to meet her gaze.

He continued staring down.

"I thought we reconnected last night. Or was that just a sympathy fuck?"

He looked up now, and there was genuine hurt in his eyes.

Sharon was happy to see it. She was sick of wearing that expression all by herself. "Why do I still want to be with you?" Touching her diseased breast, she said, "Is it because I've got cancer? Because I'm about to turn forty-five and I'm scared to death of approaching fifty and suddenly being alone?" Finally, she realized that her voice was rising with each rhetorical question. Could Patsy hear her in the outer office? Deciding that she didn't give a damn, Sharon thundered on with, "Is it because I've got twenty-two years invested in this joke of a marriage and I'm too blind to know when it's time to pack it in?"

"It's not a joke," Heath said quietly. "You know that I love you."

"Oh, you love me." Her tone mocked him. "I should feel lucky, I guess. Imagine how things might be if you felt anything less than that." She paused a beat. "What's her name?"

"Don't do this, Sharon."

"No, I think I should know the name of the woman my husband is fucking this week. Are you going to answer my question, or am I going to have to ask Patsy?"

Heath simply watched her, his face a masterpiece of misery. "Holly," he said finally.

"Holly," she repeated softly. "I hope you use protection with *Holly*. I don't need whatever she's carrying. I've got enough health problems. Wouldn't you agree?"

He ran a hand over his chin and down his neck, smoothing the stubble of his two-day beard growth. "She doesn't mean anything to me."

Sharon clucked. "And therein lies the problem, Heath. She *does* mean something to *me.*" She crossed over to the window, watched the players in action for a moment, then spun around to lean against the sill. "But I didn't come here to talk about Holly. Believe it or not, there are more important issues—our daughter, for example. She's in trouble."

"I called Kit Jamison," Heath put in quickly. "She's going to take Katie out for a burger and talk to her about this decision to quit the soccer team."

Sharon buried her face in her hands, shaking her head. Heath didn't have a clue. Only once did she break down in tears as she told him everything that she knew about Katie's sudden affinity for the Goth look and her newfound fear of breast cancer.

"Jesus Christ," Heath whispered gravely.

Sharon drew in a deep breath. "We have to tell her the truth about the adoption. She's worried about a genetic history that's not hers, and I don't know anything about her birth heritage. All these years I've been trying to pretend that the adoption never took place." She hit the wall with the bottom of her fist. "I was so selfish. I was so insecure. I should've listened to you, Heath. You've wanted to tell her for years. I remember when you told me that the truth was not something we could block with a TRESPASSING sign, that it was Katie's right to know. That visual image has always stuck with me. You had better instincts about this."

She stepped over to the credenza and picked up a framed photograph of Katie. "What color are her father's eyes? Does her mother have a bad temper? Is there a history of heart disease in her gene pool? I don't have the answers to any of these questions." She turned to her husband, seeking—and needing—his support.

"It's okay, Sharon. We'll talk to her together. And when it's time to seek out those answers, we'll do it as a family."

Instantly, Sharon felt the heat of her anger begin to cool. It never took much for her to put Heath back on the road toward forgiveness. And today was no different. "I'll contact Peyton Drake and Dr. Ridgeway in California. Their records should help us get started. Katie will have so many questions."

"Katie can handle this," Heath said confidently. "I know she can."

Sharon reached into the side pocket of her sweatpants, pulled out the letter from Georgette Tucker, and, reluctantly, handed it to her husband. "There's more."

Chapter Twenty-three

"You're like a lot of my patients," Keri Ward was saying. "With the kids and the career and the successful husband, you don't have time for breast cancer. But *your* health has to come first now."

Sharon nodded stoically.

"I suggest that you look into the possibility of hiring some help, perhaps a day nanny."

Sharon experienced a tremor of alarm. Would she not be able to take care of her own children?

"Radiation treatment will require daily visits to the hospital for at least six weeks. You'll likely experience fatigue, weight loss, and stiffness in your back and right arm. Are you prepared to cut way back on your time at Bliss?"

"No," Sharon answered quickly, amazed that such an idea would even come up. "I couldn't leave the store for that long."

"Then get some help at home. How women structure their lives after receiving this kind of diagnosis is very important. It plays directly into their recovery success.

You're blessed with a fortunate financial position. Hiring someone won't be a problem. Take advantage of that."

Sharon nodded her agreement, though she hated the idea of a stranger caring for Liam. Like a bolt from the blue, Linda Moore came to mind. Yes! She would be the ideal day nanny. Liam had responded to her right away, and, Sharon reasoned, having someone there when Katie arrived home from school would be a comfort, especially now.

"In the event our lab tests reveal something unexpected, this treatment plan will be revisited. But I don't anticipate any surprises."

"I don't understand," Sharon said, feeling a sudden uptick of her pulse.

Keri's thin fingers formed a tent. "If we discover cancer cells in the lymph nodes, the prognosis changes."

"Will you be able to tell right away?"

"After surgery, there's usually a wait for those test results. Most of my patients consider that their worst time. Prepare yourself for it."

Even with the distraction of a whirlwind day, Sharon missed Antonio like a drug. She had ushered Liam to school, dashed to Stone Mountain Ranch to meet with Heath, raced to Keri Ward's office . . . and still found the time to mourn the loss of their standing espresso appointment.

So here she was, in the middle of the afternoon, seated at a tiny table in java.com with the man who'd instantly become a stabilizing force in her life. It was with no reluctance that she told him about almost everything—her upcoming surgery and radiation treatment, Heath's latest affair, and Katie's disturbing behavior. The adoption issue she kept to herself. After all, Katie didn't even know yet. To tell someone outside the family would be unconscionable.

"What worries you the most?" Antonio asked.

The question jarred her. They'd been sitting in companionable silence for several moments. When Sharon thought about it, the answer that bubbled to the surface embarrassed her. "I'd rather not say."

"Come on," he prodded gently. "There's something on your mind. And I hereby grant you full immunity." He flashed her a you-can-trust-me grin, his uncannily white teeth gleaming.

She stared at him. What a fantastic smile he had.

"It's just between us," he whispered, pulling at her desire to confide.

"I worry about meeting someone who will want me. Heath has slept around for so long. I've tried to compartmentalize that, treat it like *his* weakness, *his* character flaw, but it's become my own cross to bear. I've realized that each time he strays I feel less desirable, not just to him but to any man. And on top of all that, I now have to factor in breast cancer and permanent scarring from my surgery. It's . . ." Sharon trailed off, feeling exposed.

Antonio's gaze was locked onto hers, the sincerity in his eyes like a safety net. "Go on."

She no longer felt the least bit awkward or repressed, but her eyes were misty with emotion. "I'll survive the cancer. I believe that now. But I don't think my marriage will make it. Whatever Heath does to see me through this period . . . it just won't be enough. I know that. I'll be left wanting more from him. Not exactly a new turn of events." She laughed a little and killed a tear with her knuckle. "I'm angry, and I'm so sick of being angry, Antonio. That's become a cancer all its own. It's no longer enough to stay in this for the kids, you know? I look at Katie and see how messed up she is. My daughter's smart. She knows what goes on. I used to think that Liam was too young to sense all of this, but I'm not sure of that anymore. He says things, my two-year-old angel, that make me want to cry. Sometimes I think he knows more than all of us."

Sharon halted, wondering if she'd said too much. She curled her fingers around the java.com cup. The espresso was still warm, begging to be drunk. "I must sound like a fool."

Antonio tipped his head to one side and reached out to take her hand. "Not a chance. You're my buddy, and my buddy's no fool."

She let out a deep, contented sigh. A feeling of coziness spiraled over her. He was a flamethrower, his touch like fire, and it was the safest feeling she'd known in a long time. She closed her eyes, as if to seal this moment in, the warmth it provided as comforting as sunshine on a spring morning. To have a strong shoulder to cry on, to have a friendly face to open up to—it felt so good.

"It's been years since I've had a close friend, Antonio. If I lean on you too much, please tell me. The last thing I want to do is drive you away."

"Wild horses couldn't."

And Sharon believed him.

Chapter Twenty-four

Kit Jamison missed her son.

Watching a flock of parents pick up their kids at Riverside Central High, she wondered if she would ever see Cameron again. Her need to mother was so acute that she'd jumped on Heath's request to talk to Katie the same day that he'd tendered it.

No, it couldn't be, Kit thought to herself, watching a teenager similar in size and features to Katie stalk out of the school, heading for the bus.

"Dead girl walking!" someone in the crowd shouted.

A couple of jock types were in hot pursuit of this Goth girl, led by a rich-looking white guy who posed a tough stance. Kit groaned. Suburban kids with serious gangbanger fantasies were so annoying.

"I don't care if you dress up like a vampire, baby, as long as you suck what I want you to suck," he taunted.

His entourage cracked up with macho bursts from the gullet.

The accosted girl attempted to move around them, but

the leader blocked her path. "Come on over to my house, Katie."

Now certain that this was indeed Heath's daughter, Kit moved fast to intercede. "She's not interested, creep. Start moving. *Now.*"

Katie made instant eye contact with Kit, then, as if considering the implications of her visit, looked away.

"Who's this bitch?" He directed the question to his posse.

"Kit Jamison. Who are you, punk?"

He cocked his head and bellowed, "Thomas Prewitt," as if the name would actually mean something to her.

The raw arrogance was infuriating. She wanted to slug this bastard.

"Hey," he laughed, cupping his crotch with an ink-smudged hand, "I got nothing against the elderly. A hole's a hole. Why don't you come over, too?"

Kit fought hard to reign in the anger. It amazed her that she'd once seriously considered going into teaching. With mutants like these she'd last one day in the classroom.

"I'm not going home with you, sport," Kit began in a voice belying her true fury. "I'm going to do you one better and tell you your future, so pay attention." The tone she adopted next was one of educator to dense pupil. "If you're as stupid as you look and sound, then your SAT scores will only get the attention of junior colleges. But I'm betting your father is an accomplished man, so you'll probably snake your way into a respectable university, where you'll pledge the fraternity of your choice. Being the idiot that you are, you'll lean back in a stolen barber chair at a postgame fraternity house party one night and proceed to funnel enough beer to cause a normal person death by acute alcohol poisoning. But you're not normal. You're an extraordinarily obnoxious animal, so you will survive the beer binge and proceed to get behind the wheel of the late model SUV that your father paid for, wrap it around a telephone pole, spend a night in jail, and get charged with your first DUI. College requires more discipline than you're capable of, and after two years of grade reports so embarrassing that people begin to wonder if you sustained brain damage in the accident, your family will cut you off financially in an effort to force you to behave like a responsible adult. This is called tough love. Too late to make a difference, if you ask me, but it's a start. Then you'll look around and realize that your high school buddies have moved on and that most of your frat brothers are able to drink themselves into oblivion *and* pass classes. And there you will be—flunked out of school, stripped of your allowance . . . and delivering pizzas."

Kit rubbed her temples with her fingertips, feigning deep concentration. "I can only see you to age thirty, Thomas. But you're still delivering pizzas. And just think, if you'd treated Katie with the respect she deserves, things might've turned out differently. It's all about karma."

Thomas stared back, dumbfounded.

Katie cracked a smile.

Kit reached for her hand. "I'm starving. How about you?"

They tumbled into Kit's Jeep Cherokee and headed for Johnny Rockets to fuel up on cheeseburgers, fries, and chocolate malts.

Katie's mood seemed to have been lightened by Kit's haranguing of Thomas Prewitt, but she was still unusually quiet. Finally, the girl said, "The way you shut him up back there was cool."

"Does that guy give you trouble on a regular basis?"

Katie didn't answer.

"You don't have to put up with that. He could get suspended, maybe expelled." She paused a beat. "Is this why you quit the soccer team?"

Katie shrugged. "I just want to disappear. You know, fade into the background and be by myself."

"Don't take this the wrong way," Kit ventured carefully, "but dressing like that doesn't make you the Invisible Girl. When we walked in here, you got a double take from almost everyone in this restaurant."

Katie drew back defensively. "You don't care about me. I bet you're just here because my father sent you. What's he doing now—screwing a cheerleader?"

Kit regarded the teenager carefully. If Heath was aware of the depth of his daughter's problems, he certainly hadn't warned her. Quitting the soccer team was barely a blip on this girl's trouble screen. "I'm here because I want to be, Katie. I don't work for your father. What do I look like, the waterboy?"

Katie relaxed her adolescent porcupine quills, almost cracking a smile.

"Heath is a friend. I came to you as one, but if you want me to get lost, just say so."

"Some stuff is going on that I don't want to talk about."

"That's cool," Kit said easily. "I can respect that."

Katie gave Kit a long stare, as if determining her trustworthiness before moving forward. "Sometimes it's hard to know how to act. I used to flirt a lot and wear clothes that were tight and sexy like the women in the magazines and on MTV. When I get a boyfriend, I don't want him to hook up with other girls like my dad does. That's what my mom puts up with. I don't want to be like her."

Kit sipped the last of her malt, worried that she was way out of her league. Katie needed a licensed therapist, not a sports-radio broadcaster. "What made you stop dressing like that?"

Katie dropped her gaze to inspect her black fingernails. "Have you ever had a day that changes everything?"

Kit nodded somberly. Her personal waterloo was the day she realized that Leslie, her lover, the biological mother of their son, had taken Cameron into hiding. "I know how that feels. It's like your life is suddenly divided into the way you used to feel before that day and the way you now feel after it."

"Yeah," Katie agreed. She reached out to dip the last fry into a pool of ketchup, soiling the sleeve of her black shirt in the process. "Shit." As she cleaned up the damage with a napkin, her sleeve pushed up, revealing the skin on her forearm.

Kit took in a fast breath. She knew those marks. The sight sent her mind back to her own troubled youth—the cruelty of her peers, the confusion about her sexuality, the yearning for relief. "What happened to your arm?"

Katie's body tensed. "My cat scratched me."

Kit nodded sadly. That had been her old lie.

Chapter Twenty-five

"Cossar, Wexler, and Green," the polished, female voice said.

"Peyton Drake, please."

A pregnant pause, followed by the awkward, "Um . . . Mr. Drake is no longer with us."

Sharon cursed silently. She didn't have time to track down this man. After fifteen years, he could be anywhere in the country. "Do you have a number where he can be reached? I'm a former client."

"Mr. Drake is no longer with us."

Sharon sighed impatiently. "I understand that but—"

"He's dead," the receptionist blurted.

"Oh . . . I-I'm sorry." Sharon thought back to the two days she and Heath had spent in Stockton, California. Peyton had been barely ten years out of law school, same for Dr. Ridgeway, the obstetrician. She remembered thinking how young and smug they were. "When did this happen?"

"A month ago. He was murdered. Don't you read the newspaper or watch the news?"

"I'm calling from Atlanta," Sharon explained distantly. "Is there someone else I can talk to, someone who can access his client records?"

"Tom Wexler took most of Peyton's cases. Hold on."

A moment later. "This is Tom Wexler."

"Mr. Wexler, my name is Sharon Driver. I'm very sorry to hear about Peyton Drake."

"Thank you. What can I do for you?"

"Peyton handled an adoption case for us fifteen years ago. I need as much information from that client file as possible. It concerns a delicate medical matter."

"That would've been nineteen . . ."

"Eighty-six," Sharon finished. "Heath and Sharon Driver." She glanced down at the letter from Georgette Tucker in her hands. "The birth mother was Georgette Herring."

He put her on hold for what seemed like forever, forcing her to think back on the event. She had been so desperate, after all the fruitless attempts at natural conception, after all the failed infertility treatments. And then Heath had been passed a tip from a colleague in Los Angeles about Peyton Drake, the Sacramento-based lawyer who—for the right price—could get you the baby of your dreams. It had been a quid pro quo operation. He represented the parents; he represented the young mothers, too.

Sharon allowed the wave of revulsion and shame to pass over her. She knew how sleazy it was, even back then she had known. But the joy of holding a sweet baby in her arms, her naked need to be a mother, the amended birth certificate that would tell the world that Katie was hers and hers alone, had superseded all the second thoughts. And nothing else had mattered. Until now.

Tom Wexler was back on the line. "There's nothing here. Sounds like that case was from the private practice he ran before the firm got started. Those records were probably at his home office."

"Wait," Sharon broke in, hearing the desire to end the call in the partner's voice. "The hospital was St. Joseph's in Stockton. A Dr. Ridgeway delivered the baby. Any idea if he's still in the area?"

There was something eerie about the silence that followed.

"Mr. Wexler?"

"I'm here," he said tonelessly. "But I'm afraid luck is not on your side, Mrs. Driver. Dr. Ridgeway is dead, too."

Chapter Twenty-six

Sharon's mind was in tumult all the way to Phipps Plaza. She could scarcely believe it. Peyton Drake and Dr. Ridgeway had been murdered within days of each other Around the same time that she had received the letter from Georgette Tucker. The coincidence left her cold.

So deep in thought, she missed a stop sign in the parking lot and nearly collided with a Mercedes. Braking just in time, she stalled a moment to collect herself, then took the next available space. *Get a grip,* she told herself.

Seconds after Sharon approached the Chanel cosmetics counter at Saks Fifth Avenue, Linda Moore announced to her coworker that she was taking a break. And off they went.

"I'm so happy you called," Linda said. "I was bored out of my mind."

They headed for the food court and settled on pizza, each going for a slice of plain cheese with a Diet Coke. Sharon prattled on about a number of insignificant things until they finished eating, then got down to business. "I think I have a temporary solution for your career slump, assuming that you're interested."

The look on Linda's face indicated that she was up for anything that didn't include selling lipstick and night cream. "I'll take it."

Sharon smiled. "You don't even know what it is!"

"No offense," Linda began cautiously, "but retail sucks."

"None taken, but trust me, if you owned the place, your perspective would change."

"Maybe. So what's your solution?"

"Temporary solution."

"How temporary?"

"A few months."

Linda sighed relief. "That's like dog years in a job like this. What would I be doing?"

"Working for me . . . our family . . . as a day nanny."

Linda beamed instantly. "Oh, I would love it! Liam is such a doll. When can I start?"

"I have a fifteen-year-old, too, who needs a different kind of care, more like policing."

"Sounds like me at fifteen."

"There's so much going on in our household," Sharon said. "In fact, we have a family meeting tonight that I'll fill you in on later." She took a final sip of soda, her body humming with nervous energy at the thought of telling Katie about the adoption. "If I gave you the details now, you wouldn't take the job." She laughed a little.

"Why the sudden need for help at home? Are you going to start putting in more time at Bliss?"

Sharon shook her head. "Doctor's orders." And then she told Linda about the breast cancer, her morning radiation treatments, and her need to have someone at home in the afternoon while she tended to matters at Bliss.

Linda regarded her with amazement. "You're so calm about this."

"It's all an act. My kids need me, so I only allow myself to freak out between midnight and five o'clock in the morning."

"What about your husband, Sharon? You don't talk about him much."

"Things are strained between us . . . but he's dedicated to the kids."

"I want to help you," Linda said matter of factly. "I'll start right away. Make me an offer."

"Six hundred a week."

"How about tomorrow?"

"Tomorrow," Sharon repeated, surprised by the sudden response. Granted, she had to do a reference check, but that was just a formality. Deep down, she knew that Linda Moore was the perfect choice.

Chapter Twenty-seven

Katie washed off her ghoulish makeup, closed the blinds, cranked up the radio, and meditated in the throbbing darkness. She tried to identify at least one part of her life that was going right . . . and couldn't.

Grrl Talk was a bust. Everyone at Riverview Central High knew she was behind the zine now, and without the excitement of mystery, she'd lost interest in putting it out.

Derek Johnson wasn't a hot senior guy; he was a cruel, perverted creep who'd ruined her reputation. The boys at school were taunting her; the girls were shunning her. Even Mamiko had pulled away. Angel was loyal but kept pressing for details. Why couldn't she understand that Katie didn't want to talk about it, that she wanted to pretend like that horrible day never happened?

The telephone jangled.

She peered at the caller-ID screen, read Angel's name, and made no move to pick up. It would roll over to voice mail, but her friend wouldn't leave a message. Angel never left messages. She always called back—in five-minute intervals.

Katie's stomach fluttered. Her grades were slipping like never before, but the initiative to crack a book just wasn't there. All the stress had brought on a feeling of constant sickness. And now there was her mother's health to worry about. She closed her eyes, wishing she were someone else.

Kit Jamison crept into her mind. The way Kit had dealt with Thomas Prewitt was so cool. Katie wished she could handle her enemies like that, too.

The telephone buzzed again.

Groaning, Katie picked up. "Hi, Angel."

"Are you mad at me?"

Katie smiled to herself. It was just like Angel to internalize a personal crisis that had nothing to do with her. "It's not you. I've just got a lot going on."

"Like going Goth and not telling me?"

"It was an experiment," Katie said, secretly admitting that her mother and Kit were right—the look attracted more attention than it deflected.

"Everybody's talking about how that lady went off on Thomas Prewitt. I told people to bring lots of pizza coupons to school tomorrow. We're going to stuff them in his locker and call his cell phone all day to complain that our pizza hasn't arrived yet."

Katie laughed in spite of her dark mood. "He deserves it."

"I know that Mamiko's being a real bitch—"

"I don't want to get into it, Angel," Katie said. "I have to go. I'll see you tomorrow."

There was a soft rap on the door just as the phone hit the cradle. Her mother and father flicked on the light and stepped inside.

Katie's gaze zeroed in on their hands, the areas around their pockets, searching for the hot-pink pages of *Grrl Talk*. If they didn't know about her zine, then they certainly knew about the afternoon with Derek Johnson. Why else would her parents insist on showing up here *together?* They looked serious as hell. Even worse, she could tell they were on the same side, and that was almost never the case.

Dad twisted down the stereo volume, phasing out Third Eye Blind while Mom perched herself on the end of the bed to say, "Katie, there's something very important that we have to talk about."

It suddenly occurred to her that they appeared more nervous than she was. Could they be getting a divorce? She knew a girl at school who said it was great for parents to divorce when you were fifteen because they usually felt so guilty about it that a new car on your sixteenth birthday was a sure thing.

"This is something we should've been open about a long time ago," her mother began, a slight tremor in her voice.

Dad put his arm around Mom, a gesture that looked forced and caused her to stiffen.

Katie sat up, mindful of her posture. Usually she barely took notice of either parent talking, but this time they had her full attention.

Sharon didn't know where to start. Most adoptive parents explained the finer points to their children as soon as they were old enough to understand. Yet here she was, laying it on a fifteen-year-old the day after a cancer announcement.

The guilty, almost fearful expression on Katie's face pulled at Sharon's heart. "Relax, honey," she said soothingly, "you're not in any kind of trouble."

"So what's going on?" Katie asked.

Sharon looked to Heath, then back to their daughter. "I guess there's no way to say this other than to just come out with it. We've debated the issue of telling you for years, but yesterday, when you expressed your fears about breas cancer, something clicked. I knew that it was time."

"Time for what?"

"To tell you about . . . your adoption."

"I'm . . . adopted?" Katie stammered. She was thunder struck. "I don't understand. You're not my real parents?'

The words stung. Speechless, Sharon turned to Heath who looked equally hurt.

"Of course we're your real parents, Katie," he said, "jus not your biological ones."

"But you can have children. You had Liam."

"We adopted you after a series of failed infertility treat ments. We wanted a baby . . . we wanted *you* . . . so badly. Years later, when we discovered that I was pregnant with Liam, it came as a complete shock."

"He looks like you," Katie said flatly. "I've always noticed that. I've always felt the way you respond to it."

"You don't have our genes like Liam, Katie," Heath put in. "You don't have our hair, our noses, or our eyes. But you have our hearts, and that's all that really matters."

Katie rolled her eyes. "Oh, please. I hope you come up with better lines than that when you're cruising the cheerleaders."

Sharon watched the shame color Heath's face. It was almost scarlet. She felt an odd impulse to defend him. "What your father said is true. It's how we feel. Don't disregard that."

"Why not?" Katie challenged hotly. "*You* disregarded the truth for fifteen years."

"We had our reasons for not telling you," Heath said. "Maybe they weren't the right ones, but we based our decision on how much we love you."

"I was scared, Katie," Sharon said. "I've read about adopted children growing up with a sadness that never goes away. I've heard about the kids who seek reunions with their birth parents only to be rejected."

"Not all reunions are that way," Katie argued.

"That's true. I was selfish. I wanted you to be ours com-letely and not have to worry about losing you to someone i the future."

"What do you know about my real mother?"

"Your real mother is sitting in this room," Heath said.

Sharon smiled and felt her eyes begin to tear. "Your irth mother was eighteen and unwed. We took you home om the hospital the day after you were born. You were beautiful . . . and such a good baby."

"I'll never forget seeing the IT'S A GIRL sticker on your assinet in the hospital nursery," Heath put in. "Our last ame was printed neatly under it. That's when I realized ou were ours. I talked to you through the glass over and ver again, saying, 'You're my little girl.' "

Katie stared back coldly. "What was my birth mother's st name?"

Sharon tensed. "Her name was Georgette Herring."

"Give yourself some time to process this," Heath said. When you're ready to find out more, we can do that ogether . . . as a family."

"Yeah," Katie scoffed. "We're so close that way."

"We're not perfect," Sharon said, threading her fingers hrough Heath's in a show of solidarity. "We have prob-ems. Every couple does. Every family does. But we're here o support you. If anything is bothering you—anything at ll—please come to us."

Katie stood up and folded her arms tightly, staring down t the carpet. "I've got homework to finish. Do you mind?"

Instinctively, Sharon decided it was better to take Katie's ead and drop the issue. There would be easier, more asual times to touch on it again. Heath was reluctant to eave, but she quietly urged him out of the room with her. They headed downstairs to the kitchen, where he grabbed a beer and she started some water for tea.

"I thought she'd ask more questions," he said. "I don like the way she's withdrawing from us."

"Katie's a fifteen-year-old girl, and she's going to reje what she needs the most, especially if that's being offere by her parents. I feel good about it. I think it went reasor ably well." She reached out to stroke his forearm. "Th things you said were sweet."

Heath pulled her in for an embrace, holding her tightl rocking her from side to side. "I'm sorry, Sharon. I'm sorr for the way I am. I feel like I've let my girls down."

She closed her eyes and just accepted the comfort h was offering. His words communicated the apology, bu not the promise to change. Heath would disappoint then again. She knew that.

And so did he.

Katie stared at the algebra homework without actuall seeing it. Why had she been given up for adoption? Wa she the progeny of some wild, passionate forbidden love Who did she look like?

Chills ran down her arms, and her stomach did a flip The part of the story that stuck with her was the fact tha for fifteen years, her birth mother had never tried to locat her. Did she even remember having her?

Abandoned as a baby.

Unable to relate to her parents.

Abused by guys.

Taunted by her peers.

Everything added up to the way she felt—unwanted alienated, and unreal. There was only one way to mak these feelings disappear. She had done it once before— after the incident with Derek and his cousin. The act ha provided only temporary relief, but for that short time, i had done the job of chasing away the pain.

Katie pushed her books and papers aside to reach int

er nightstand for the razor blade and towel she kept idden under a small stack of magazines. Then she pushed ack her sleeve and with her fingertips, swept over the nooth, unblemished skin surface of her arm.

She began to cut. It hurt. She cut a little deeper. It hurt ıore. But when the bleeding started, she felt the relief. eeing the blood flow down her arm proved that she was eal, and slowly, the pain inside subsided in a way that made ıe pain outside bearable. Once the bleeding stopped, she overed the new wound with a bandage and cried herself sleep.

At six o'clock the radio blasted her awake. Teenagers ere calling in to the station with shout-outs to their iends. They sounded so happy and carefree. What was ıeir secret?

She showered, carefully treated her cuts with antibiotic intment and new bandages, and dressed quickly in hiking oots, baggy jeans, and a bulky sweatshirt.

Halfway down the stairs she could smell French toast nd bacon wafting from the kitchen—obviously, her moth-r's way of overcompensating for last night's bombshell. ut the mere thought of eating made her feel sick.

Liam was already seated at the breakfast table, happily unking his sweet toast into a sweeter pool of syrup. "This good, Mommy."

"It's Katie's favorite," her mother said, flashing a smile.

"Katie's favorite," Liam echoed.

"Sit down, honey. A new batch is coming right up."

"I'm not hungry," Katie snapped. "And you don't have o go to all this trouble to prove that you love me. God, hat's so phony!"

Her mother seemed to be fighting against another esponse when she said, "I wanted to do something nice for ou. There's nothing phony about that."

"Well, forgive me for not wanting the crappy breakfast. Besides, bacon is gross, and you make the French toast too mushy. Give it all to him,'' she said, throwing a hosti look toward Liam. The anger she felt for her brother rig now was almost frightening. All he did was serve as a livin reminder that she was not like the rest of them. An urg to knock him to the floor rose up within her. She cam very close to giving in to it. Too close. She had to get o of there.

Katie stormed out the kitchen door, down the concret path, and toward the sidewalk, hearing her mother's foo steps behind her.

''Katie!'' her mother hissed.

She spun around to face her, scowling. ''What?''

''Our talk last night changes nothing about how we tre each other under this roof. Is that clear?''

''Crystal.'' She turned to go. Her mother grabbed he arm and held fast. The tight grip squeezed last night fresh cut, and the pain was murder. But Katie willed herse to not so much as wince.

''There's more.'' Her mother's voice was softer nov more vulnerable. ''My radiation treatments for breast ca cer start soon. I'm not going to be at one hundred percen for awhile, so someone will be helping out at home, most to tend to Liam. But she'll be here when you get hom from school, too. Her name is Linda Moore. I think you' like her.''

Katie shook her arm free and started down the walk ''Just what I need, another mother.''

A Ford Focus pulled into the driveway just as Sharo was returning down the walk. Linda Moore stepped ou with a big smile and a mock salute. ''Day nanny, reportin for duty.''

''Mother of fifteen-year-old, ready to quit,'' Sharo replied lightly.

Linda offered a look of understanding. "A fight before chool?"

Sharon nodded. "You'd think we could get through five ninutes in the morning peacefully but—"

"You're her mother," Linda cut in.

"And she's fifteen," Sharon finished, then felt a twinge of guilt for making light of Katie's angst. "I shouldn't say hat. There's more to it. She's going through a really bad ime. Don't expect much this afternoon. I imagine that fter school she'll just seal herself off in her room."

"Sounds intense. Anything I should know?"

Sharon hesitated a moment. "It's a delicate family mater. Just give her plenty of space."

Linda gave a dutiful nod. "Then space it will be."

Upon entering the house through the kitchen, Liam ounded toward them like an excited puppy. "Mommy!" ne chirped, clutching her leg and gesturing to be picked up.

Sharon heeded his request, amazed at how heavy he'd ecome. "You're a big boy," she said, brushing back his urfer blond hair. "Do you remember Linda?"

"She took me down magic stairs."

Linda tapped him on the nose. "No, silly, I took you *up* he magic stairs. You went down all by yourself."

"No, you took me *down,*" Liam said forcefully.

"Do you remember buying me a cookie?" Linda asked.

Liam's eyes went wide. "*You* bought *me* the cookie!"

Linda smiled. "Did not."

Liam giggled. "Did to!"

"Boo bear, Linda is going to help take care of you during the day while Mommy goes to some very important appointments."

"Okay," Liam said.

"We're both going to take you to school and pick you up today, but tomorrow it will just be Linda."

Liam turned to his new caretaker. "Daddy coaches th
Infernos."

"Wow. You must be really proud of him."

He held up three fingers. "I have this many shirts."

"That's great."

"My Dipsy's broken."

"One of his Teletubbies needs a new battery," Sharo
explained, placing him down. "I believe the two of yo
are going to get along just fine."

Absently, she began clearing the breakfast table. Wha
a waste. Only Liam had bothered to eat. Tomorrow's su
gery had Sharon so nervous that her appetite was nonexi
tent, Katie had stormed out, and Heath had simply grabbe
a cup of coffee and left.

A sudden loneliness pierced her heart. She couldn't wai
to join Antonio for their morning espresso. Besides Liam
he was the only one who brought lightness into her world

Linda stepped toward the sink. "I'll take care of thi
mess later. It's almost time for Liam to leave for schoo
and I know you have more important things to do."

And then it finally dawned on Sharon that relief ha
arrived. A sense of calm passed over her. "You're a good
luck charm, Linda. First you rescued Liam. Now you'r
rescuing me."

Chapter Twenty-eight

The preoperating room was cold. One moment there were so many people around—the reassuring presence of Dr. Keri Ward, the wisecracking anesthesiologist, and a trio of friendly nurses. But the next moment Sharon was alone.

She lay there, in all her existential solitude, trying to determine which was worse—the trepidation before surgery or the defeat after hearing Keri announce that one word . . . *cancer.* It was amazing how six letters could disrupt a life, provoke such clarity, and all within days.

Sharon didn't feel like superwoman anymore. Usually, she exercised control over the details. That had been her way throughout her life, calling the shots. On her lavish wedding to Heath, the regime of infertility treatments, the decision to go with a baby broker rather than wait out the uncertain adoption agency process, and the direction of Bliss. She had orchestrated all of that and more.

But then cancer appeared and changed everything, usurping command of almost every facet of her life. For the first time ever, Sharon wasn't making things happen; things were happening to her. And that scared her most of all. *I'm a lame duck,* she thought.

She felt for her right breast, experiencing only numbness. The local anesthetic had done its work. Nothing belonged to her anymore—not her body, not her feelings, not her schedule, not even her family. Cancer had staked a claim on all of it.

Sharon once had a lock on the way she dealt with Heath's fooling around. Now the subject was like an exposed nerve, so excruciatingly painful when touched, conjuring up at once a maddening anger and a storm of insecurity. Before cancer, she'd never considered leaving him. Now she couldn't bear the thought of staying with him.

The Infernos were losing game after game in their worst season ever, and Sharon was taking quiet pleasure in it. Heath had become obsessed with turning the team around, which meant more time away from home than usual. He hadn't bothered to ask about her surgery or treatments, so she hadn't offered the information.

But Antonio had asked, again and again, and at first, she had resisted his offers of support, but in the end her need to feel protected and cared for won out. Antonio had held her hand on the way to the hospital. Right now he was standing vigil in the waiting area. Yet the sad truth was, his presence only intensified her loneliness . . . because he wasn't Heath. No matter how much had disintegrated between them, she wanted her husband there.

Her thoughts floated to Katie and Liam. With Linda Moore at the house, Sharon had nothing to worry about. Strangely, she resented Linda for that, the way she had so quickly captured the rhythm of the household and earned the acceptance of the family. Liam adored her. Heath raved about her, too, if only because she relieved him of responsibility. Even Katie appeared to be warming up to the day nanny. The whole scene made Sharon feel replaceable.

She closed her eyes to the sterile room, her mind racing, thinking of the thousand and one things she must see about upon her release. And then it hit her. The conversation with Tom Wexler in Sacramento. The murders of Peyton Drake and Dr. Ridgeway. As soon as she was able, she wanted to know how and why they were killed. It was odd, but she needed an explanation, like a robbery or a crazed lover, for her own peace of mind.

Sharon sensed movement and opened her eyes.

Keri Ward stood over her, smiling. "We're about to get started."

She knew what to expect. They would remove the lump and some lymph nodes from the area around her breast and under her arm, and then the node samples would be sent to the lab for cancer-cell testing. This was do or die, more telling about her future than the biopsy. Granted, the lump was cancerous, but if the nodes were as well . . . suddenly her mouth felt very dry. "I hope I'm luckier than my mother and grandmother."

Keri patted her hand. "I hope so, too."

There were others in the room now. The funny anesthesiologist was back. He cracked another joke. Something about a tabloid headline. She laughed at the right moment, but her mind was elsewhere.

She thought of Heath's weakness, Katie's anger, Liam's innocence, Antonio's comfort . . . and Georgette Tucker's rage. The weirdness of the latter registered. Why had she thought of her in those terms?

It was a feeling deep in her gut, she realized, as her body went warm with alarm. Then the strong sedative kicked in, taking her under, drifting her away. But somewhere in her semiconscious mind, the telepathic danger remained.

They were rolling her out of the room now. Antonio

dashed to her side, took her hand, and whispered that he would be waiting.

"Stay away from us," Sharon murmured.

Almost instantly, the look of worry on his face transmuted into hurt.

No, she wanted to say, but the words wouldn't push past her lips.

The nurses rolled her forward.

Antonio stayed behind.

I didn't mean you . . . I meant Georgette. And then Sharon closed her eyes. She needed all the strength God could give her. She needed control again.

It had been a good day at Riverview Central High. For the first time in weeks, people left Katie alone. She had a brief conversation with Angel during lunch, but other than that, she kept to herself, no hassles.

"Hi," Linda said casually as Katie came in from school and started up the stairs toward her room.

She halted on the third step, turning to see Linda and Liam sprawled across the floor, playing with a Fisher Price Main Street set.

"We're going to make a Sonic run for sundaes in a few minutes. Want to come?"

Her rote response was a terse "No thanks."

Linda shrugged diffidently and placed one of the little people in the barbershop. "Suit yourself."

Katie respected Linda because she didn't try too hard. This prompted her to reconsider. Besides, the thought of another afternoon and night alone in her room gave her a lethargic feeling. "Well, I guess I could go."

"Whatever. No biggie," Linda said absently.

Katie continued upstairs to deposit her books and came back down to pile into Linda's cramped economy car. They grooved to Ricky Martin all the way to Sonic, laughing as Liam waved his hands to the beat of "Livin' La Vida Loca."

They parked; ordered strawberry, caramel, and peanut butter fudge sundaes; and promised to share with each other. The conversation was perfect in its silliness—talk of cute movie stars, busted Hollywood marriages, and Liam's occasional chime in about something *Star Wars* related.

When he fell asleep, Katie sat in comfortable silence with Linda, enjoying the sunny weather and the peacefulness of the outing. She couldn't recall the last time she had felt so relaxed.

But a carload of high school guys rolled into the drive through and killed the serenity. They screamed out their orders in unison, jockeyed violently for speaker position, and shamelessly flirted with the Sonic girls.

In a nanosecond, Katie's misery kicked in again.

Linda seemed to pick up on it. "Teenage boys are just one notch above apes on the species chain. Did you know that?"

Katie tried to suppress a chuckle but lost the battle. "Yeah, I'm pretty aware."

Another patch of silence.

"You know, your mom had surgery today. I hope everything went smoothly."

Katie thought of the Internet research on breast cancer treatment that she'd promised but never delivered. Pushing the guilt from her mind, she announced, "I was adopted. I just found out, like, a few days ago, but only so I wouldn't freak out about getting cancer myself. Otherwise I never would've known. Anyway, she's not my real mother."

"You mean she's not your birth mother," Linda said.

"Whatever."

"That must be a tough thing to deal with."

"It's weird. Sometimes I feel as if I always knew. I mean,

I never felt like I belonged. I don't look like them. When they told me, I was more angry than surprised."

"Maybe you'll find your birth mother one day."

Katie rose to toss out the empty sundae containers. "Maybe she'll find me."

Chapter Twenty-nine

Kit downed her third cosmopolitan at Cozy's, a watering hole that failed to live up to its moniker. But she was legend here. Her father had been Georgia Tech's most beloved coach, and he'd celebrated his victories and drowned his losses on this very stool.

She turned to Heath, who watched in misery as ESPN replayed footage of the bloodbath that been the Infernos game against Phoenix earlier that day. He shook his head slowly and signaled the bartender for another.

"Why did we come to a sports bar?" Kit asked. "A strip club would've been fine with me."

"I'm a masochist, I guess." He paused a beat. "What were those motherfuckers doing on that field?"

"Losing . . . badly."

Heath poked her ribs with his elbow. Stuffing a handful of stale popcorn into his mouth, he muttered, "Bitch."

"Are you up for a serious talk?"

"About what? My future in the NFL?"

Kit took a long, serious sip of cosmopolitan number four. "About your daughter."

"Well, as it turns out, quitting the soccer team is the least of her problems. We just told her that she was adopted." He sighed wearily and started in on a fresh bourbon. "My wife likes to procrastinate."

"There's more to it, Heath. Katie's in trouble. Serious trouble. If I were in your shoes, I'd get her into counseling right away. Her problems are more than I can handle with a friendly ear and a burger and fries. I think there was an incident with a boy at school. She's shut herself off from her peers. Some of them are harassing her. You know how cruel teenagers can be. I—"

"What kind of incident?" Heath cut in, his tone carrying a defensive edge.

"I don't know. She wouldn't talk about it. But my guess would be a sexual one."

"Come on," Heath scoffed. "Katie doesn't even date."

"Your daughter's a very grown-up fifteen."

Shaking his head, he said, "I appreciate you taking the time, Kit, but what gives you the right to come to these grand conclusions after one afternoon? You were a parent for what, two years, before your dyke friend ran off?"

Kit merely sat there, as if experiencing the moment outside of herself. A sudden, ferocious flash of anger almost sobered her up—but not quite. She was still drunk enough to say more than she wanted to. "This isn't about me, you son of a bitch." Her voice was an exterminating hiss. "This is about Katie, your fucked-up daughter." She considered the quarter inch of liquor that remained in her glass. It wasn't enough to throw in Heath's face, and the thought of ordering another to do the honors crossed her mind.

"I'd say you're the fucked-up one. At least Katie's a teenager. What's your excuse?"

Kit stepped off the stool and ransacked her purse for

the cash to cover her drinks. She threw twenty-five dollars on the counter, hating herself for taking pity on this bastard and inviting him out tonight. "This is bullshit, Heath. Don't make me your punching bag just because you've lost control on the field *and* in your own house. Remember, I'm just the messenger." She started out, passed two tables, then doubled back, deciding against letting him off so easy. "Is there any brain activity in your head, or does your dick do all your thinking? Katie knows about your affairs. At one point she believed dressing like a video vamp was the ticket to getting and keeping a boyfriend. She told me that she doesn't want to end up like her mother—married to a guy who sleeps around like you."

Heath turned on her, the enormity of her words all over his face, the shock clearing his bloodshot eyes.

"And she doesn't even know about this actress from *Score*. Yet. But the news will filter down. Like it always does."

He looked perplexed. "I'm discreet."

"You call screwing in your office before lunch discreet? What's risky by your standards—getting blown as part of the half-time show?"

Heath just sat there, taking it all in.

Kit pushed up the sleeve of her sweater and thrust her forearm in Heath's face. "Do you see those scars?" She spat the words, adrenaline surging.

He drew back at the ghastly sight, his face a portrait of quiet horror.

"When I was Katie's age, I lived with so much emotional pain that the only way I thought I could release it was to cut myself. If I bled, that meant I inflicted just enough hurt to chase away the other pain." She paused, locking her gaze onto his. "Go home and look at Katie's arm."

Heath's lips parted, but no words came out.

"She told me that her cat scratched her."

"We don't have a cat."

"I know." Kit's voice softened when she said, "Katie's

way out there, Heath. Pull her back in.'' She watched him as he wearily combed his fingers through his thick hair. For the first time since she'd known him, he gave off vibes of a man whose better days were behind him.

''She used to tell me everything, ask me what I thought about things. We barely talk anymore.''

''So what are you doing in this dump? Go home and see about your family.''

He gestured toward his last drink. ''I will. Soon.''

''Don't be an idiot. Call a cab if you need one.''

Heath grinned. ''I bet the other lesbians love your way with sweet talk.''

Kit grinned back and muttered, ''Asshole,'' under her breath as she started out again, with every intention of leaving this time. Reaching the door, she felt someone take her arm. It was Heath.

He looked desperate and anxious, like a man on the verge of losing something very important. ''Those things I said,'' he began tentatively, ''I didn't mean them. I know how much you miss Cameron. It was a cheap shot.''

Kit shrugged, even though his digs were still ringing in her ears. That Heath possessed the capacity for such cruelty would alter their friendship. Ultimately, she would forgive him. But she would never forget.

''Thanks for kicking my ass tonight. I needed it.''

''Glad to be of service.''

''Seriously, Kit . . . I'm sorry.''

''No harm done.'' The smoke in the bar was irritating her throat. ''Go home, Heath.'' She pushed open the door and darted out, engulfing as much of the fresh air as her lungs would allow.

Kit sat in her car for a moment and pondered the hours ahead. This night would end like so many others. Dinner from a drive through on the way home. Video from Cameron's last Christmas. Tears until sleep.

* * *

"Hey, aren't you the dip shit who coached those pussies to a twenty-one point loss?"

Heath stopped short of sliding back onto his stool. To finish his last drink in peace was obviously too much to ask. He had a pretty good read on his mood tonight—not to be fucked with—and as he spun around to face the liquor-charged voice, Heath wished that he'd left with Kit.

The heckler was the only one standing at a fully occupied table for four. He looked about thirty with greasy, already thinning hair, a doughy middle, and bad skin. His aura did everything but spell out NOTHING TO LOSE in neon.

Heath decided to dump the drink and get the hell out. The longer he stayed, the greater the chance of needing ice for his knuckles. He snatched two twenties from his money clip and gave the bartender a good-bye nod.

"Don't leave on his account, coach. Say the word and the asshole's gone."

"Thanks, but I'm calling it a night anyway." Heath tried to avoid eye contact as he passed the offending table on his way out, but the bar jerk blocked his path.

The low rumble in Cozy's cooled considerably. In fact, Heath could almost *hear* the silence.

"I asked you a question."

Heath's team had been clobbered up and down the field just hours ago. No way was a redneck in a sports bar going to get the best of him. "The real pussy in question is the Monday-morning quarterback I'm looking at."

Silence reached epic proportions. It was after dark; it was high noon.

The disgruntled Infernos fan, easily six inches shorter, looked up, pulsing with aggression, nostrils flaring.

It happened so fast that Heath didn't see it coming. The bastard rocked back and upward, gaining uncannily furious momentum. Like a human battering ram, he used his head to slam Heath to the floor.

Heath's chin throbbed, shock waves rippled up, and he could actually feel his own brain shuddering.

"Come on, old man!" the bar rat shouted, emboldened by striking the first hit.

The rage rising up in Heath worked fast to ameliorate the bourbon haze. Standing up was slow . . . and painful. It wouldn't be long before he turned fifty, and he felt that number right now like never before.

The scumbag charged again, shoulders wedged beneath his head for straight-line support, but Heath managed a fast and powerful punch, getting in nose, cheek, and mouth damage—all in one shot.

The guy fell backward onto his own table, which flattened under the force of the sudden weight. Then cheap wood, broken glass, blood, and a loser with a bad attitude crashed to the floor in one messy heap.

Heath yanked him up by his sweatshirt collar and jabbed a knee into his groin with such impact that the punk lost his breath. He told the bartender to bill him for the damage and swaggered out, feeling a little less old.

Getting into his Durango, Heath felt home call out to him like a siren. He knew that he should go there, to be with Sharon, when she got off work at Bliss, to check on Katie. But it was late, he reasoned, not to mention he was close to drunk. Tomorrow he would start fresh. Tonight he would get laid.

He reached for his cell phone and punched in Holly Ryan's number. She was there. She was always there. God bless Australia. "I'll be there in fifteen minutes," Heath said.

He ignored the speed limits all the way to Northside Parkway. Turning into Riverside by Post, an expensive planned community that worked hard to bring a small-town sensibility to metro Atlanta, he wondered how Holly paid the rent on a third-tier actress's salary. Certainly the producers of *Score* weren't putting her up. That project was low budget all the way, a surefire straight-to-video junker. Maybe she'd been smart with her earnings from the Australian soap. But Heath didn't figure the girl for an investment whiz.

She showed up at the door wearing nothing but a short silk robe—untied. From that moment on thoughts of her personal finances faded into oblivion. He pulled Holly against him and went straight into a shocking, soulful, ravenously passionate kiss.

"What happened to you?" she asked, stroking his swollen jaw line tenderly.

"Some barfly insulted my team. He hit me. I kicked his ass."

Holly giggled. "You sound like a dockworker or something. It's kind of sexy."

Heath pawed her breasts with one hand and with the other fondled a trail down the crack of her ass. "Oh, yeah?" He nipped lightly at her deliciously plump lower lip. "Are you going to give me some drinking money and keep the rest of my paycheck?"

She giggled again. "This is such bad role-play."

Heath laughed, too, popping her butt cheeks with both hands. He walked away from her to check out the bar in the split-level apartment, pleased to find it fully stocked. "Want a drink?"

"No, thanks. I just had my tongue down your throat. I feel like I've had a fifth of bourbon already."

Heath ignored the complaint and twisted off the top of a new bottle, splashing some into a crystal highballer and chasing it down fast. "So put something else down your throat."

Holly closed her robe and tied the flimsy belt. "Ooh, that's a turn on. Cheap porn dialogue. You're either too drunk or not drunk enough. Which is it?"

Heath's fuse was lit. He felt frustration boiling, rising, like lava in a mountain. The losses that could very well cost him the head coaching job. Sharon's illness. The fractured state of their marriage. Katie's problems. The expression on Kit's face after he hurled those terrible words. His duel with the redneck. Everything boiled together in the heat of the moment. Now it pissed him off that he was taking shit from some B-list actress who was supposed to be an easy lay and nothing more. Gripping the neck of the bourbon bottle, he heaved it against the living room wall.

Holly stood stock still, watching it smash and splatter, never flinching. "I prefer my booze in a glass."

Heath regarded her with contempt and headed for the door. "I came here to escape my problems, not start a new one."

She stopped him as he flipped the deadbolt, molding herself to him from behind. Rucking up his shirt, she untied her robe, pressed her breasts to his bare back, and brought her hands around to his crotch.

He got hard right away and stood frozen in place, eyes shut tight, feeling her nipples distend against his skin.

"Okay, I'm a bitch. So what else is new? Don't go. Take what you came here for."

Heath fought against it, trying to visualize himself opening the door, starting the car, and driving home. But the image didn't materialize. Slowly, he turned around and slipped the robe off her shoulders.

Her tongue—wet, warm, eager to explore—found its way into his ear. "Don't use a condom tonight," she whispered boldly. "I want to feel you inside me . . . completely . . . no barriers."

Heath started to lead her upstairs to the bedroom, but Holly dragged him down onto the carpet. And all was forgiven.

Fifteen minutes later he was satisfied and on his way

home to his wife and kids, thankful for the diversion that was Holly Ryan.

Sharon noticed that Mary Payne had just checked her watch for at least the tenth time that hour. It was Saturday night, and Bliss business was anything but. No real shoppers, just people hanging out at the mall and cruising in for a quick browse.

"So what are your plans later on?" Sharon asked.

"Some friends from college are in town for the weekend. We're hitting a few clubs."

"Sounds like fun." Sharon remembered her own gal pal days at Pepperdine. All the smoke, beer, and loud music she hardly longed for. But she did miss the constant laughter.

Mary Payne looked ambivalent. "You know, it's strange. I'm not *too* old for that scene, but I don't feel young enough for it, either. If I'm still clubbing at thirty, shoot me dead." She shrugged. "There's a guy I'm scoping out." Leaning in, she whispered, "A lawyer. And a good one. He doesn't have an ad in the Yellow Pages or a police scanner to listen for bad accidents. He's with a big firm."

Sharon smiled. Mary Payne was a constant source of amusement, plus she was trustworthy and reliable. Leaving Bliss in her capable hands for several days, even a week or more, could be done without a second thought. "Take off. I'll shut things down."

Mary Payne's body seemed reluctant, but her eyes gave away her zeal to grab her purse, sign out, and make a fast exit. "Are you sure?"

"Positive. Antonio's closing tonight, too. We'll probably have a cup of coffee before we head out."

"Be a bad girl," Mary Payne suggested, heading for the office, "and have it with cream." She spun around and winked.

Sharon, feeling the flush of embarrassment start at her neck, turned away quickly. The truth was, Mary Payne wasn't far off the mark. She entertained such thoughts about Antonio often—and with increasingly less guilt.

Earlier tonight she'd spotted him delivering a latte to one of the java.com tables set up in the center of the mall. It had been impossible for her to take her eyes off him, so handsome in his white turtleneck, dark blazer, and slim-cut black pants. She loved his beautiful olive skin, his perfect mouth, and the slight natural curl of his thick black hair.

When they enjoyed their espressos together, she often found herself staring at his hands, admiring his long fingers, clean nails, and meticulously groomed cuticles. They were the hands of a lover, she fantasized, a giving lover. Briefly, scornfully, she thought of Heath and how selfish he was in bed. Antonio would be different. Sharon knew that . . . and she wanted to experience it, too.

Admitting this triggered a surge of joy. The surgery had been only days ago, yet here she stood, the specter of radiation treatment still looming, but having a sensual thought nonetheless. Life was still there! Her nodes had tested negative for cancer cells, and the tumor was small enough so that the lumpectomy would leave behind only modest scarring.

But the fear of recurrence lay buried fathoms deep. This time she'd been lucky, if you could call a malignant tumor that. The fact that no nodes were involved made her more fortunate than most, but the big question remained. Would the cancer come back? And if so, how soon?

The past few weeks had changed her forever, Sharon realized. Never would she think of herself as disease-free again. Throbbing deep inside her would always be a painful awareness, a worst fear, that next time the treatment would not be so simple, the prognosis not so optimistic.

Knowing this, she spent the few quiet hours she could

find scrutinizing her life and the people in it, wondering if she was living it right. She ruminated hard on the subject. With the exception of her children and the pleasure she found in running Bliss, only Antonio stood out as a positive force that she declared essential to her new future. Heath failed to register.

To be diagnosed with cancer put the mind on a spiritual track. She had read that and discovered it to be true. So she wondered if Antonio might be an angel sent down to protect her. Without him, she didn't know what she would do. Heath was never home to hear her fears, and Katie hardly spoke at all. But Antonio listened, sometimes made her laugh, and always insisted that she put herself first.

As if on cue, he stepped into the boutique, a vision of youth, kindness, and sex appeal, grinning mischievously. "My watch says nine o'clock."

Sharon checked hers. "You're fifteen minutes fast."

"I like my time zone better."

She smiled. "Me, too."

Antonio leaned against the counter and just looked at her, still grinning.

The intense focus of his gaze unsettled her. "So who's minding the store?"

"Justin. He knows the place better than I do. A retail fact—overachievers in high school make the best employees. But you grow to depend on them, and they go off to college. Do you think I could start hiring seventh graders in the gifted class?"

Sharon laughed, wondering if her lipstick had faded. "I think there are laws about that."

"Oh," Antonio replied with mock dimness. "Would you mind if we skipped coffee tonight?"

Sharon worked hard to conceal her disappointment. "No, that's fine."

"I'm hungry. Let's go out for a late dinner instead. If you can, that is."

Her heart picked up speed. "Let me check on things at home first." She stepped behind the counter and dialed. Katie picked up on the second ring.

"Hi, sweetheart. How are you? How's Liam?"

"He's asleep."

"What time did Linda leave?"

"Around five."

"Is your father home?"

"What do you think?"

She paused a beat. "I'm going to have a late dinner with a friend. Can I bring you home something special? Maybe a yummy dessert?"

"My legs are fat enough."

"Don't say that. You've got a beautiful figure."

"Everything's fine here. Go have dinner with your *friend.*" Click.

Sharon opened her mouth to speak but realized that Katie had hung up. For several seconds, she stood there with the receiver in hand, trying to read as much into her daughter's answers and tonality as she could.

"Is everything okay?" Antonio asked.

"No, it never really is," she said distantly, then returned the phone to the cradle and faced him, "but it's okay enough to have a meal. I'm starving. What are you in the mood for?"

"How about the Cheesecake Factory?"

"Perfect." A sudden wave of doubt crashed over her. "I have to ask you something. Promise to be honest."

"I always am."

"It's Saturday night in Atlanta, a city that's filled with beautiful women. So why is a man with your options taking a withered-up old broad like me out to dinner?" She grinned in an attempt to soften the edge on her self-esteem meltdown.

Antonio reached out and cupped her face with those

remarkable hands. His gaze had the heat and intensity of a laser. "Don't talk that way."

All her insecurities and emotional frailties seemed to surface at once. Tears formed in her eyes. "Look at me. I've got cancer, my marriage is falling apart, and my daughter hates me. If I'm not an impossible bitch yet, it's only a matter of time. I'm a sinking ship." She looked down, then up, unable to hold his gaze any longer.

He killed a tear with his thumb. "Right now your mind is like a bad neighborhood, Sharon. You shouldn't go into it alone."

She laughed in spite of herself.

"I know what my options are. Believe me, I've been out there. I know what's available. Some are younger, some are prettier, some are less damaged." He kissed his fingertip and then touched it to her lips. "But I'm choosing to spend time with the best."

The sudden longing she felt was so overwhelming that it frightened her. If he asked her to run away with him right now, she knew that her answer would be perilously close to yes. What the hell was she doing? How far could she allow this to go?

"You're in the Saks parking garage, right?"

She nodded, imagining Liam in his youth bed, surrounded by his stuffed animals, snug in his blankets. The image pulled at her heart, played the strings of guilt and shame, but she still wanted to be with Antonio tonight. "I'll follow you to the restaurant."

Sharon didn't bother with the ritual closing procedures. It was five minutes early, but she secured the mall entrance gate anyway. Instead of counting and balancing the cash drawer, she shoved it into the safe and cut off the lights.

They slipped out the back door and walked briskly to the garage. There was a bridge of awkward silence. She didn't quite know how to act, what to say. It was just dinner, yes, but it was so much more.

Upon reaching their cars, she busied herself with the task of finding her keys.

Antonio lingered at his BMW.

Sharon noticed a figure approach but thought nothing of it.

"Give me your fucking money."

Barely registering the words, she looked up. A gun was inches from her face, the hand holding it steady and certain.

For one fleeting moment, the terror didn't seem real. Her body began to shake involuntarily. She dropped her purse. It hit the floor hard. The sound echoed.

Sharon met the crazy eyes of her assailant. He was young, not much older than Katie. But anxious as hell. Whatever he needed tonight, he needed it bad.

"Pick it up, bitch. Take off your jewelry, too." His finger moved on the trigger.

With trembling hands, she removed the diamonds from her ears and slipped off her Tank watch from Cartier. She tugged at her wedding ring, but it wouldn't budge.

"Get that fucking ring off."

She pulled and pulled but couldn't get it over her knuckle.

"Come on!"

Hard steel pressed into her forehead. She shut her eyes. One more yank and the marital symbol that had lost all meaning to her gave way. Her relief was total. She dropped everything into her purse and lifted it up, her eyes never leaving the ground.

"I should kill you so you won't scream."

Sharon stopped breathing and started praying.

Chapter Thirty

It was the second time Georgette Tucker had watched Heath Driver make love to a woman. But there was nothing loving about his treatment of Holly Ryan. His moves were rough and urgent, selfishly designed to meet the only goals that mattered—his satisfaction, his release. And without so much as a promise to call, he was gone.

As soon as Holly locked the door behind him, Georgette emerged from a patch of darkness at the top of the stairs. "And the Oscar goes to . . ."

Holly jolted violently. "Jesus Christ, you scared the shit out of me. How did you get in here?"

"It's called a key. I pay the rent, remember? Now that's what I call acting—pretending to enjoy a romp with a pig like him."

Holly smiled, suddenly at ease. "He's not so bad. Try blowing four producers twice a day for a month. That's what I did to get my last movie role."

Georgette made a slow descent to join the hired help on the first floor. Holly had played the role of the erotically compliant actress to the hilt, making her Heath's perfect go-to girl morning, noon, and night.

He was so mind-numbingly predictable. All Georgette did was factor into her plan his overblown ego and hunger for illicit sex. Heath did the rest, moving through her plot like a mouse in a maze.

Holly gave her a puzzled look. "Why the skullcap, rubber suit, and gloves? You look like a cat burglar."

"I can't be seen here. You know that." Georgette picked up a dagger sharp slab of broken glass from the smashed liquor bottle. "I was hoping he'd get mad enough to smack you around a little, but this is good enough," she murmured.

"How did Chad perform?" Holly asked.

Georgette smiled. "Like a dream. You were right—he gives good barroom brawl."

"He gets steady work as Creepy Guy Number One in lots of B movies. The leading man usually beats him to a bloody pulp somewhere in the second hour."

"Heath worked him over pretty good, but I made it worth that cretin's while. He's already on a plane back to Los Angeles."

Holly smirked. "It's amazing what wallet-enhancement therapy can do."

Georgette fingered the shard of glass as if it were a work of art.

"Why did you want him to fuck me without a condom tonight? I assume I'm supposed to turn up pregnant now."

Georgette answered with a prolonged, hostile glare. "Never assume anything." And then she lashed out with a quick and lethal fury, lancing the sharp end of the makeshift dagger into Holly's neck and ripping the skin from left to right and up and down in one merciless, violent motion.

The actress-model-tramp tried to scream, but it died in her slashed throat.

Holly sank to her knees, hands clutching her neck, blood seeping through her fingers. The murderous red stained the plush cream carpet. Her heart stopped beating, but her eyes remained wide open, frozen with the shock of her demise.

"Good death scene," Georgette said to the corpse.

Chapter Thirty-one

In Sharon's peripheral vision she captured Antonio's black Prada lace-ups on the other side of her Range Rover. *Oh, God, please don't play action hero,* she thought, hoping he would remain out of sight until this monster took off.

"Facedown, bitch!" He jabbed her temple with the gun. "Facedown!"

An arc of pain shuddered through her head. She moved to flatten herself on the cold floor of the parking garage. Still weak from the surgery, her right arm buckled, sending her down fast. She slammed her chin and bit her tongue.

Antonio crept closer to the rear of the vehicle.

Somewhere in the distance there were voices and laughter.

Sharon watched her attacker case out the surroundings. When his blazing eyes fell on Antonio, her heart did a free fall.

"You want to play Superman, motherfucker?" The veins on his neck were bulging as he took aim at Antonio's chest.

Antonio stood statue-still, wide-eyed, his face stark white with fear. His hands were turned up, one holding his wallet, the other his keys. "There's at least two hundred in cash right here," he said in a hushed, remarkably calm tone. "Take my car, too. No one has to get hurt."

He tossed Sharon's purse at Antonio's feet. "Throw in the wallet."

Antonio dropped it inside, only taking his eyes off the gun for a brief moment.

"Get down like her! Now!"

Antonio hit the floor, locking his gaze onto Sharon. "Are you okay?"

She nodded frantically.

A moment passed without a threat or a hostile movement. And then another moment passed.

"He's gone," Antonio said. He craned up his neck to be absolutely certain. "He's gone."

The relief she experienced transcended all meaning, yet she didn't know whether to start celebrating or start mourning.

Antonio swept her up in his arms . . . and he kissed her. There was desperation in his lips, a hungry grab for the moment.

Suddenly nothing mattered. Sharon only felt a greed for the taste and sensation of his mouth, for the invasion of his tongue. It knew no bounds. Alive with panic, she twined her fingers into his hair, kissing him back with a savage, intense lust.

Antonio molded her to him, painting himself against her with arms like tight bands. "My God, Sharon, I thought I was going to lose you. I felt so goddamn helpless. I didn't want him to see me because when a punk like that gets scared. . . ."

Her mouth parted in lust and wonder. She was so thankful to be alive. She was so thankful for him. Her heart felt light as she realized she couldn't care less about anything but the mind melting kisses of Antonio Miguel. No matter, the practical part of her managed to say, "We have to call the police."

And then the flesh for flesh fantasy moment died, giving way to the extra-strength reality of random crime. The sensual spell was officially broken. He retrieved a spare key from a little magnetic box underneath his car and tumbled into the vehicle to punch in 911.

Chapter Thirty-two

"911 Emergency. What are you reporting?"

Georgette spoke in a frightened and breathless voice. "Something's wrong at Riverside by Post off Northside Parkway. I heard a man and woman fighting, then a loud crash. He ran out and got into an SUV. I think it was red." There was a silence as she contemplated saying more . . . and discarded the idea. Satisfied, she pressed *END*.

Recalling the look on Holly Ryan's face when she stabbed her in the throat, Georgette felt an exquisite, full-body tingle, almost like a sexual aftershock. The thrill of death to the deserving—those were the moments she wanted to stretch out forever. Holly Ryan was nothing but a dumb whore. The bitch had served out her term as a useful ally, so the best place for her was the grave.

The other killings moved inside her mind, a collage of delicious, bloody memories. She remembered the melodious crack of Ed Tucker's neck as he tumbled down the stairs of his own home in the Hamptons. He had been her first, the virgin kill, the one who gave her the strength, power, and cunning to go after the others.

Like Peyton Drake. The scumbag attorney who represented her and the Drivers during the adoption, playing both against the middle to decrease his workload and increase his bottom line. Wasting him had been easy. She'd just approached him at his car one dark night as he was leaving a bar and uttered the same words he'd thrown at her in the hospital: "This will be over soon. Trust me." The bastard had stared at her for one long, puzzled moment. There was a faint glimmer of recognition in his eyes before she'd shot him in the face.

And Dr. Ridgeway. The sleazy obstetrician who turned her baby over to the Drivers and cut out the core of her womanhood without her consent. Murdering him had been more complicated. She'd actually tracked his hospital schedule for several days, waiting for that brutal twenty-four-hour shift that would send him home bone tired and craving sleep. He hadn't heard her shatter a window, slip inside the house, pull one of his own golf clubs from the front closet, and enter the bedroom where he slept atop his comforter, still in his pale green scrubs. The first bash to his head had triggered a violent jolt. Then he'd simply laid there like a sack of garbage as she pummeled away. Only when his face was unrecognizable had she stopped.

Oh, God, it felt so good to rid them from the earth. So purifying. So cleansing. At first, she feared the fact that they hadn't suffered would haunt her. But thankfully, their quick and efficient murders had her brimming over with pride. She had shrewdly budgeted the torture for Sharon and Heath, those checkbook adoptive parents who for the past fifteen years had experienced every precious moment with her baby. Oh, yes, they deserved all the pain she had in store for them.

Georgette turned her cheap car into the almost shabby apartment complex where she rented an inexpensive one bedroom unit. She kept it sparsely furnished and remained casually friendly with her neighbors, careful not to pique interest or curiosity.

Once inside, she started on tonight's project with a feverish longing. As she papered onto the wall photographs of Savannah from infancy to the present, she whispered, "We'll be going home soon, baby," over and over again.

There were hundreds of photographs to choose from, all of them slashed directly from Sharon's treasured collection of family albums. She found a spot for a photo of Savannah at age three, affixed it with poster-weight double stick tape, and carefully smoothed it down, turning back to the sea of snipped and ripped snapshots strewn across the bed. Not a single photograph of Savannah remained in Sharon's possession. Even the picture frames had been raided.

A soft knock rapped the front door.

Georgette shut the bedroom door behind her and peered through the peephole.

It was Stan, the pest from next door. He'd been after her to go out for a drink ever since she moved in. How many times did she have to say no?

She opened the door and smiled. "Hey, Stan."

"Tonight's your lucky night. I'm taking you out for a beer."

Observing the sight of gold jewelry on neck, wrist, and at least three fingers, she came close to gagging, but held it back in favor of a long sigh. "Sorry, neighbor. It's been a tough day. I'm too beat to party."

"Come on. One beer."

She held firm. "Maybe some other time."

He winked and smiled, revealing crooked teeth. "I'll hold you to that."

"I'm sure you will. Good night, Stan."

"Good night, Linda. You know, I never caught your last name."

"Moore."

"Linda Moore," he said in singsong, a flirtatious gleam in his eye. "That trips off the tongue nicely."

With good humor, she shook her head. "I really need some rest, Stan. I'm a day nanny, and the woman I work for is a real bitch."

Chapter Thirty-three

Sharon pretended to be asleep when Heath came into he bedroom. It struck her how estranged they were. The hasm between them was wider than ever before.

Just hours ago she had a gun in her face and a crackhead creaming obscenities in her ear. Now she lay here bruised, till trembling, unable to drift off, and fighting recurring mages of the grisly scene. Yet the comfort of her husband as the last thing she wanted.

What she craved was the comfort of Antonio Miguel. he savored the erotic fantasy of just one night with him. ut did she really have the constitution to seek it out? The normity of such an act weighed down on her. It would nean betraying the vows she made to Heath. Goddammit! Ie constantly ignored those vows. Why couldn't she just nce?

The shower jets gushed into action. Who is he washing ff tonight? Was it the "actress"? Or maybe he's already umped her for some other bimbo. She stewed in her ilent fears, tortured by the terror of the night and the

certain breakup of her marriage. For the first time in weel
cancer didn't top her list of worries.

She remained rigid in pretend sleep as Heath join
her in bed. Part of her wanted to feel the safety of h
strong arms around her, but she resisted the temptatio
A terrible sadness registered. The tears that follow
seemed to go on and on. Sharon cried as quietly as sh
could, but she knew Heath could hear her muffled sobbi
and feel the slight shaking of the bed. She could sense h
awareness, imagine his open eyes staring at the ceilin
Would he reach out for her?

They were inches apart in their bed, yet miles apart
their hearts. After waiting what seemed like hours for th
touch that never came, she finally began to feel the hea
ness of sleep. *Soon,* she thought groggily, *I'll ask him to lea
soon.*

"Daddy!" Liam had just started to eat his breakfast b
lost interest the moment Heath shuffled into the kitche
In a nanosecond he was in his father's arms, hugging hi
planting kisses on his cheek, beaming like crazy.

"Who's my boo bear?" Heath asked in his thick ear
morning voice, moving slow and looking terrible.

"I am!" Liam replied proudly.

"Coffee," Heath remarked to no one in particula
"Lots of coffee." He glanced at Sharon and did a doub
take. "What happened to you?"

She eyed him distantly, touching her bruised chin, dee
in her own thoughts. Liam's need for Heath was almo
ravenous. She watched her son's tiny hands pat his father
chest with loving abandon. Scenes like this twisted th
rheostat of her courage. How could she even think
breaking up the family?

"Your face, Sharon," Heath said, intense concern in his yes. "What happened?"

"I was mugged in the parking garage last night."

He put Liam down and even dismissed the idea of coffee. Jesus Christ! When?"

"After closing."

"Why didn't you call me?"

"It's just a bruise, Heath. I'm fine."

He looked helpless for a moment, then annoyed. "What id the police say?"

"Not to expect much. The kid wasn't much older than atie, probably looking for drug money." Then she took otice of bruises on his face and right hand. "What's your xcuse?"

Heath groaned and turned around to pour his coffee. Bar fight. Some asshole got under my skin." He sipped lowly. "Hell, maybe I was the asshole for giving him the ime of day."

As far as Sharon was concerned, there was no maybe bout it.

"Daddy," Liam interjected, tugging on Heath's underhirt. "Wanna play with my *Star Wars* toys?" The smile on is face indicated that the deal being offered was very good ndeed.

Heath softened immediately and stroked the boy's hair. 'Let your old man finish his coffee. I'll join you in a ninute."

Liam took off for the play room.

Sharon looked at his untouched breakfast and frowned. 'I don't know where he finds the energy. He hardly eats."

"Has Katie been downstairs yet?"

Sharon cleared the table of Liam's food. "It's Sunday. f she's feeling ambitious, she'll be up at the crack of noon."

"I had a long talk with Kit Jamison last night. She's vorried about Katie."

Sharon noisily scraped food off the plate and into th sink. "That makes three of us."

"When Kit was a teenager, she had a lot of emotion problems, too. She used to cut herself with razors, and sh thinks Katie's doing the same thing."

She left the faucet running and spun around to face h husband.

Heath was stroking the inside of his forearm. "She worn long sleeves for days now. I can't say for certain th this isn't true. Can you?"

Self-mutilation. The very idea that Katie could har herself intentionally made Sharon feel sick. She wanted strike out, to tell him that his lesbian friend didn't kno a damn thing about their daughter . . . but something he her back.

"Kit believes there was a sexual incident with a boy school. She witnessed firsthand Katie being harassed."

As waves of guilt and self-loathing crashed over he Sharon buried her face in her hands. What kind of moth was she when a stranger had to point out warning sign in her own daughter's behavior?

"Of course, we don't know if there's any truth to thi It's just Kit's—"

"But I don't know that it's not true, Heath. That's th sickest part of all. I've been so self-involved lately, conten to just let Katie exist in her own world. She's withdraw from her friends, from us . . . these are textbook signa of trouble."

The doorbell chimed.

Heath went to answer it, muttering aloud that it wa probably a kid selling candy or a yard man looking fo work. But he found a man and a woman—both in the midthirties—staring back with grim, intelligent faces.

"Heath Driver?" the woman asked, her tone clippe and official.

Sharon was behind him now, her brow crinkling, a distinct feeling of uneasiness coming over her.

"That's me," Heath said.

The woman flashed a badge; her partner did the same. "I'm Detective McCarthy. This is my partner, Detective Wagner. We're with the Atlanta Police Department," she said. "May we come inside and ask you a few questions?"

Sharon's brain went hyperactive, trying to pinpoint a reason for the visit. Only one answer came to mind—maybe the jerk from the bar was pressing charges.

"Sure," Heath said easily, stepping out of the way to allow them entry. "What's this about?"

Wagner held up a slickly produced eight by ten glossy. "Do you know this woman?"

The photograph displayed a glamorous Holly Ryan. Sharon's stomach did a death drop.

Heath turned to Sharon, then back to the detectives. "I've seen her a few times. She's an actress, I think."

McCarthy fixed a steely gaze on Heath. "When did you see her last?"

He shot an uncomfortable glance toward Sharon. "What's this about anyway?"

Wagner took a step forward. "We'll get to your questions later. If you don't mind, answer ours first. When did you last see Holly Ryan?"

"I don't remember exactly. A few days ago, maybe," Heath said.

Sharon watched her husband in profile. He was lying. Of that she was sure. She could tell by the pattern of his blinking.

"Since your memory's not so good," McCarthy began, "is it possible that you could've seen her as recently as last night?"

"No," Heath said firmly. "It's not."

McCarthy shared a look with her partner. "We'll be back

in touch if we have any further questions. Thank you f
your time."

"Has something happened to Holly?" Heath asked.

"Yeah," Wagner said. "You could say that. Someo
murdered her."

Linda Moore arrived just as the detectives were leavin
Heath seized the opportunity to disappear, headi
upstairs, bailing on his promise to play with Liam.

Sharon broke the latest crime statistic, explained h
bruise, and confessed how happy she was that Linda h
arrived to lighten the day's load. As she talked, Linda
gaze was intently focused behind her.

"What happened to the family photos?" Linda fina
asked.

Sharon turned back to scan the picture gallery on t
antique hutch. Astonished, she stepped closer, as if h
eyes were playing a deceptive game. But what she saw w
disturbing fact. Every frame had been invaded, its pictu
crudely ripped or cut to remove Katie's image. The symb
ism triggered instant anguish. This was her adopted daug
ter's way of saying she didn't belong.

Slowly, Sharon reached for one of the family albu
nestled on the shelf. She opened it somewhere in t
middle, caught sight of the butchered contents, and sh
her eyes.

"Katie did this," Linda said quietly.

Sharon remained silent.

"She told me about the adoption."

With dread in her heart, Sharon checked the conditio
of the other albums, opening and closing each one, h
despair almost unbearable. Every page had been mangle
beyond repair.

"I think you should leave," Sharon said. Her voice w

quiet but firm. "I'll pay you for the full day, but I think you should leave."

"Sharon, I—"

"It's not just this. There are other issues, too. You should go. I don't expect the day to be a pleasant one."

The rebuke registered on Linda's face. "If that's what you want. . . ."

"Heath and I need a day to deal with private family matters. You're a tremendous help, but you're an outsider. I wouldn't feel comfortable with you here. I don't think you'd feel comfortable either."

Linda nodded solemnly. "Maybe you're right." She moved into the kitchen and gathered her things to leave.

Stunned by the sum total of it all, Sharon merely stood there. Last night's mugging. The possibility that Katie could be mutilating her own body. Holly Ryan's murder. Now the systematic destruction of every family photograph. Part of her wanted to escape, to run to Antonio, the only comfort and happiness she knew. But she had to stay, to face it all down. She sensed Linda lingering in the doorway and looked up.

"There's something I need to tell you," Linda said. She glanced upstairs and brought her voice down an octave. "About Katie."

"What is it?"

Linda hesitated. "Have you ever suspected that she might be on drugs?"

"Drugs? Not *my* daughter," Sharon said defensively. Then after a moment, she asked, "What makes you say that?"

"She's cut herself off from her friends. She's lost interest in her favorite activities. She's secretive. She's moody. These are common signs."

"Katie has her share of problems, but drugs isn't one of them."

Linda averted her eyes for a moment. "Most paren refuse to believe it at first."

Sharon said nothing. The truth was, if Katie was o drugs, she would be the last to know.

"Demand a urine sample. Take it to a lab. It's the onl way to know for sure."

Sharon thought of herself at Katie's age. She had bee so happy, so carefree, enjoying the freedoms of a nurturin home, a safe environment. When did everything change Why was growing up so different now?

"She'll hate me even more," Sharon finally whispere imagining Katie's reaction to this invasion of privacy, th breach of trust. But Linda was right. She had to know.

"You stupid son of a bitch. " As he excoriated himse aloud, Heath brought the razor over the curve of his ja line and tested the smoothness with his free hand.

Avoiding the truth, he realized, had hardened into sinister trend. He lied to Sharon. He lied to any woma he slept with. He lied to the owner of the Infernos. Now h was lying to detectives involved in a murder investigatio "Why the fuck did you lie to the police?"

For Sharon. Instinctively, Heath had known she was clos to leaving him. And if she ever found out that he'd bee getting laid while she'd been getting mugged, then h could kiss it all good-bye. The marriage. The family lif Everything that kept him grounded.

He thought of Holly Ryan. Beautiful Holly. Sexy Holl Dead Holly. Jesus Christ, he could hardly believe it. Les than twelve hours ago, she'd been straddling him lap dancer style, with her ankles resting on his shoulders, urg ing him on with dirty talk.

Come on, Heath. Fuck me. Harder. Faster. Don't ever stop.

Her voice was so clear and fresh in his mind. He coul almost hear it. Right here. In this room. As he finishe shaving, his mind roamed over every moment with her. Without a doubt, she was the best sex he'd ever known. That she could be gone seemed impossible.

The towel around his waist was slipping. He tightened it and stared into the mirror. Those tight-ass detectives hadn't told him shit about the murder. How was Holly killed? When was she killed? And goddammit, why was she killed?

He tried to think of discreet friends in high places, and Kit Jamison popped into his brain. Her great grandfather had been a congressman, her grandfather a beloved country singer, and her father a legendary football coach. With lineage in politics, entertainment, and sports, she knew someone in every pocket of the city. Heath grabbed the phone and punched in her number.

She answered with a sleepy voice.

"Hi, it's Heath."

Kit sighed. "I'd rather you insult me in bars than call me before eleven on Sunday."

"This is important. Do you have friends at the police department?"

"I have friends everywhere, Heath. Unlike you."

"Holly Ryan was murdered last night."

"Who's she?"

"That actress from *Score.*"

"What?" If Kit hadn't been sitting up before, she was definitely doing so now.

"Two detectives were just here asking questions, but they didn't give away much as far as details. Can you ask around?"

"Sure." Kit paused a beat. "You sound scared, Heath. What's going on?"

He pondered confessing his predicament, then thought better of it. What good was another voice telling him how stupid he was? His own inner voice had that area covered. "Just find out what you can. I'll wait by the phone."

"Give me a few minutes." And she hung up.

He watched the clock, the wait stretching out for what seemed like forever. Finally, he busied himself with getting dressed. After that, he tried to watch ESPN but couldn't concentrate. When coverage of yesterday's game hit the screen, he turned the TV off before the asshole commentators got a chance to weigh in.

The shrill jangle of the telephone played like sweet music. One ring and he was on it. "Kit?" he answered.

"What I found out isn't comforting. Her throat was ripped open with a shard of glass from a broken liquor bottle. No sign of forced entry. No robbery. They think Holly knew the murderer. There was physical evidence of recent intercourse and no sign of vaginal tears or bruising. That poor girl. She was only twenty-five years old."

Key phrases echoed in Heath's mind. *Broken liquor bottle. Recent intercourse.* He was responsible for both. A crazy fear stirred inside him. The dumbest move he made was lying to the detectives. But his story was on the record. He would have to stick to it.

"Daddy said he would play *Star Wars* with me," Liam whined.

"I'm sure he'll be down soon, boo bear," Sharon said, so distracted about Katie that she didn't know what to do with herself. Part of her wanted to march upstairs, shake her daughter awake, and demand answers to all the questions swimming inside her head.

The phone jangled for the second time that morning. After two rings, she realized Heath wasn't picking up and answered it herself.

"How are you?" It was Antonio. His voice carried her away, if only for a moment.

"I'm fine," she replied softly. There was a distinct intimacy between them now . . . beyond friendship. Her heart pounded with guilt, danger, and promise.

Antonio remained silent, as if questioning her veracity.

"Really," she assured him.

"I couldn't sleep last night. I just kept thinking about you. I wondered if you were safe." He paused a beat. "I wanted to hold you, Sharon. I craved it."

She was taken aback, unable to speak or even breathe. Last night had been one of the loneliest ones she could ever remember, and her own husband had been beside her for most of it.

The familiar tone of call waiting flashed.

"Hold on, Antonio. Someone's trying to get through," she said, thankful for the escape chute.

"Sharon!" Mary Payne exclaimed, obviously near tears. "The store is a wreck! Almost every piece of inventory has been slashed! Horrible words are spray painted all over the walls!"

"Slow down . . . what—"

"It's a nightmare!"

Sharon tried to picture the scene in her mind. Something deep within her, something self-preserving, wouldn't allow her to. "I'm on my way." She remembered Antonio and clicked back, her mind in tumult. "Are you still there?"

"Of course I am."

"I have to go. That was Mary Payne. Bliss has been vandalized."

"I'll meet you there," Antonio said.

She hung up and cast her eyes for Liam, who sat in the corner, his mouth settled into a firm pout. Now Sharon regretted sending Linda home. But who knew this would happen? "Come upstairs with Mommy and get dressed, angel. We're going to Bliss."

"I wanna play with Daddy!" His voice brooked no compromise.

Sharon hated to pull the bribe card, but she didn't have

time for any other negotiations. "We'll buy a new *Star Wars* toy. Anything you want."

Liam shot up and raced over to take her hand.

They trotted upstairs and into his room, where Sharon dressed him in the first items of clothing her hands could find. Then she dashed to the master bedroom and threw on a sweatshirt and jeans, ignoring Heath as he sat on the edge of the bed, almost catatonic.

Finally, he looked up. "What's the big rush?"

"Bliss has been vandalized."

"What?"

"Mary Payne just called. We'll be back later."

"I'll watch Liam."

"That's okay. You need time to mourn." Without a glance in his direction she scooped up her son and walked out, closing the door behind her.

"Daddy looks sad, Mommy," Liam said.

"He is sad, sweetheart. He's very sad."

BITCH OF ALL TIME.

BABY WHORE.

MOTHER FROM HELL.

DISEASED CUNT.

The depravities screamed out at her in murderous red. It was so awful, so full of hate. Sharon couldn't fathom anything, not the who, not the why. Turning away from the angrily scrawled words, she walked the store slowly, inspecting each fixture, examining every shelf. Nothing could be saved. There were violent rips to garment after garment, as if jungle tour guides with machetes had hacked their way through.

Mary Payne stood at the counter, pale-faced and distraught.

"Don't cry, Mommy."

Sharon hadn't even noticed the tears trailing down her

cheeks. She looked at Liam, who was hoisted onto her hip. "Sometimes you can't help it, boo bear."

"Nothing was stolen," Mary Payne said, holding up a clipboard stacked with inventory forms as she approached. "The safe wasn't touched. Not so much as a paper clip is missing. Whoever did this got their kicks out of the destruction."

"Sharon!"

She spun around to face the soothing voice.

Antonio stood at the mall entrance, his fingers looped around the security gate. He stared at the vulgar walls in disbelief. "My God."

Steeling herself, she wiped her cheeks with her fingers and nodded for Mary Payne to let him inside the store.

He stroked Liam's head affectionately with one hand and discreetly massaged the small of her back with the other.

"There's nothing left," she whispered. "Everything's ruined."

"The guys who helped me with java.com are fast and dependable. I'll have the walls cleaned up today."

"The insurance agent will—"

"Take Polaroids," Antonio cut in. "And if that's not good enough, I'll pay for the work. I won't have you looking at this filth any longer than necessary."

Sharon turned to Mary Payne. "Will you take Liam into the mall for a cookie or something?" She smiled weakly. "I need some nervous breakdown time."

She waited until they were out of sight to collapse into Antonio's arms.

"It's going to be okay," he whispered. "Don't let this wear you down. This isn't important. What's important is your first radiation treatment tomorrow."

Sharon leaned back and gazed at him in amazement. *Radiation. Cancer.* She'd actually forgotten. And this beautiful, kind, supportive, and devastatingly sexy man had remembered for her.

He waved his hand as if to say the store meant nothing. "This can be fixed, yes? With insurance, a little cash, some sweat. Your health is what matters. And people—like that fantastic kid of yours who's stuffing his fat little face with cookie about now."

She laughed. A real laugh. And it felt good.

Antonio touched her nose. "I like to see you laugh."

Sharon closed her eyes. "I'm so blessed to have met you." Now she met his gaze. "I don't know what I'd do without you right now."

"You'd survive."

"Maybe. But not as well."

He grimaced as his eyes fell on the wall emblazoned with MOTHER FROM HELL. "Who did this?"

Sharon swallowed hard. Katie had access to the keys and knew the entry code. It was difficult to form the words, but she knew what the truth was. "My own daughter did this."

Chapter Thirty-four

It was one o'clock in the afternoon when Katie finally forced herself to get out of bed. There was really nothing to rise for. All she could think of to do was to mark time until Monday morning, which started another miserable week at Riverside Central High School.

Despite meticulous treatment before turning in, last night's cuts had bled in her sleep. She hoped the white sheets weren't ruined. Just after slipping on a long sleeve T-shirt to cover her arms, she stripped the bed and headed downstairs to the washroom.

Thankfully, the house was quiet. Still as a tomb, really. Her mother had a load of Liam's clothes ready to go. Katie snatched them out of the machine and onto the floor, replacing them with her bloody sheets.

Her father was in the kitchen, sitting at the counter with a cup of coffee, looking like a lost soul.

"Good morning," he said lightly. "It's still morning somewhere in the world, I guess."

"I was tired," Katie said archly. Sometimes it exhausted

her to take every little comment personally, but she just couldn't help the way she responded. The deafening quiet of the house unnerved her. "Where is everyone?"

"Bliss was vandalized. Your mother took Liam with her to see about the damage."

"How bad was it?"

Her father shrugged. "I don't know."

She noticed the bruising on his face and neck. "What happened to you?"

"I got into it with a jerk at a bar." He smiled. "Don't worry. You've got your mother's brains."

Katie saw his desire to edit his words after they hit the air, and she wasn't about to let this opportunity slip away. "Which one?"

"You know what I mean." He stared at her, as if trying to make up his mind about something. "What's on tap for you today?"

"Nothing," Katie said, grabbing a Pop-Tart and shoving it into the toaster oven.

"I haven't heard much about Angel and Mamiko lately. How are they doing?"

"Fine, I guess. They're around." Katie hated conversation like this. It was too little too late. Her father had lost interest in her life a long time ago. Now wasn't the time to get back in the game.

"You seem to be spending an awful lot of time alone lately," he said.

She busied herself by checking the browning element on the toaster oven. "Maybe I prefer it that way."

"I'm your father. I know better." He strode over and moved to embrace her.

Katie hugged him stiffly. *You know the least of all,* she wanted to tell him. But she held her tongue and allowed herself to take comfort in his sudden attention. She would never admit this, but it felt good. No matter what, he was still her daddy.

He drew back, taking both of her hands in his. "Your other and I don't know how to talk to you anymore. It ems like everything we say is wrong, and we know the loption isn't the only reason. There's more to it than at."

She felt a flutter beat in her chest.

"You're so grown up. In a few years, you'll be off to llege, then start your career, get married, have kids. If could do it all over again, I wouldn't worry so much about inning football games. I'd spend more time at home."

"I don't think being a coach has anything to do with it. ou'd find a way to turn the rest of us into background enery no matter what you did."

Her father's face registered hurt and shame.

Like she gave a damn.

He released her hands. "And you'd find a way to piss n anyone who tried to meet you halfway."

The tightness in his voice alarmed her. He'd never talked her that way before. It was angry. It was adult. Had she one too far?

"If you don't tell us what the hell is going on with you, ien we'll send you to a shrink. One way or another, you're oing to get some help." He grabbed her wrist and yanked p her sleeve.

The horror was all over his face. She saw the fresh cuts s he must see them. Sick, ugly, crazy marks.

"There's no one to blame for this, Katie. I don't care ow fucked up our family is. Jesus Christ, nothing could e so bad that you have to resort to carving up your own ody to cope."

Katie pulled her arm free. She'd kept everything under raps. Her privacy had been her sanctuary. Now everything as coming undone. She felt borderline psychotic. "You on't know anything!" she screamed. "Just leave me lone!"

"That's the last thing you want. Everything you do cri out for attention."

Her mother stalked through the kitchen door, Lia zonked out in her arms. She moved past them in all h female fury, not a look, not even a glance, to either them.

Katie started to back out of the room.

"Stay right there until your mother comes back dow We're not through yet."

She glowered at him. Why did he have to be home toda Why couldn't he be at some stupid slut's house trying get laid?

Her mother stomped back into the kitchen, taking t temperature down yet another ten degrees.

What was her problem? Katie thought.

Sharon stopped just inches from her, staring lasers wi open contempt. The slap across the face came fro nowhere, hard, ruthless, and mad as hell.

"Sharon!" her husband cried.

Katie almost lost her balance from the shock. She place a hand to the throbbing cheek of impact, still stunned.

"Do you have any idea how much damage you've caused her mother screamed.

Katie could barely string two thoughts together. Th was insane. What was she talking about?

"I should have you arrested," her mother threatene

"For what?" Katie cried.

"Don't play innocent, you destructive little bitch!"

"Sharon!" Heath interjected once more. He put a fir hand on her arm and pulled her back a few feet. "Wh the hell are you talking about?"

"Get your hands off me!" she spat. "Katie vandalize Bliss last night. And yesterday she cut up every family phot graph in this house. Go look around. Even the albums a destroyed." She turned back to Katie, more furious tha er now. "I think you're on drugs, and I want a sample your urine to find out for sure."

"You're crazy!" Katie yelled. She wanted to cry, but all e could do was boil.

"Show me your arms," her mother said evenly.

Katie looked to her father. Maybe he would jump in and ve her from this madness.

But he just stood there.

"Show me your arms," her mother repeated.

Katie made a move to bolt from the kitchen.

Her mother blocked her path.

"I didn't do any of this! You're crazy!"

"You spend all of your time alone in your room. You on't have any friends. And you mutilate your own body. m not crazy, Katie. You are."

"I hate you!"

"Go to your room. Because right now I'm close to saying ose words back to you. And meaning them."

Katie broke free and raced up the stairs to her room, amming and locking the door. Her tears were flowing. er head was spinning. Without thinking she opened her oset and pulled out the suitcase.

Kit hung up the phone feeling downright giddy. For the rst time since Leslie had taken Cameron away, she was ptimistic about the possibility of his return. Yes, it was a ng shot, but an attorney with the National Center for esbian Rights in San Francisco had just told her that her articular case benefited from "good facts." That is, a tuation not burdened by a nonbiological mother's unfit ehavior.

Take my case, she prayed, knowing the organization's ght budget restricted it to only taking on situations that ere potential precedent setters. *I want my boy back.*

Kit's buoyant mood crashed as thoughts of Leslie Tolly-

son smoked her brain. How could she have been with h
for all those years and not realized her capacity for cruel
The bitch just left one day—without warning—aware th
she held all the cards. At least the legal ones. She w
bankrupt on the moral front.

There were other women in the world like Kit. Lots
them. Nonbiological mothers involved in lesbian fam
splits. They were, in fact, legal strangers to their own ch
dren, unrecognized by the law. Most women in Kit's po
tion decided against making a public stink because pissi
off an ex only made matters worse. But she had nothing
lose at this point. Leslie had already done the unthinkab

It hurt that people didn't fully comprehend what s
was going through. Most of her friends concentrated
the breakup with Leslie, urging her to get out there a
start dating again. They seemed to believe that she w
missing Cameron like an aunt might miss a nephew.

Why couldn't they see that it was so much more th
that? Her pain was unbearable. Sometimes she found h
self eying the bottle of Halcion, wondering if she had t
courage—or perhaps the cowardice—to swallow them
at one time. With Cameron, she had shared labor a
nurture from day one, changing his diapers, preparing h
meals, wiping his tears.

The agonizing days since Leslie's disappearance h
turned to weeks, then months. Once Kit had enjoyed
close connection with Cameron's caretakers, teache
pediatrician, and some mothers of his preschool frien
But time had eroded all those relationships. In the ey
of the world, Kit wasn't a parent anymore. Maybe she nev
had been. After all, society offered so little support to sam
sex families. Yet a straight man in her position would g
thrown a legal bone, at the very least some sympathy.

She opened a can of Campbell's Healthy Request sou
and shoved it into the microwave. A five-star lunch. Th
soup was bland, the crackers stale, and the newspap

ɔring. Suddenly the rest of her solitary Sunday loomed ıt like time served for some heinous act.

Things could be worse, she thought, *as in sliced up and ; the morgue like Holly Ryan.* Kit ruminated over Heath's ıxiousness about the details surrounding the actress's ɛath. Had he left Cozy's for an interlude with Holly? Was ɛ the sex partner in question, perhaps the next to last ɛrson to see her alive?

All of this brought up a sore professional point, and that as the decision to report on the sometimes seedy off-field ves of players and coaches. Kit hated doing it. She wasn't tabloid bloodsucker; she was a sports journalist. But leave to a certain number of fast-living subjects to blur the ne.

Denny, the bartender from Cozy's, had called her last ight to fill her in on Heath's brawl with a bigmouthed atron. She worried about him, what with this Holly Ryan usiness, a crappy season for the Infernos, his daughter's emons, and the cesspool of hostility that must be his ıarriage. There was already noise about firing him if the ɛam didn't turn it around. He'd been a damn good coach, ut you were only as good as your current season. It was story, she hated to admit. And friendship, empathy, and nderlying attraction aside, she would have to cover it. oon.

Just as she settled onto the couch with a Butterfinger nd the remote, she heard someone coming up the stairs to er apartment, then two knocks hit the door. She groaned, ɛaring it might be a friend showing up to whisk her away ɔ the Sunday social at Cheetah's, a popular lipstick lesbian ar.

"Katie!" Kit exclaimed, shocked to find Heath's daughɛr on her doorstep. It was clear the teenager had been rying.

"I didn't know where else to go."

Kit's gaze fell to the suitcase in the girl's hand. The sight

of Katie's desperation pushed every maternal button ins
of Kit. Before Cameron had come into her life, childr
were always other people's problems. But he changed
way she thought about everything. A kid was in trouble
takes a village, she thought wryly.

And then she hugged Katie Driver and told her eve
thing would be okay. Even though she knew it would
be. Heath Driver was going down, and life would get wo
before it got better.

Chapter Thirty-five

Sharon wondered if Katie would ever forgive her. For riking her. For lashing out with those horrible words.

She hated herself for losing control. On the way home om Bliss, the rage had built in the car, simmering, bub-ling, then erupting the moment she placed Liam onto is youth bed and started downstairs. It infuriated her that atie was capable of so much destruction—to their family ementos, to a family business, and, most maddening of l, to her own body. Whether by cutting or drugs or both, e was abusing it.

Sharon, outside on the deck and wanting desperately to e alone with her regrets, heard Heath approach. She idn't acknowledge him. Her nerves were on edge.

Pop!

Oh, God, she hated that sound his lips made when he ok a healthy swig from a beer bottle. The truth was, she ated a lot about Heath these days.

"Sharon, I think—"

"I don't want to talk about it, Heath," she cut him coldly.

"It's the only subject on my mind."

"Then talk to yourself. You're always the smartest pers in the room anyway. The conversation should go well.

Heath just stood there a moment, sighed heavily, a took another swallow of beer. "This is about Katie. May you could put your problems with me aside for right nov

She glared at him. "That's a taller order than you realiz

"You're a big girl."

"I'm married to you. What choice do I have?"

"You lost it back there. You lost it bad, and you feel li shit. Don't take it out on me."

"But that's how bad of a husband you are, Heath. matter how much I screw up, there's always you to bla for something."

"Goddamn you!" He raised his Corona as if to thr it. Beer spilled out and splashed onto the deck. Then regained his cool and gripped the neck of the bottle, ho ing it by his side. "I'm trying here, Sharon."

She stood up to face him, unfazed by his outburst. " you do is try, Heath. Maybe you should follow throu once in a while."

"I saw her arms. What she's done to herself . . . it's it's sick. There were cuts all over. Kit Jamison was rig Katie's got deeper problems than we can handle. She nee help. She needs a therapist."

"Do you know how ridiculous that sounds? *Kit Jamis was right.* Who the fuck is Kit Jamison? She takes Katie c for lunch, and suddenly she has all the answers? Nobo has all the answers. That's the scary part. If you had se the words she spray painted on the walls of Bliss. Thin like *bitch of all time* and *diseased cunt.*"

Heath grimaced.

"I've never felt so hated. I started thinking about th teenagers in Columbine. Their parents never suspect anything. I've always harbored such contempt for mothers whose kids do terrible things. I figure they must wear blindfolds while raising them. I mean, how could you not know that there's a monster in your own home? I thought I had a good read on Katie. I thought I knew our daughter, the girl who's lived with us for the past fifteen years. I don't feel that way anymore. I don't trust her. I love her, but I don't think I like her."

Heath's expression was apoplectic. He stared at her as if he didn't know her.

Sharon lifted her cheeks and shut her eyes for a moment. "There's so much wrong with our family. There's so much wrong with us. I survived a mugging last night, and the odds are on my side to survive breast cancer. But I'll probably die . . . trying to fix this. I have to think about myself. I have to think about Liam."

"What are you saying?"

She wasn't exactly sure, but she found herself thinking about Antonio, imagining what could be. In a strange way, her cancer diagnosis had given her a second chance at life. Did she have the inner strength to take that chance? And then the words came out so clear, so declarative, that they surprised her. "I want out of this marriage."

Heath was genuinely stunned. "You don't mean that."

Sharon stared him down for long, thoughtful seconds, never blinking once. "I do mean it. If my wedding ring hadn't been stolen last night, I would give it back to you right now. That's how much I want out."

He couldn't believe it. They'd been together for twenty-two years. Granted, he wasn't husband of the year, but she'd never made noises about divorce before. His head felt hot, like he had a fever. "Come on, Sharon. You're talking crazy."

She looked back at him in amazement. "This is the sanest I've been in a long time."

It seemed as if everything were about to fall, like he was

under the shelf of a mountain of snow. He thought of the current season that would likely get him canned from the Infernos, Holly's murder, and Katie's psychological meltdown. The last thing he needed in his life was more change, more shit to deal with. He rolled the Corona bottle between both hands, examining it, wondering how the weekend could get any worse. "You're not in a good place right now."

"We're through, Heath."

He closed his fist, experiencing a sudden flash of wild anger. "How does splitting up solve anything, Sharon? Does it change the fact that you've got breast cancer? Stop Katie from hacking herself with razors? Erase the experience of being mugged last night? Jesus."

"Those are new problems. This one I've been wrestling with for a long time."

The telephone rang.

Heath didn't hesitate before making a move inside to answer it. Maybe it was Kit calling with more information from the police. Sharon could stay out on the deck all day and dream up settlement demands. Right now he didn't care.

It was Kit. Only the news she reported had nothing to do with Holly Ryan's death. "Katie's here, Heath. I didn't want you to worry."

"Katie's *there?*" His tone was incredulous.

"With a suitcase," Kit confirmed. "She's in pretty bad shape."

He fell silent. "I didn't even know she'd left the house."

"Teenagers are talented that way."

"I'm sorry about this. I'll be right there."

"Maybe she should stay here. Just for the night. Give everyone a chance to cool off."

Sharon stepped inside.

Heath placed a hand over the receiver. "Katie snuck out of the house. This is Kit. She showed up there."

Sharon threw him a look of disbelief and headed upstairs, ostensibly to check their daughter's room.

Heath returned to Kit. "Can I talk to her?"

She put Katie on, and he could hear the sound of muffled tears. A helpless feeling came over him. He wanted to help, to make everything better. But he didn't know how. "Hi, sweetheart."

"Daddy, she's crazy. I didn't do any of those things. I didn't!"

"Take it easy," he comforted her. "We'll work this out." But he didn't know what to make of it all. Here he was, smack dab in the middle, of a daughter on the edge and a wife who wanted out. As much as he hated to admit it, he didn't believe Katie. Her behavior had taken such a bizarre turn. She had lied so many times. And Sharon always kept a cool head. As a mother, she had only truly blown her top on a single occasion. This one.

Katie continued to sob and deny everything.

Sharon came back downstairs. In her hand was a can of red spray paint. "Most of her clothes are gone. I found this in her closet."

"Kit's offered to let Katie stay there. Just for tonight."

"That's fine," Sharon said coldly. "Because until she has a drug test, I don't want her back in this house."

"How about you stay with Kit tonight, sweetheart? A little bit of space would be good for everyone right now. We'll pick you up in the morning."

"I heard what that bitch said!" Katie half spat, half cried.

"We'll all get a good night's sleep and feel better about things tomorrow," he said soothingly.

Katie started sobbing.

Heath closed his eyes.

Suddenly Kit had the phone again. "Hi," she said quietly. "Don't worry. We'll rent some scary movies and binge on junk food. Tomorrow's another day."

He looked at Sharon. He heard Katie in the background.

He thought about Holly Ryan. The idea of tomorrow made him cringe.

Until she has a drug test, I don't want her back in this house.

The words ricocheted inside Katie's mind. Her mother was crazy. Just plain crazy. But then again, Sharon Driver wasn't her *real* mother. Now more than ever, Katie felt the unyielding urge to find the woman who gave birth to her.

"You're staying here tonight," Kit announced, returning the cordless phone to its base. "Your parents will pick you up in the morning."

"Yeah, to take me to get some stupid drug test. I hate them both! Why did they even adopt me in the first place? She only cares about her real child, and he's too busy screwing around to pay attention to anybody!"

Kit joined her on the roomy couch and sat in the same position—with her knees tucked up to her chest. "That's bullshit, Katie. Your mother raised you for thirteen years before your little brother came along."

"But—"

"But shit. As for your father, I know how much he loves you. Yes, there's the problem with his weakness for other women, but that's got nothing to do with you. Your father's like most men—he's either acting his age, or he's seventeen years old."

Katie felt a smirk snake onto her lips. Kit treated her like a real person and didn't sugarcoat or dumb down things just because she was fifteen. "I don't want to go home with them tomorrow."

"Too bad. You have to. I'm helping out a friend for the night. This isn't a runaway shelter."

"My mother thinks I'm on drugs."

"Are you?"

Katie felt a flush of anger. "No!"

"So have a test run and prove her wrong. You'll show up clean, and she'll feel like crap."

"It's not just . . . she thinks I'm doing all this horrible tuff!"

"Listen, Katie, the world you're growing up in is brutal. It's not *The Brady Bunch* anymore. You've quit doing things hat you used to love, pulled back from your friends, gone o school dressed like a freak, and basically moped around he house biting everybody's head off. Am I right?"

Katie merely stared, her mouth slightly agape.

"Hell, if you were my kid, I'd think you were on drugs, oo."

"Thanks."

"Don't mention it. You want some popcorn?"

She answered with a shrug.

Kit went into the small kitchen and threw some popcorn into the microwave. She kept talking over the noise of the oven. "Your parents are scared for you, and fear brings out the worst in mothers and fathers."

Katie thought of Georgette Herring, her birth mother. Who was she? Where was she? Did she ever wonder about the little baby she had given up?

"And nothing instills fear more than a teenager."

Katie regarded Kit carefully. She seemed to be the kind of woman who knew everything. "What do you know about adoptees searching for their birth parents?"

Kit got quiet, grabbing two cans of Pepsi from the fridge and reaching up to the top shelf in one of the cabinets for a large bowl. "I know that if you're not eighteen, you'll only be able to seek out those records with your parents by your side."

Katie pulled a face.

"And I know that no matter how it turns out, it's still an emotional roller coaster. Why does that interest you?"

"It just does."

Kit ripped open the steaming popcorn bag, filled up

the bowl, and returned to the sofa. "What do you expec
to get out of it?"

Katie grabbed a handful. A few kernels dropped and
disappeared between the cushions. She started to search
for them.

"Don't bother," Kit said. "Besides, there's no telling
what you'll find."

Katie grinned and took in a mouthful of the butter
snack.

"By the way, this is dinner. But don't tell your parent
that."

Katie grinned again. Her mood was lifting.

"Seriously, what do you expect to get out of it?"

"Well, I'd like to ask her why she gave me up, and I'd
like the chance to connect with her."

"What if she tells you to get lost?"

The question stunned her. That thought had never
occurred to her. She was getting used to Kit's straight talk
but this was just mean. "She wouldn't do that."

"How do you know?"

"I just do. She was only eighteen, and she didn't have
any money. Otherwise she would've kept me."

"Maybe she moved up in the world, married well, and
had her own family. If so, you might be the last thing she'd
want to find on her doorstep."

Katie fought to keep that scenario out of her mind. Her
vision was one of open arms, hugging, lots of tears, and
promises to never let her go again. She shook her head
stubbornly. "No, that wouldn't happen."

Kit leveled a get-real look. "You can't romanticize this
It's complicated. There's so much you don't know. Besides,
it's too soon to search, and you're not the least bit ready."

"Yes, I am!"

"You can't get it right with the two parents you've known
for the last fifteen years. The last thing you need is another
parent to deal with."

Katie glared. She usually managed to get the last word
n, but Kit stumped her at every turn. "You're a bitch."

"So are you. That's why we like each other. What do
ou say these two bitches make a Blockbuster run for some
cary movies. We each get to pick one."

"Scream!" Katie suggested.

Kit pondered her choice for a moment, then announced
in a fiendish voice. *"Halloween."*

Katie felt an eagerness, a girlish excitement that she
adn't known in a long time. Maybe everything was going
o be okay after all.

Georgette Tucker watched the news with increasing irri-
ability. Holly Ryan's death was being reported as an unsolved
nurder. The police were morons. Would she have to spell
out for them in a child's big letter storybook?

The day was passing like Chinese water torture. She'd
lanned to have a front row seat for the emotional carnage.
ut it wasn't happening that way.

I'll pay you for the full day, but I think you should leave.

If the bitch only knew. That the maid's salary she offered
or a month's work would barely cover Georgette's weekly
ardening bill in the Hamptons. That caring for her two-
ear-old brat brought Georgette one step closer to child
nurder every day.

She touched her heart. It was pumping wildly. Breathing
leeply, she concentrated in an attempt to calm her emo-
ions, to contain her hatred. She knew that, at this point,
eing too impatient and taking too much for granted was
he worst thing she could do. When she vibed in on the
act that she'd never in her wildest dreams envisioned
aining such intimate access to the Driver home, her agita-
ion leveled off.

She thought back to that day in Phipp's Plaza. Watching
rom a distance, she had witnessed an unexpected gift—

the boy wandering into the mall. Stealthily, she had scooped him up playfully, promised him a cookie, and whisked him down the escalator.

Her story of past day nanny service had been nothing more than inspired spontaneity. What she'd hoped to get from that was, after a forced acquaintanceship with Sharon, perhaps the odd chance to baby-sit. And then the bitch had announced her cancer woes. Poor baby. No one deserved the disease more.

Being inside that house was at once exhilarating and painful. To just see her baby girl took Georgette to peaks of joy she never knew were possible. But she forced herself to pull back from every natural instinct toward Savannah. To never take her eyes off her. To hold her tight and never let go. To buy her anything she wanted just to see her smile.

Savannah was a smart girl. Her eyes gleamed with a fierce intelligence. But she was still young. If Georgette played every second with computer cool, then Savannah would fall into line. It was so excruciating to allow Savannah her space and to lavish all that attention on the brat. Still, there was no other way. Because the idea to seek out Linda Moore as an ally had to be Savannah's alone. Only then would the bond be strong, meaningful, and unbreakable.

Georgette's eyes fell upon the red spray paint can resting atop the counter. She smiled. Dropping the bit about the possibility of drug use had been a stroke of genius. Talk about insult to injury. First the bitch would blame Savannah for the family photo slashings *and* the vandalism at Bliss, then accuse her of being a druggie. Like any freaked out soccer mom who's seen one too many *Dateline* stories on teens and drugs, her suspicions would drive her to snoop. And nestled inside Savannah's closet was a can of spray paint just like the one used to graffiti Bliss.

Her plan was slow moving . . . but richly rewarding. After all the false allegations and privacy invasions, the bitch's relationship with Savannah would be battle scarred beyond repair. A house divided. Indeed.

Georgette stepped into the bedroom to gaze at the wall enshrined to her child, from baby to little girl to young woman. As tears rained down, fury piled up. She had missed so much. The first smile, the first step, the first day of school, the first crush, the first period. They had robbed her of every precious moment. That's why they would pay so dearly.

The bitch.

The bastard.

Even the little boy.

Georgette Tucker had plans for all of them.

Drew Barrymore was hanging from a tree with her guts ripped out.

"That is so gross!" Kit wailed. "I've never seen this before. It's good. It's scary."

Katie managed a weak smile. She'd seen *Scream* at least a dozen times. The inaugural excitement had worn off. *Halloween* had been fun, but the truth was, she didn't want to spend her time with Kit watching stupid girls in tight sweaters run away from masked killers. She wanted to talk. Kit helped her see things in a different light, and there was plenty of crap inside her head that needed a new view.

Once Skeet Ulrich jumped into Neve Campbell's bedroom by way of the window, Katie could take no more. She reached for the remote and pressed PAUSE. The screen froze on Neve. "Do you mind if we watch this later?"

Kit's face registered a flash of disappointment. She was totally into the movie. "Not too much later. It can't be the last thing I do before I go to bed. I'll never get to sleep." She leaned back and tossed a celestial throw blanket onto her lap. "What's on your mind?"

Katie didn't know where to start. "You're cool. I wish . . . I could be more like you."

"I'm cool?" Kit asked with self-deprecating doubt. "Don't make the mistake of thinking I've always been this way. You're much more together than I was at your age."

Katie scoffed. "Like I'm together."

"Compared to me back then—yes, you are."

Katie was instantly intrigued. "What was your deal?"

"For starters, I was the only gay girl in my high school. I don't recommend that if popularity is your key objective—or a date to the prom—because it's pretty much after high school that boys start fantasizing about lesbians."

Katie tried to take in Kit with a more critical eye without being too obvious. She was a near dead ringer for Heather Locklear, only not quite as thin and more casual in her style. "I didn't know."

"I don't alert the media every ten minutes like Ellen and Anne. My sexuality is a small percentage of who I am. It's no one's business."

Katie pointed to a photograph of a little boy about Liam's age. "Well, who's that? I assumed he was your son."

Kit stared at the picture for a long time. "That's Cameron. He is my son."

"I don't—"

"Katie," Kit began, cutting her off gently but firmly, "I'd rather not talk about this right now. The wound is too fresh. Okay?"

"Sure."

"Besides, I was fine watching a bunch of smart-ass teenagers get killed, but you turned the movie off."

"So you hated high school, too?"

"Who doesn't?"

"I could name several people who seem to love it at Riverside Central."

"Well, they're either good performers and full of insecurities like everyone else, or they're the kind of people who peak in high school. It seems life or death right now, Katie. What some asshole says to you in front of a big group in the cafeteria. A rumor about you that starts in the hall and ends up in every classroom before the last bell. But once you leave all that shit behind and start your *real* life, it will seem as ridiculous as it is." Kit pointed a firm finger at her. "Listen to me when I say this: Never give a bunch of jerks power over you. Tell them to fuck off and keep moving."

"I can't think that fast, like the way you did with Thomas Prewitt. People heard about it, and they were calling his cell phone to complain about their pizzas being late for a whole week!"

Kit laughed so hard that she snorted like a pig.

Katie laughed, too, though more at the noise Kit had made than the situation. "I just can't think that fast on my feet."

"Bullshit. Give those fuckheads half the hell you give your parents, and they'll need a diaper just to pass you in the hall."

Katie giggled at the image.

"I'm serious. It's in you. I can see it."

"Is that how you handled it when you were my age?"

"Hell, no," Kit replied with a severe shake of her head. "I passed all that frustration onto myself." She rucked up the sleeves of her Georgia Tech sweatshirt and thrust out her forearms.

Katie stared at the scars, the hideous hacking marks going this way and that, starting at her wrists and stopping just before her elbows. It suddenly occurred to Katie that her own arms would look the same one day.

"Needless to say, summer's a pain in the ass. It's a bitch wearing long sleeves in Georgia heat."

A few beats of silence passed between them.

"Show me yours," Kit said.

Katie regarded her for a prolonged moment as it dawned on her. "You told my father."

"I sure did. I saw your arm at Johnny Rocket's and knew right away. Especially when you gave me that line about your cat scratching you. I used to say that too, but at least I had a cat. You're the worst kind of cutter, Katie. Just like I was. I didn't do it for the attention. I did it for relief. I was so secretive about it that my parents didn't find out for months."

Katie felt that familiar stirring. If she were alone right now, the razor would be slicing into her skin. There was so much pain inside her, and she wanted to feel the blood flowing down her arm. It's not that she wanted to die. It's that cutting had become her way of staying alive.

Kit hesitated a moment, as if her mind had taken her to a deep, dark, and sad place. "I always did it at night, when everybody was asleep. Once my parents found out, they made me sleep in their room. I couldn't even go to the bathroom without one of them following me and standing outside the door. They made me feel like a crazy person. So did my therapist. I still don't think I was crazy, though. I was just coping. The best way I knew how at the time."

Katie wondered what her parents were going to do. Her mother had looked her dead in the eyes and called her crazy. What if they sent her away to some kind of hospital? That's what happened in the Winona Ryder movie *Girl, Interrupted*. A helpless fear swept over her. "I'm not crazy."

"I know that," Kit said softly. "But convincing the rest of the world isn't always easy. I remember once my therapist tried to tell me that my cutting was a symbolic substitute for self-castration because I perceived my sexuality as dangerous." She delivered the doctor's theory in the kind of crisp, dry tone that an out-of-touch research scientist might employ.

Katie pulled a face. "What does that mean?"

"To me, it meant nothing. For him, it meant that he spent too much time with his face buried in psychiatric journals. I knew that it wasn't being a lesbian that made me hate myself enough to take a knife to my own body. I think it was all the assholes around me. I started to believe what they were saying."

"How did you stop?"

"My therapist wasn't a total quack. He helped me to realize that by cutting myself, I was just disguising my rage and substituting my body as the real target for my pain and anger. That might sound like a lot of psychobabble, but for me, it was a big breakthrough."

Katie thought hard on that one. Slowly, it began to make sense to her, too. When she marked her own skin, it didn't just provide relief, it made her feel in control.

"What are your talents?" Kit asked. "You must do something that makes you feel really good about yourself. Is it soccer?"

"Soccer's fun, but . . . it's not, like, the main thing."

"Well, what is?"

Katie hesitated, then reluctantly told Kit all about her *Grrl Talk* zine project. She talked about writing it, designing it, and getting the critical rave from the San Francisco-based zine review *Factsheet Five.*

Kit listened with wide-eyed amazement, especially when Katie told her how she and Angel used to cut class in order to distribute it randomly in lockers throughout the school.

"This is incredible!" Kit finally exclaimed. "You're a fifteen-year-old publishing diva!"

Katie grinned and put her face in her hands. The praise embarrassed her. But it also made her feel fantastic.

"You've got to get me a copy of the latest issue."

She stiffened a bit. "I'm not doing it anymore."

"What made you stop?"

The question kicked up a storm of terrible memories. The erotic column *Her Fantasy*, namely that particular one detailing a sexual adventure with Derek Johnson. The frightening incident at his cousin's house. And then the humiliating aftershocks at school. Her eyes began to sting.

"This has something to do with those guys harassing you, doesn't it?"

Katie nodded. A silent tear rolled down her cheek, and she stopped it with her knuckle.

"Why don't you tell me what happened? You can trust me. This will stay between us. I swear to that."

Katie was ready. Living alone with the experience had brought her nothing but pain and loneliness. If she were going to take the scary leap in the dark to share it with anyone, then Kit was that person. "I had a crush on this guy, a senior football player named Derek Johnson. He reminded me of Will Smith. I wrote an erotic story about him once in *Grrl Talk.*"

Kit was watching her, but not judging her. That gave her the courage to go on.

"We used to flirt a lot, and one day after school he invited me back to his house. It was a stupid thing to do, but I jumped into his car and went with him. He ended up taking me to his cousin Ty's house. Derek took me to one of the bedrooms in the back and started coming on really strong. I tried to get him to slow down, but he locked the door." Her voice quivered at the end, then halted altogether.

"What happened next?" Kit asked.

The memory was snare drum tight in Katie's mind. "He kept telling me how much I wanted it, that if I'd just give him five minutes I'd be begging for it."

The expression on Kit's face was total disgust. "Did you tell him to stop? Did you say no?"

Katie shook her head. "I didn't say anything. I didn't do anything. I just kept thinking how it was nothing like the fantasy I wrote about. I only wanted it to be over so I could go home." She shut her eyes to the image of Derek's jeans around his ankles and his thick gold chain banging against her chest. "It hurt really bad, and I felt sick. I wanted to take a shower. Then his cousin knocked on the door, and Derek let him in."

Kit's lips parted in fear.

Katie fought against the sense memory of Derek's stale breath and the room's dank carpet. "Derek said I was good and told Ty he should get some from me, too. Ty asked him how old I was. When Derek told him, Ty said, 'A fifteen-year-old will get me fifteen years. But there's no crime in me watching while she sucks you.' I begged them to let me go home, but Ty kept telling me that I couldn't until I proved what a good girl I was. Finally, I just started doing what he wanted. It seemed like the quickest way out of there. Ty sat in a chair and played with himself. He told Derek to make me swallow but I didn't. I spit it out in the bathroom sink and got out of there as fast as I could. I felt so cheap and dirty. All the way home I kept thinking that it was my fault. I thought maybe I had asked for it with the things I wrote and the way I dressed."

"That's not true," Kit said sharply. "You didn't *ask for it.* Don't ever think that way."

"The trouble at school started right away. He told some of his friends." She sighed heavily and rolled her eyes. "Word travels fast at Riverside Central. I became the slut of the century overnight."

"Did he use protection?"

"No, but he pulled out. There's no way I could be pregnant."

"It's the risk of sexually transmitted diseases that I'm worried about. You should get tested for HIV. Who knows where this creep has been?"

Katie stared blankly, suddenly feeling incredibly stupid. Never once had she bothered to think about that. She'd taken the lunkhead coach's health class and listened to him prattle on about AIDS, herpes, gonorrhea, and other crap.

"You're guilty of poor judgment here, Katie, but I've seen girls much older than you get themselves into far more dangerous situations. You've learned a hard lesson early on. If you don't know a guy really well, you always have to keep the upper hand. Athletes can be the worst. I've dealt with them my whole life. I know. My father was a football coach, and now I work in sports. Sometimes I'm in the locker room with these pigs. And remember, the animals I'm dealing with have at least been to college. This Derek guy is just one big teenage hormone. Have you thought about turning him in? I mean, this sounds like date rape to me."

"Fuck no," Katie said, feeling like it was something Kit might say. She loved everything about Kit—the way she talked, her confidence, her ability to detect bullshit a mile away. "I've seen all the TV movies. It's not like I was some sweet innocent girl on a movie date. I had written a soft-porn story about this guy. I was dressed like Mariah Carey. I jumped into his car, let him take me to a strange house, and willingly headed into one of the bedrooms with him right away. Who's going to feel sorry for me? Stories like mine do more harm than good. I'd set date rape cases back ten years by going forward."

"So what are you going to do?" Kit eyed her with a steely gaze, throwing down the question like a gauntlet.

Katie stared back, uncertain how to answer.

"What you just said is true. It sucks big-time, but it's true. You're no bimbo, Katie. You know the score, and you're tougher than you give yourself credit for. If getting traditional justice is so unlikely, that doesn't mean you can't get your own kind."

"What do you mean?"

"Don't let that son of a bitch get away with it. Make him pay."

"But how?"

"What makes you feel strong and powerful and capable?" There was a gleam in Kit's eyes, as if she already knew the answer.

Katie searched her heart, soul, and mind. Creating *Grrl Talk* took her to another world. She missed the feeling it gave her. But if she went back to the zine, it wouldn't be the same. Because she wasn't the same. Her spirits lifted as the art of the possible flew in and out of her brain. "My zine!" she shouted, like some game show contestant.

Kit grabbed her hands. "Damn straight!"

Katie beamed. She threw her arms around Kit and hugged her tightly, then drew back, flashing a diabolical grin. "What's the old saying? The pen is mightier than the dick?"

Kit put a hand over her mouth and laughed, shaking her head. "I've created a monster."

Katie felt a surge of adrenaline. She couldn't wait to get started. She couldn't wait to call Angel. "*Grrl Talk* is back in business."

Chapter Thirty-six

The days of Sharon forgetting that she had breast cancer were over, at least for the next six weeks. Starting today, radiation therapy would become part of her weekday routine.

Antonio had wanted to accompany her this morning, but she'd insisted on coming alone. After all, he was consumed with clearing the obscentities off the walls of Bliss. She couldn't have him tending to her medical needs as well. Allowing him to do both would make him, what, her husband? In theory, he did qualify for the title, more so than her real one at home.

Which is why she had been so stubborn about tackling radiation treatment alone. Heath no longer held a monopoly on marital infidelity in their house. Sharon may have staved off a physical affair with Antonio, but the emotional one was hotter than ever.

Could it be that Antonio seemed so good because the rest of her life was so bad? *No,* she decided, *he is that good.* In fact, he seemed to get better each day. Before she became aware of it, Sharon had wandered too far down and discovered that a door had silently closed behind her. She was trapped now, in that make-believe room, with Antonio. And she was in love.

"Are you wearing antiperspirant?" Suzanne asked, stepping into the treatment room and cutting into Sharon's inward distraction. She was part of the radiation therapy team that Keri Ward had assured her would become like family.

Sharon nodded. "Secret—it's strong enough for a man. . . ."

The nurse laughed. "I'll be right back."

A few minutes later she returned with a basin of warm, soapy water and instructed Sharon to cleanse her underarm area thoroughly. "Antiperspirant can interfere with the radiation. I'd stop using it until your treatment cycle is complete," she explained.

Everyone on the team was warm and compassionate, showing great concern and taking special care. They were meticulous with measurements needed to determine the correct angles for aiming the beams, even making ink marks on her skin to focus on the right area. The procedure itself was short and painless, almost like an extended X ray. In a few minutes it was over.

Keri Ward had cautioned her that a likely side effect of radiation would be fatigue. Muscle stiffness in the back and upper arm had been mentioned, too. Sharon wondered if it was starting already, or if her body was simply reacting to the horrific weekend.

"You did great," Carrie said. She was heavy, with a round face and sweet brown eyes. "That wasn't so bad. Now you're done."

Until tomorrow, Sharon thought. *And the day after that. And the day after that. . . .*

She said her good-byes, gathered up her things, and left quietly. Heath weighed on her mind. Checking her watch, she realized that he was probably on his way to Kit Jamison's apartment to pick up Katie. The next stop was to the hospital for a drug test. After that, he would deliver her to school.

Sharon had insisted that Heath take on these tasks alone. She didn't want to see Katie right now. She didn't want to be with her husband either. There was so much to deal with, so many feelings to sort out.

Deep inside her Prada bag, Sharon's cellular phone sang to life. She scooped it out and checked the screen. The ID function identified the caller as A. Miguel. She experienced a distinct uptick in her heartbeat as she clicked the button to bring him into her life.

"How did your treatment go?"

The sound of his voice soothed her instantly, and whatever fatigue she'd been feeling just slipped away. "It was quick and painless." She paused a second. "Unlike the rest of my life. There should be radiation treatments for bad husbands and impossible teenagers."

"What about cyber cafe guys who refuse to honor the wishes of a beautiful boutique owner?"

"I'll get back to you on that. It's not exactly a disturbing trend yet."

"I couldn't stay away. The thought of you coming out of here alone really messed with my mind."

Sharon was still in the outpatient center parking lot. She stopped in her tracks, directly in front of her Range Rover. His use of the word *here* had captured her undivided attention.

"Turn around," Antonio said.

She spun quickly to see him leaning against the trunk of his BMW, one leg crossed over the other, his cell phone cradled to his ear, an incredibly sexy smile planted on his face.

"I'm not a stalker. I promise."

"Even if you were, a girl could do worse."

"I'm taking you out for breakfast. If you're not hungry you can watch me eat. I'm starving."

Sharon thought of Heath and the potential irony of this role reversal. While he was taking care of their family, she was contemplating an outing with a gorgeous, younger man. She knew it was wrong. She knew this getaway would lead to more of the same. She knew that their emotional affair might one day turn physical.

But she walked across the parking lot anyway.

"Shit," Heath hissed. "This fucking traffic is worse than L.A." He fought it all the way to Kit's apartment, and the stop-and-go crawl gave him ample time to think about his life.

He wondered how serious Sharon was about calling it quits. Over the last twenty-two years, they'd hurled some pretty cruel words to each other, but neither had ever thrown talk of divorce into the air. Until she did yesterday.

There were strong signals that Sharon meant business. Talking about giving up her wedding ring. Refusing to sleep in their bed last night. Announcing the AIDS fund-raiser at the Swissotel as their last public appearance as a couple. If she was trying to get his attention, she had it.

He tried to imagine life as an almost fifty single man, and it scared the hell out of him. Married men with the right package could have the best of both worlds—a cozy home life and an outside sex life. But for divorced men, the planets always shifted a bit. A guy could get tagged as pathetic real quick.

Heath played the point out in his head, thinking how lonely it would feel to set up his own household. Not to mention what a hassle it would be. Then there was the issue of joint custody to consider. And holidays. Jesus Christ, the holidays. He rubbed his tired eyes, depressed by the realizations. All that freedom would probably kill his sex drive. It seemed to thrive on the illicitness of his encounters.

He pulled into Kit's complex and vowed to work his ass off to get Katie in line again. If that happened, maybe Sharon would calm down. His right knee throbbed with pain as he climbed the single flight of stairs. Shit, he was falling apart.

Kit answered the door, dressed for work and looking anxious to get there. Sometimes her beauty just smacked him between the eyes. Like it did this morning. She was scrubbed clean and golden—the ultimate California girl.

"I hope you didn't teach my daughter any of your bad habits," Heath cracked.

Kit scanned him up and down. "You look like shit."

"That would be one of them."

She grinned. "Katie! Your father's here."

His daughter emerged from the bedroom carrying her suitcase. She embraced him and kissed his cheek. "Hi, Daddy." Her voice was soft, calm, and conciliatory. She shot a quick look down to the empty Durango. "Where's Mom?"

Heath just looked at her for a second. "She started her radiation treatment today. Head on down to the car, sweetheart. I want to talk to Kit for a minute."

Katie put down her suitcase and hugged Kit tightly. There seemed to be a silent, secret exchange as they locked hands in a show of female solidarity.

"Another burger, fries, and malt pig-out—soon," Kit said.

Katie smiled and started down the stairs and to the car as instructed.

"She seems better already," Heath observed.

"You've got a fantastic kid there."

He turned to see her sitting in the front seat, watching them.

"Anything we discussed is confidential. So don't ask.

But I will say this: Katie maintains that she didn't vandaliz Bliss or cut up the family photos, and I believe her. W shared a lot. She wouldn't lie to me."

"You don't know teenagers."

"I know that one."

"I'll pass your faith along." He sighed, filled with drea in triplicate. At the thought of taking his daughter to th hospital and ordering up a drug screen. At the idea o going through a divorce. At the possibility of facing thos tight-ass detectives again.

"Denny called me. He's the bartender at Cozy's. Th idea of a bar fight is passé. People get shot now. Haven't yo heard? How will your daughter get to her drug screenings i you get killed by some jerk?"

He looked down, then up again sheepishly, with a hin of a grin. It was his vulnerable man look, shamelessly stole from George Clooney. But he had the move locked down Even Kit seemed affected by it. "He called my team bunch of pussies."

"I was at the game. He's right."

For some reason the truth didn't hurt coming from her It gave him a charge. They could laugh, drink, talk sports tear each other apart, get pissed, and come back to the same place like nothing ever happened. If only they coulc fuck, too. Then their relationship would be perfect.

"You're becoming a story, Heath. The Infernos are shi this year. People are blaming you. I have to cover this, and I won't give it the soft touch."

He stared at her, finally deciding to say exactly what was on his mind. At this point, what could it hurt? "I want to sleep with you."

Kit didn't say yes. But she didn't say no, either. She just stepped inside her apartment and closed the door.

* * *

They sat in the emergency clinic waiting area. Heath watched the twenty-inch television across the room. A bunch of freaks were pushing and throwing punches on Ricki Lake.

Katie thumbed through a battered issue of *People.* "It's going to come back negative." This was the third time she'd declared her purity. Once on the way over, once before she produced the urine sample, and now as they sweated out the results. "What's next, then?"

Heath didn't have an answer for that one. He just patted her knee . . . and waited, taking in the people around him. Soccer moms with sick kids. Old people with broken bones. Professional types with the flu.

"Mr. Driver, if you could come back with me for a few minutes. We'll bring Katie in shortly." The black nurse looked young enough to still be in school, but her large eyes projected confidence and competence.

Heath's heart lurched. Why would they split up the parent and child for good news? He followed her down a corridor and into an examining area. It wasn't a room. She just pulled a curtain for privacy. Babies were wailing. Kids were coughing. He finally got close enough to the nurse to read her badge. Her name was Denise.

"Your daughter's not on drugs."

He felt instant relief.

"But we always screen for STDs in girls her age as well. Katie tested positive for chlamydia."

At first, Heath couldn't believe it, but the nurse continued on.

"Luckily, we have the benefit of early detection here. This can be treated with oral antibiotics. But we recommend testing every six months. Twenty percent of girls become infected a second time."

Stunned, he sat down on the examining table. The butcher paper made a loud crinkling sound. He tried to wrap his brain around the news. How could it be true? It just didn't seem possible.

Katie had contracted a sexually transmitted disease.

Sharon and Antonio were tucked into a booth at a Waffle House. It was cheap, dingy, packed with workers just off the all-night shift, and exquisitely romantic.

He cleaned up the last of a big plate topped with eggs, bacon, grits, and pancakes.

A tired waitress refilled their coffees and put down a ticket. "Ya'll have a great day now, you hear?"

Antonio smiled his thanks as she shuffled away. He sipped the fresh coffee and murmured, "Mmmm . . . what does it say about java.com when Waffle House makes a better cup of coffee?"

Sharon grinned, feeling her own eyes twinkle, content to just sit here and watch this man eat and listen to whatever he had to say.

He became aware of her focus. "What?"

"You're so wonderful. I can't believe any woman would let you get away."

Antonio appeared suddenly uneasy. "Believe it. I walk in with a lot of gloss and polish, but once that wears off, the flaws are there."

That was a point she wanted to explore when her cell phone rang. She retrieved it from her purse and checked the ID screen. It was Heath. Her heart sank. Gesturing for Antonio to hold that thought, she answered.

"Katie's drug screen came back clean," Heath announced without preamble.

Sharon sensed something more.

"But she tested positive for chlamydia."

"Chlamydia?" It came out as a shriek.

Antonio was startled.

The patrons sitting in the tables and booths around them obviously heard. They lobbed over strange looks. Some of them laughed.

"I'm at the drugstore now," Heath was saying. "We're on our way home."

Sharon heard a certain despair in his voice that touched her. Despite everything else, he loved Katie and Liam fiercely, wanted the best for them, worried about them. In that way, he was an ideal husband. Maybe it was the only way . . . but she had to at least give him that much. "I'll meet you there."

Antonio's eyes were on her, waiting for an explanation.

"It's my daughter," she said, retrieving her keys and returning the phone to her purse. "I have to go. I'm sorry." She started to rise, then realized that her Range Rover was at the cancer outpatient center.

"I'll take you to your car," Antonio said.

Sharon didn't utter a word during the drive back. Her silence was deliberate, and instinctively, he seemed to know not to break it with small talk or concerned inquiries.

"I'll call you," he said as she exited the car.

Sharon hesitated before closing the door. She wanted to tell him not to. Everything was so complicated, and her feelings were all over the place. But his interest provided a quiet comfort that she didn't have the strength to let go of. "My life is such a mess. What makes you want to stick around?"

"That's an easy question. You."

She swung the door shut and climbed into her vehicle. His answer was so poignant that her heart responded to it immediately. And then a decision came to her quite easily. After the AIDS benefit, she would ask Heath to move out. She promised herself that she would go through with it.

No matter what.

* * *

Katie hated Derek Johnson, and he was going to pay. Big-time.

In all honesty, she owed her mother a debt of thanks for suspecting her of being on drugs. The nurse at the clinic had said that most girls with chlamydia don't show any symptoms and that an untreated infection could trigger pelvic inflammatory disease, which causes infertility. The domino effect was amazing. That horny thug could have possibly ruined her chances of having a family of her own!

She sat at her desk, in front of her computer, brainstorming about the next issue of *Grrl Talk* as fast as her fingers could type out the thoughts. For the first time in months, she actually would prefer being at Riverside Central High School. After all, that's where Angel was, and they had so much work to do on the return of the zine. What she had planned would shock the shit out of the entire student body.

A soft knock broke her concentration.

Katie activated the screen saver to hide her notes and unlocked the door.

Linda Moore stood on the other side. "Hi, there." Her eyes zeroed in on the suitcase in the middle of her bed. "Going somewhere?"

Katie shook her head. "Coming back. I stayed with a friend last night. She's the coolest woman I've ever met. Her name's Kit Jamison, and she has her own radio show called *Adrenaline.* She's pretty, smart, and funny—a real ball buster. I want to be just like her."

Linda's eyes widened with interest.

Katie realized how badly she wanted to share her incredible experience with Kit. Angel was trapped in Mrs. Larson's

Spanish class, and her father was too freaked out by the idea of her having sex to have a real conversation.

"Your little brother's napping," Linda said. "I'd love to hear about it." She settled on the edge of the bed and looked up expectantly.

Katie told her all about Kit's apartment, the movies they watched, the junk food they ate, and how the two of them stayed up half the night talking and sharing intimate secrets.

"That sounds like fun, but Kit's an adult. Don't you think you should be doing those things with girls your own age?" Linda asked.

Katie gave her a strange look. Since when did the nanny get off policing her friends? "Kit's sort of a big sister. She's smart about things that girls my age don't have a clue about—like trying to find my birth mother. Kit says it's way too soon. She thinks I need to sort out all the chaos with my adoptive parents first. I mean, they reached out and took me in as their own. I owe them that much. Plus, how do I know my birth mother even wants to be found? She could reject me. And Kit doesn't think I could deal with that right now, not on top of everything else."

Linda reached out and stroked Katie's hair.

The gesture took Katie by surprise.

"You're a beautiful girl, Katie. No mother in her right mind would turn away from you."

"Who knows for sure? And what if *I* reject *her*? I mean, I struggle enough to get along with the mother I've known since I was two days old! Why should I believe that meeting my birth mother will mean instant love? Kit says that's *Fantasy Island* thinking. This is the real world. It's tough. Sometimes shit just doesn't go your way."

Linda stared back at her, nodding intently. "This Kit Jamison has been a strong influence on you. She sounds interesting. I'll have to make a point to meet her one day."

* * *

Through the French doors, Sharon watched her husband stand outside on the deck, his lips on a beer bottle, his eyes on the trees. This was the place where she'd told him that she wanted a divorce. It would go down on record as the setting for one of the strongest and most difficult moments in her life.

Heath sensed her presence and turned to look at her, raising his Corona in mock toast.

She stepped outside to join him. Clouds covered the sky. A wind was picking up, and the threat of rain hung in the air.

"I couldn't talk to her. I didn't know what to say." He shook his head. "Our fifteen-year-old daughter's out there having sex, and she doesn't even have a boyfriend."

"My concern is that she's not using protection."

"So the sex isn't a problem?" He was instantly hot, brazenly rhetorical. "You just want her to use condoms?"

"Look at the culture she's living in, Heath. Sex is inevitable. Yes, I would prefer that she wait, but how realistic is that? I just want her to be safe about it."

"Maybe we should put a basket of Trojans near the front door."

"Sounds good," Sharon said, annoyed by his bitter sarcasm but up to swing back some of her own. "That would be convenient for you, too."

He gave her a cold stare.

"What? There's no sweet young thing waiting in the wings to help you get over the grief of losing Holly?"

"No . . . not yet. But there will be." He turned up the bottle and drank deep, a nasty expression on his face. "And who can blame me? It gets cold sleeping next to you."

Sharon fought hard to remain calm. It was a cheap shot and he knew it. Even in the beginning, their sex life had never really caught fire. The years of infertility had wreaked so much havoc. And then there was her sense that he brought other women into bed with him. Whenever they made love, she always got the same disconcerting notion—that he thought of someone else, a movie, an erotic fantasy . . . anything but her. It always left her feeling inadequate and unsatisfied. Now here he was, all but threatening to seek out another, justifying his cheating by calling her frigid. She hated him for it.

"I'll talk to Katie," she said quietly. "You go to hell."

Sharon knocked once and tried the door, distressed to find it locked. Katie's days of ironclad privacy were about to end. As much as the idea disturbed her, she considered doing a full-scale snoop of Katie's room. She still lived under their roof, and the ability to trust her had faded to almost nothing. It was time to seize control of their daughter. Assuming it wasn't too late.

Katie opened the door, gave an impassive glance, and returned to her desk.

"Your father's beside himself. He doesn't know how to talk to you about this."

"The subject is sex. That shouldn't be a stretch for him."

Tentatively, Sharon sat down on the edge of the bed. "How long have you been active?"

Katie didn't take her eyes off the computer screen. She was scrolling through clip art files. "I'm not. That was my first time. Maybe my only time until Enrique Iglesias makes himself available."

"Who was the boy, Katie?" There was an edge to her tone that she couldn't hold back.

"I'm not telling you."

Sharon took in a breath, hoping to keep her cool. "He needs to know. So do his parents."

"Believe me, I'll let him know about it." Katie's voice carried an ominous quality.

"I want to talk to his parents."

Katie scoffed and swiveled to face her for the first time. "Like his parents could give a shit. First of all, there's no father to speak of, and his mother would probably blame me. This guy was a crush, the kind that grosses me out when I think about it now. You know, a big mistake. But look at the bright side—I'm fifteen-years-old and my bad-boy complex is over. How many girls can say that? If nothing else, it will prepare me for that rogue Italian on my first trip abroad."

Sharon was taken aback. Underneath Katie's trademark insolence, something new existed. Her daughter sounded strong, feral, and forthright. In a strange way, it worked toward abating Sharon's worry. But there were other issues at stake. Her self-inflicted cuts. Her destruction of Bliss and the family photographs. "I think you should talk to someone, Katie. A professional who—"

"Hold on," Katie cut in. "If you believe that I had anything to do with vandalizing Bliss and cutting up those pictures, then *you* need the professional."

" 'Mother from hell' was spray painted on the wall." Sharon spoke in a low, modulated tone, her stare tracking her daughter's reaction with laserlike intensity.

"I don't necessarily disagree with the sentiment, but I didn't have anything to do with it. I'd hurt myself before I hurt anybody else." Katie pushed up her sleeve and thrust out her forearm. "And I have."

The marks were hideous. Sharon wanted to turn away, but her gaze was riveted.

Katie covered her scarred skin. "But that's all over now."

It disturbed her that Katie could be so compelling and convincing in a face-to-face lie. She actually wanted to believe her. "You have access to my keys," Sharon accused. "You know the security code, too."

"So does Mary Payne. Maybe she hates working for you. Ever thought of that?"

"No. Her behavior has never been so bizarre that I could even begin to suspect her of anything so awful."

"Oh, I get it. But since I'm the child you bought and not the one you gave birth to, you can suspect me!"

Sharon rose up in anger. "That's so unfair! You've been secretive and hateful for weeks. One day you're trying to walk out of the house dressed like some video starlet, and the next day you look like a Marilyn Manson groupie. What am I supposed to think?"

"I don't know! But it wasn't me! Maybe you pissed someone off! Maybe you have a stalker!"

The suggestion stunned Sharon into a deep, probing silence. A stalker? Her body went cold. She thought long and hard on the matter. Suddenly the murders of Peyton Drake and Dr. Ridgeway popped into mind. That news had unsettled her when she heard it weeks ago. It had the same effect today. A premonition of danger enveloped her. Sharon continued to be on edge about the possibility of Georgette Tucker finding her family. An idea occurred to her. Maybe she should find Georgette Tucker.

Chapter Thirty-seven

Tara Daye, Inc. was discreetly nestled inside a midtown Atlanta office building. Sharon had heard about the private investigator from a regular customer at Bliss who'd employed her to get the goods on a suspicious husband. As it turned out, he was spending most of his business hours on the Internet, luring gay teenage boys into meetings at cheap motels.

Sharon passed through a door that looked like it would lead to a dentist's office in Anywhere, USA. But inside it was half-science-fiction movie set, half-sleek-fashion funhouse.

High-tech ruled, from the flat-screen computers and space age office equipment to the glass and chrome do-it-yourself spy center, which offered for sale everything from bugging devices and night-vision goggles to truth detector phones and secret cameras disguised in push-up bras.

A statuesque blonde sat at the reception desk, fielding incoming calls on a headset phone. She crisply informed those on the outside to "hold patiently" and smiled. "You must be Tara's ten o'clock."

"I'm Sharon Driver."

A few clicks of the mouse and the live video image of a beautiful young black woman filled the receptionist's computer monitor.

"Tara, your ten o'clock has arrived."

"Send her back." The tone was all business, supremely confident.

Sharon walked down a short corridor and entered the last office on the right. One look at the decor—leopard-print wallpaper, black carpet, and oversize, ultra-modern furnishings—and she knew that this woman's wild reputation was more fact than fiction.

Tara stood up to offer her greetings. She was poured into a red leather cat suit zipped down to there. It fit like scuba gear. Her body was as lean as a jungle cat's. Only a woman who put herself through two hours of daily workouts could pull off an outfit like this, and the power hungry glint in Tara's hazel eyes told Sharon right away that this girl had the iron discipline to do it.

"Thanks for seeing me on such short notice."

Tara grabbed a yellow legal pad from her desk and gestured for her to sit in a cozy visiting area. "There was a cancellation. Walking through that door takes guts. The ones who actually do it really want answers to certain questions."

Sharon laid out the scenario, beginning with the adoption, showing her the letter from Georgette Tucker, explaining her discovery of Peyton Drake and Dr. Ridgeway's deaths, and detailing the mutilated family photographs and vandalization of Bliss.

Tara's brain computer downloaded every word, her face a masterpiece of total concentration.

"Katie's behavior has been so erratic lately. My first instinct was to blame her, but she's so fiercely denied any involvement, and . . . I'm actually starting to believe her. I was up most of the night thinking about it, and that feeling never wavered. It's strange."

"Is it a gut thing?"

Sharon nodded.

Tara speed-read Georgette's correspondence a third time. "There's something disturbing about this letter . . . I can't really articulate it yet . . . maybe it's the syntax . . . or the subtext. But I get a distinct sense of . . . entitlement."

"Exactly!" Sharon exclaimed, thankful to hear the appropriate description that had eluded her for so long. "Remember, this was a closed adoption. All the records were supposed to be kept confidential. And we've moved several times in the last fifteen years. This letter arrived out of the blue. I keep wondering how she found us."

Tara jotted down more notes. "Maybe she hired someone like me."

The thought chilled Sharon. "I'd like to know more about this woman. If nothing else, it will put my mind at ease."

Tara stopped writing and looked up, her expression cautionary. "Not necessarily."

Chapter Thirty-eight

Dice were rolling. Toes were tapping. Local stars were glad-handing.

Sharon could hardly believe the AIDS fund-raiser had come together so well. Yet here she stood at the Swissôtel, encased in a snug Vera Wang number, accepting air kisses and deflecting praise from Atlanta's elite.

The Las Vegas theme was hardly original, but money was flowing like beer at a stag party. Infernos players Doug Conover and Adonis Waters had played nice and agreed to serve as blackjack dealers. Their tables were packed. The bodies lined up behind those lucky players indicated they would stay that way.

Missy Conover, Doug's newly pregnant wife, rushed over to say, "Oh, Sharon! You've done such a fabulous job. It's amazing. Heath must be so proud."

She felt sorry for Missy—just into her thirties and pregnant for the first time, with a self-image entirely wrapped up in being the wife of an NFL quarterback. Her big grin was simply a mask for a bigger hurt. Word had spread fast that her husband's hot-then-cold affair with a sexy country music star was back on the burner. In fact, the singer—in town for a sold-out concert at Lakewood Amphitheater—was rumored to be ensconced in an upstairs suite.

And then across the room was Adonis Waters's wife, April, watching with contempt as a trio of exotic dancer types giggled at any syllable that escaped her husband's mouth at the high-rollers table. To get all three of them into bed—even at the same time—would be no gamble at all for the star player.

But Missy and April would accept it, look the other way, bury the pain, because being the unhappy *wives* of pro football players sure as hell beat being the unhappy *ex-wives* of the same. Thankfully, Sharon had never been sucked into the empty vortex of the Coach's Wife Syndrome. Instead, she'd lost herself in more psychologically lucrative pursuits, like raising great kids and building something of her own—Bliss.

"I think this losing streak is over," Missy was saying. "Doug told me the team had a great practice today. They're more focused than ever and hungry for a win."

"Really," Sharon said, hopelessly bored with the conversation. It was rare that these women, these players, anyone on this circuit, didn't bore her. "In all honesty, I hope they continue to get their asses kicked."

Missy stared back in horror.

Sharon realized that the bitter thought inside her head had actually pushed itself past her lips. But the damage was done, so she made the rash decision to press on in order to explain herself. "Missy, we're constantly being humiliated by these bastards, and I find it rather pleasant to watch them suffer through a losing season. Of course, it's not the same kind of embarrassment. I mean, we're not openly fucking younger men or anything. But I'll take whatever cookies I can get."

Shocked silent, Missy continued to stare. After several long seconds, she murmured, "How can you talk like this?"

She tossed a gaze around the room in search of Heath and found him near the swing band, chatting up the slinky singer on a break during one of the instrumental numbers. "It would take me twenty-two years to answer that."

Sharon suddenly felt something amiss and turned to witness a stir at the entrance to the ballroom. Detectives McCarthy and Wagner, flanked by a cluster of uniformed police officers, were charging through. They pointed at Heath and marched toward him.

Every instinct within her sensed a certain doom. Her heart began to pound like an insane drum. She weaved through the crowd, hoping to reach him first.

A severe brunette with acne-scarred skin and an unfortunate face-lift was now marching with the invaders as well. Sharon recognized her as Louise Glickson, the controversial district attorney who many joked would eat her young for a guilty verdict.

They reached Heath first, startling him with their appearance. His face turned a ghostly white.

The band stopped playing. A ravenous hush seized the affair.

Sharon pushed through the stalled bodies, imploring them to let her pass.

"Heath Driver, you're under arrest for the murder of Holly Ryan," Detective McCarthy announced in an official tone.

There was a collective gasp.

No!

"What?" Heath cried.

In all the years that she'd known him, Sharon had never heard her husband sound so frightened. "Get out of my way!" she screamed, shoving more aggressively now. She was almost there.

"You have the right to remain silent. . . ."

The handcuffs clicked with a toneless finality.

"Heath!" Her heart tripped faster still.

He craned his neck to meet her gaze, his eyes pure panic.

They were taking him to jail. None of it seemed real. Sharon rushed to Louise Glickson. She seemed to be the one in charge. "This is insane! My husband didn't kill that woman!"

The district attorney returned a cold, hard stare. "Our evidence will prove otherwise." Her voice carried a peevish edge.

"You're wrong!"

"I'm never wrong."

Sharon watched them walk out, trying to sort it out logically. How could this be possible? Cancer, a mugging, all of the problems with Katie, the destruction of Bliss, an impending divorce. Now it seemed as if God, careless at the end of a busy day, decided to see how she would cope with the father of her children going away on a murder charge!

"I know a good criminal defense attorney."

She turned to the source of the voice.

It was a visibly shaken Kit Jamison with a cell phone to her ear.

Her words cut right through to the morose shell of Sharon's thoughts, but that didn't lessen the resentment Sharon felt for this outsider's friendship with Heath, for her rapport with Katie. On reflex, she snapped, "We'll find our own attorney."

"You'll need the best," Kit said. "I just heard from my source at the department that they found the murder weapon in Heath's car, along with a large sum of cash and his passport. It doesn't look good for him."

Sharon felt a burning sensation inside her skull.

Kit stared at her resolutely. "Jack Newcomb is the best

man in the state." She raised her phone. "And I've got him on speed dial."

Sharon held her head in her hands. It was throbbing now. "Call the son of a bitch." Keri Ward had cautioned her against taking on too much, as the radiation would gradually wear her down. She was well into her treatment, enduring more fatigue each day. But giving in simply wasn't an option. Not now. Especially not now.

Kit seemed to pick up on her inner thoughts. "You're in no shape to drive. I'm going to the Fulton County jail. Ride with me."

While Kit secured the counsel of Jack Newcomb, Sharon called Linda Moore and dispatched her to the house. Who knew when she might get home? It would have to be before morning, though. The arrest would no doubt lead the news and scream across the front page of the newspaper. Katie had to be talked to before she hit the school grounds.

Kit smiled faintly, a gleam of relief in her eyes. "Jack's on his way."

Jack Newcomb emanated a fearsome power. He was tall and wildly charismatic with a stocky build and an intelligent, square-cut face that hypnotized you with its strength. Even at the stroke of midnight, he showed up immaculately dressed in a Brioni suit. This man appeared as if he could never be caught off guard. Not even for a millisecond.

Right now he sat before Sharon and Kit, having already met with Heath, Detectives McCarthy and Wagner, and the district attorney. Between gulps of bad coffee, he shot straight. "Heath lied to the police the morning they came to the house to question him about Holly Ryan." He fixed his eyes on Sharon. "Your husband was with her the night of the murder. They had an argument, he threw a liquor bottle against the wall, he fucked her, and he was out of there within fifteen minutes." Jack opened his hands. "That's all he knows."

Jack was watching her, Kit was watching her, but Sharon remained stoic.

"Their case against him is solid," Jack went on. "Heath was drunk as shit. Even he admits that. Some patrons from Cozy's came forward with a report of him beating up an obnoxious fan just before he left to go see Holly. Then there's an eyewitness at the apartment building who recognized him as he arrived, and an anonymous call to 911 that reported a commotion inside Holly's unit a short time later. The murder weapon was a shard from that broken liquor bottle. They searched his Durango and found it buried in a sports bag with his passport and ten thousand in cash. The D.A. will fight bail on that point and probably get her way."

Sharon was breathing with rapid, shallow gasps.

Jack fixed a ray gun gaze on her. "Prepare your kids. Their father won't be home until after the trial."

Kit leaned in, massaging her hands, looking worried. "You're scaring the hell out of us, Jack."

"This is going to be a media circus that will paint Heath guilty all the way to the jury verdict. But in the end, we'll win. Heath will walk away."

Sharon drew strength from Jack's almost superhuman confidence. It felt like a current flowing straight up her arms and diffusing throughout her body.

"It will cost him dearly, though," Jack continued. "In fact, I bet the Infernos will drop him this week." He glanced at Kit.

She shut her eyes and nodded.

"This defense is going to get expensive," Jack announced. "What's your cash situation like?"

Sharon's head felt feverish again. "I'm not sure. I don't handle those matters."

"Do you own your house?"

She shook her head. "We've got a mortgage. I know that much. I'll check with our accountant."

"I know a literary agent who might be interested in brokering a quick publishing deal for Heath, a quickie jailhouse book like O.J. Simpson's *I Want to Tell You.*"

A rage to flee surged through Sharon's nervous system. "That's disgusting!"

Her revolt didn't faze Jack Newcomb. "Just a suggestion. But it could make the difference between staying solvent and going bankrupt."

"Daddy!" Liam chirped, pointing to the television.

Georgette watched in rapture as the Stone Phillips clone reported the arrest of Atlanta Infernos coach Heath Driver for the stabbing death of actress Holly Ryan. When a rough cut of the bimbo's sexy shower scene filled the screen, Georgette had to suppress a yelp. As producer of *Score,* she'd made the footage available, knowing that the media would pounce on it, realizing that the advance publicity would only do the movie good.

"Daddy!" Liam chirped again.

The NBC affiliate was showing a clip of Heath on the sidelines during last week's game.

"Your daddy's a very bad man," Georgette said as she flipped the channels, delighted to see that Heath's arrest had garnered lead story status on every station.

Liam frowned. "No, no."

Georgette got in the little boy's face. "Yes, he is! He hurt that pretty lady. He cut her up and made her bleed!"

"No!"

"Yes, he did!"

It was way past this brat's bedtime, but Georgette had encouraged him to drink an entire can of Coke, hoping the caffeine would keep him wired enough to stay up for the eleven o'clock news.

"Your daddy's going to jail for a long time!"

"No!"

"Go to bed!" She left the room, bored with the game He'd seen what she wanted him to see.

Liam started to cry.

"I said go to bed!" Georgette screamed, doubling back rushing menacingly toward him.

His eyes widened in fear. He started to run.

But she grabbed his arm and yanked it roughly to prove she meant business.

Liam was wailing now.

"Shut up!" Georgette hissed, dragging him upstairs to his room. She threw him onto his youth bed and turned off the light.

"You're mean, Nanny Linda! I'm telling mommy!"

She lowered her voice to an evil, snakelike hiss. "If you do that, then I'll tell the police not to ever let your daddy out of jail. You want him to come home again one day, don't you?"

His whimpering nod was all the answer Georgette needed.

"So if you tell Mommy anything, it better be that Nanny Linda is the sweetest thing you've ever known." The smudge of soft blue light from the night-light helped her make out the fear in his eyes. "You like to sleep with that on, don't you?"

Liam nodded again.

"Night-lights are for babies," Georgette spat. She ripped it out of the socket and shut the door, leaving him in the dark.

Heath's arrest had buoyed her spirits, but not enough to erase her foul mood. Savannah had ignored her all night, stepping out of her room just long enough to moan about the fact that Kit hadn't called.

Kit Jamison. Georgette shook her head and compressed her lips. The report from Investigative Group International had just arrived. She knew exactly who this bitch was. Even better, she knew exactly how to deal with her.

Heath was hunched forward, his nose against the glass. He watched Sharon walk inside the visiting area and sit down. She looked worn down.

He touched the glass with his fingers. There was a thick layer on his side, a thick layer on hers, and a stout sheet of clear plastic in between. Though only inches apart, they could only talk through the telephones mounted on the wall.

"How are you?" Sharon asked, her voice low, barely audible.

"I've been better." It was the understatement of his life. The barracuda D.A. had gone after him like a woman possessed.

"Bail denied!" the judge had thundered, cracking the gavel.

That media-crazed arraignment had deep-sixed any chance of seeing the outside world until after the trial. So they brought him back here to change into coarse cotton pajamas and rubber flip-flops, his mind still reeling at the turn of events. One question turned in his brain over and over: What the fuck was happening?

Heath flashed glances to a few of the inmates who shared the jail pod with him. They were parked atop bolted-down stools on either side of him. One was an intimidating, hulking black dude, the type he would sign to the Infernos defensive line in a second. The other was a shifty, back-woods Georgia redneck, using this time to have phone sex with his ugly wife.

"I want you to tell Katie and Liam how much I love them," Heath whispered.

"What?" Sharon was straining to hear.

"Tell Katie and Liam I love them!" Heath repeated

loudly. These telephones were shit. Tin cans with string would make for better acoustics. He rubbed his tired eyes. "I keep thinking I'm in the middle of a fucking nightmare, and I'll wake up any minute to see you sleeping beside me. Of course, you're in the guest room these days, but you know what I mean."

Sharon merely looked at him, betraying nothing.

Heath wanted to hear her say that all the divorce talk was just that—talk. Jesus, he *needed* to hear it. Drinking in every detail of her in the washed-out fluorescent light, he realized how truly beautiful she was. Right now he felt like Michael Douglas in *Fatal Attraction,* a man whose ego and lowest animal appetites had set off a chain of events that ruined a perfectly good life. But why seek out another when there was an Anne Archer at home? Most people who saw the movie got hung up on that point. Now he was stuck on it, too.

"You're in good hands with Jack Newcomb," Sharon said, finally.

"Yeah, the most expensive whore in Atlanta."

She didn't even try to smile. Her lower lip began to tremble, and tears formed in her eyes. "Holly Ryan cost you more than Jack ever will."

He sat there quietly, his fingers still on the glass, wishing he could hold her hand. "I'm worried about being able to afford him."

"We'll find a way."

"I've got a shot at some quick money—maybe big money, if I'm lucky. That way we won't have to take out a second mortgage on the house."

"Tell me this isn't about Jack's jailhouse book idea." She said it with an exasperated look.

"He's already got a ghost writer lined up. I don't have to write it. Shit, I don't know how to write a book anyway. I just have to talk to this guy and tell him my side of the story."

Sharon shook her head disapprovingly.

Heath felt his temper rise up. Maybe if she took the time to study their finances, she wouldn't sit there in goddamn judgment. Both of them came from working-class backgrounds. There was no family wealth to speak of, just two self-made people who financed their lives with what they made, not what they inherited. The million dollar home. The expensive cars. His aging parents. All of it cost a bundle each and every month. And the money Sharon earned from Bliss hardly made a difference. It was nothing. Hell, if there was a profit, it got reinvested back into the business. They were rich people on the edge, and one monster bill from Jack Newcomb could turn them upside down.

He stewed on the idea of a cell-block tell-all. It was sleazy, yes, but he needed the cash.

"Do what you have to do, Heath," Sharon said.

"What I need to do is keep the best defense attorney on my team. These people have me by the fucking balls. What is all this shit? I haven't touched my passport in years. And where did the ten thousand dollars come from? I've never had my hands on that kind of cash. Someone's playing games with me."

A strange expression clouded Sharon's face. She seemed to be holding something back.

Heath wondered what the hell it was.

Chapter Thirty-nine

Katie Driver was back in all her provocative glory—wearing a strappy velvet camisole, stretch cotton pants with a jacquard pattern, and platform shoes. It felt good to dress like a girl again. Because this time she was doing so on her terms. To thrill some stupid boy wasn't the point. To thrill *herself* was.

Giving her image a final once-over in the full-length mirror, she grinned. The black bead choker necklace rocked. The makeup was flawless. And the hair, oh yes, the hair. *Awesome.* Angel had come over the night before to help her. A Feria color job, some flat ironing, a little crimping . . . voila! Now she had that Britney Spears look from the "(You Drive Me) Crazy" video.

She double-checked her backpack. A thick bundle was busting the seams. The latest issue of *Grrl Talk.* Or, more accurately perhaps, the paper equivalent to dynamite. By lunchtime, Derek Johnson would be buried under the rubble of public humiliation.

Katie closed her eyes and took a deep breath. She sent

a telepathic message to her father. *Hang in there, Daddy.* This was all a big mistake. Her father didn't kill that woman. Maybe he went around screwing anything with a pulse but no way was he a murderer.

She couldn't believe all the shit her family was going through. That's why Katie had to clean up her problems at school—so she could then totally concentrate on helping her mother and little brother through this crisis.

When she stepped into the kitchen, Linda Moore insisted that she spin around like some model. "You're beautiful, Savannah. Absolutely beautiful," she gushed.

Katie made a face. "*Savannah?* Uh, did you, like, mix up the decaf and regular again? The name's Katie."

Linda's face flushed pink. "Oh, I'm sorry. I knew a Savannah once. She looked just like you."

Katie rolled her eyes. "Whatever." The microwave clock told her that Angel would be driving up any minute. And none too soon. Miss Day Nanny was beginning to give her the creeps. She stared too much, and she asked too many questions about Kit Jamison, as if she were jealous or threatened. There was definitely something off about the woman.

Liam sat at the breakfast table like the saddest boy in the world. His food hadn't even been touched.

"Hey, poo poo man," she said. Silly stuff like that usually got him going.

His glum expression didn't change.

Katie moved in to inspect his food. All he had was a bowl of lumpy oatmeal chockablock full of raisins. Turning to Linda, she said, "No wonder Liam's not eating. He hates raisins. You know that."

"I'm just trying to get him to try new things."

"Well, it's not working. Just look at him. Mom would never do this."

Beep!

Angel had just arrived.

Katie experienced a strange feeling, the nagging sense

that Liam shouldn't be left alone with this woman anymore. But she had to go to school. And her mother was at the hospital for radiation treatment. What would Kit Jamison do? *Tell this bitch who's boss,* Katie decided.

She shot a warning look to Linda Moore, stomped to the pantry, snatched a box of Lucky Charms, and slammed the cereal onto the counter. "Feed him something he enjoys. That is your job, isn't it? For as long as you have it anyway."

Linda Moore stared back at her, stunned and hurt. "I don't appreciate your tone."

Katie turned to Liam, who sat there trembling. She'd never seen her brother withdrawn or frightened before . . . until Linda Moore began taking care of him. "You won't appreciate me firing your ass, either. But that's exactly what will happen if Liam doesn't get real happy real soon."

She hit the door, feeling jazzed. This was the first day of the new and improved Katie Driver, so people had better watch out. Especially Derek Johnson, Thomas Prewitt, and Mrs. Boozer. And anyone else who threw negativity her way. Because they would all get squashed like a bug.

Angel was alone.

"Where's Mamiko?" Katie asked as soon as she fastened her seat belt in preparation for her friend's crazy driving.

"She's been riding with some other girls for the last few weeks. It's the same group that calls me Angel Food Cake. They're a bunch of bitches. I can't stand them."

"Well, fuck Mamiko!" Katie shouted.

Angel smiled at the upbeat bravado. "Yeah, fuck Mamiko!" she echoed.

And they zoomed off toward Riverside Central High.

Sharon was exhausted. The combination of going to radiation treatment and visiting Heath had done her in. Even the prospect of seeing Antonio didn't lift her energy level. *That would only make me more tired,* she thought, realizing that all the longing for him and the guilt that went with it were draining, too.

She checked in with Mary Payne first. Antonio's guys had finished painting the walls, and new inventory had been shipped over the last few days. Bliss was back in business.

Antonio sat waiting at their favorite table in java.com. When he saw her, he shot up to fetch the espressos. "How was treatment?" he asked, leaning in to spark her cheek with a kiss.

"Easier than visiting my husband in jail." She glanced around. "I haven't seen the newspaper yet. Do you have one?"

He shook his head. "I got rid of it. Besides, it would only upset you."

Sharon pursed her lips. She didn't find the gesture gallant. It annoyed her, in fact. If she could handle living through this ordeal, then certainly she could stomach reading about it.

"How are the kids?"

"I told Katie early this morning. She was surprisingly strong. Liam's too young to understand, but he's been moody. Maybe he's coming down with something." She sighed. "I don't know."

"Maybe I could take the three of you out for dinner. Help take your mind off things."

The suggestion surprised her. "That's sweet, but I don't think it would be a good idea."

"Why not?"

"Katie's very intuitive. She would know what's going on between us."

"Then that makes her unique. Because I don't know . . . and I'm not sure you do either."

"Are you asking me to define what we are to each other?" Her tone held a warning.

"Maybe I am."

Sharon regarded him carefully. "We're friends."

"The kind who can't wait to jump into bed with each other."

"Antonio, don't—"

"Then tell me what I said isn't true."

Her head started aching right away. Why was he suddenly applying pressure, insisting that what they were doing be neatly labeled? Even if she wanted to come up with one, how could she? Her brain was mush. So she just stared at him mutely.

"I guess no answer is as good as any," he said.

Maybe Antonio had tired of playing Superman, flying in whenever she needed to cry on a big shoulder. It occurred to Sharon that he never confided his problems to her. Was he above all that? Or had she not allowed it? She hated to think of herself as one of those nonreciprocal emotional leeches, someone who only knew how to take, someone who never gave back. "I wish it could be simple," she said finally.

"It can be."

Sharon smiled and drank her espresso. Antonio was a man. Of course he would think that way. How many times had she fantasized about giving her body to him? Hundreds, maybe. And each time she felt a tiny panic. It would mean letting him undress her, right? This young, devastatingly handsome man without an ounce of extra flesh on him. He was all bone and taut muscle. Even standing naked in front of Heath made her insecure. And Antonio was young enough to be Heath's son. She imagined his last lover was probably young enough to be her daughter.

She watched him watch her, a kind of exotic, erotic adoration in his eyes. It flattered her . . . but did he really know what he was getting? Oh, God, how did men Heath's age do it? Prostate worries, wrinkles, and snoring habits be damned, they didn't think twice about crawling into bed with a hot twentysomething. But Sharon did. After all, she was a real-world forty-four, not the Hollywood variety. There were stretch marks to consider. Scars from the lumpectomy. And let's not forget gravity. Nothing was as firm anymore. When seen at a bad angle, her breasts could really hang.

If Antonio were just some young stud whose job was to please her and hit the road, it might not be so frightening. But he was so much more than that. She wanted him to hold her in his arms, make love to her, fall asleep, wake up during the night and do it all over again, and stay until morning, too. It wasn't just the sex. It was the romance. And Heath's games over the years had torn her down to the point where she didn't feel worthy of it.

"I would never hurt you, Sharon. You know that, don't you?"

She nodded. It was a novel concept, and lovely to hear, but it didn't turn the tide. Her reluctance had not abated. "I'm still married, Antonio. I realize my husband ignores that fact all the time. Well . . . I can't. Is it over between us? Yes, it probably is. But he's still my husband, the father of my children. And right now he's in jail for a murder he didn't commit. I feel like I've got to stand by him, even if it's for the last time."

He stared at his espresso. "Why? He doesn't stand by you. He wasn't there for your surgery. He's never around for your radiation treatments."

Sharon grimaced slightly. It stung to hear Heath's recent track record recited out loud. "That might be true. But I don't play tit for tat."

Antonio shook his head. "This isn't fair."

Now a slow smile crept onto her lips. He sounded like a child. It was rather sweet.

"He doesn't deserve you."

Sharon stood up to leave. This wasn't the conversation she had planned on having. How could she make him understand that he meant something to her, even though she was choosing Heath? Maybe it wasn't inside him to get it. What did Antonio know about marriage anyway? Especially twenty-two years of it. He'd called it quits after only four. "I need to go. I feel like I should be at home."

Antonio got up. He was staring curiously and was close enough to breathe her breath. "Come here." And he took her in his arms and kissed her deeply. It was hard, bruising, and fantastic. Then he released her and walked away, leaving her to doubt every thought that had crossed her mind, every word that had passed her lips.

And now she wanted him more than ever.

"I want you to have the exclusive," Heath said, looking and sounding haggard.

Kit was touched. This was the kind of story that would put her on national radar, and he knew it. "I didn't come here for the official jailhouse interview. I came to see you."

"So you've seen me. Now take what I'm offering and start running before Jack Newcomb gets wind of it." He grinned. "Where did you find this guy? I'm not sure if he's my lawyer, publicist, or literary agent."

Kit tried to smile. Instead it died somewhere in her heart. She hated to see him like this. The Heath Drivers of the world rarely recovered from downward spirals of this magnitude. They were so used to winning, so accustomed to people jumping whenever they crooked a finger. "Jack's unorthodox, but he's the best. He'll get you out of here."

"To do what? I'm over. At least in here I'm still somebody. Jack thinks my book will go to auction. All the publishers want a no-holds-barred account of wild women in the NFL, plus the inside dirt on players and owners."

There was a moment of uncomfortable silence. They both knew that the road he was considering would only solve the short-term problems of cash flow and ego starvation. If he sold out with a tell-all book, then Heath Driver would be permanent league poison. No one would go near him. Granted, the Infernos had cut him loose, but once the smoke and debris of this bogus charge cleared, another team, maybe even a new expansion franchise, could conceivably take him on. After all, he was still a damn good coach. Finally she said, "You want to be the Eddie Fisher of pro football?"

Heath gave her a strange look. "Huh?"

"So you write some crap book that trashes everybody and you get your media moment, plus lots of dough. What then? After a turn like that, there's nothing left at the end of the day. Not only have you blown your load on one stupid book that's destined for the bargain table, you've pissed everybody off. That's no way to go out."

Heath gestured to his surroundings. He splayed a hand on the glass. "It beats this."

Kit gripped the telephone tighter.

"You're my best friend, Kit."

She put her hand on her side of the glass, directly over his.

"Promise me we'll never sleep together. It would ruin everything."

"That's a safe bet," she said wistfully. But in all honesty, Kit wasn't sure. She and Heath had walked a precarious line between friends and more than friends for a long time. He was such a jerk, so quick to make big mistakes and say something offensive. It made him unpredictable, and that quality attracted her.

"Who knows? Maybe you'll get your own chapter in the book. I'll title it, 'The Woman I Never Banged.' "

Kit laughed and pressed her hand tighter against the glass. "You're actually going to write this book, aren't you?"

"I just got fired. I'm a lousy saver. I've got a wife and two kids. If this goes to trial, the legal bills could cost me our home. Jack pulls out all the stops, hires all types of consultants and expert witnesses. That's how he gets his clients off. I can't put this man on a budget. I have to let him do his thing. I want the whole circus act, so I can get the fuck out of here."

There were several e-mails waiting for her when she got back to the shabby offices of WTOK-FM. One was from Sid Donner, a motor mouth who put syndication deals together. He wanted to do lunch and discuss an offer. She replied back with:

GOOD TIMING. I JUST GOT AN EXCLUSIVE WITH HEATH DRIVER.

Kit began scrolling through the rest of her messages, deleting most of them.

Sid must have been sitting at his computer because he flashed right back with:

THE DEAL JUST GOT SWEETER. YOU'RE GOING TO BE A RICH WOMAN. HOW DOES IT FEEL?

PROPERLY GUILTY, Kit thought about typing. But she didn't want to pour cold water on Sid Donner's negotiating mood. This was her big chance, and she had to go for it. Her father would want it that way. Winners didn't stop to help the fallen. They kept on running for the end zone. She pecked out: BETTER THAN SEX and sent the three words into cyberspace.

There was one e-mail left from an address she didn't recognize. The fact that it carried no subject line piqued her interest further. She started reading. Nothing existed but the words on the screen. For a moment she closed her eyes, listened to her heartbeat, and allowed the elation to sink in.

KIT,

I'M TIRED OF RUNNING, AND CAMERON MISSES YOU. I LOVE HIM TOO MUCH TO SEE HIM HURT LIKE THIS. IT'S TOO LATE FOR US, BUT MAYBE WE CAN WORK OUT SOME SORT OF SHARED CUSTODY ARRANGEMENT FOR HIS BENEFIT. I'VE GOT A NEW JOB OUT OF STATE. THEY'RE SENDING ME TO THE WEST COAST FOR EIGHT WEEKS OF TRAINING. OBVIOUSLY, THAT'S NO PLACE FOR CAMERON. I'D LIKE TO LEAVE HIM HERE WITH YOU. WHEN I GET BACK, WE CAN SETTLE THINGS. WE'RE AT THE HILTON TOWERS DOWNTOWN—ROOM 2025. I'LL WAIT FOR YOU UNTIL TWO.

LESLIE

"What's wrong, Kit?"

She looked up to see Andy Friedman, the extreme conservative who hosted a daily rant-and-rave call-in show for close-minded idiots. Kit felt her cheeks. They were wet with tears. She hadn't realized. "Everything's spectacular, Andy. *Adrenaline* is going to be syndicated, and my former lover is back with our child. Brace yourself. I'm going to be a rich and single lesbian with shared custody of a little boy. Isn't America great?"

Kit left Andy standing there with his mouth agape. She jumped into her Jeep Cherokee and drove like a madwoman, no longer aware of anything beyond her own head, which was throbbing with relief and hope and anxiousness. Traffic crawled. Suddenly she completely understood the propensity for road rage.

Finally she reached the Hilton, left her car in the care of a vacant looking valet, and dashed inside. The place was mammoth—restaurants, shops, a business center. It ook her a moment to locate the elevator. The wait dragged on forever.

Ding!

She rushed the doors before they opened and couldn't punch the button of her floor fast enough. When the number lit up, so did Kit's heart. Cameron was here. Her sweet, innocent Cameron. And she would never lose con-act with him again. Then the thought slammed into her. She'd come empty handed! Oh, shit, what did it matter? When she had him all to herself for eight weeks, she'd buy him any toy his heart desired. Cameron loved cars. She decided to spend her first big *Adrenaline* check scooping up every toy car in the whole fucking world!

Kit passed Room 2021 . . . and 2023 . . . now 2025 was right in front of her. She could feel her heart thrumming along far too fast. Taking a moment, she smoothed down her shirt and drew in a deep breath, then knocked three times.

The door opened. A stranger stared back. The only similarity to Leslie Tollyson was that she looked about the same age—thirty-three.

Kit experienced a tremor of panic. Had she read the wrong room number in Leslie's e-mail?

"You must be Kit," the woman said. "Please, come in."

She stepped inside, immediately struck by the precise order of everything, as if no one were staying in the room. There was no sign of luggage at all. "Where are Leslie and Cameron?" Kit demanded.

"They're in Mexico."

She gave the woman a hostile look. "I don't understand. Who the hell are you?"

"Do you remember Elizabeth?" The woman stepped over to the desk, opened the top drawer, and pulled out a set of photographs. "That would be Leslie's girlfriend before you. She has a beautiful place in Puerto Vallarta. That's where they are, and Cameron's very happy there.

He goes to the beach almost every day." She laughed little. "His favorite thing to do is to build a sand cast and drive his toy cars through it. He never thinks abo you anymore. I'm afraid you're just a distant memory. She handed over the pictures.

Kit sifted through them, feeling assaulted. Everythin this woman said appeared to be true. There was Camero standing on the beach, the water up to his ankles. Th sight of him triggered a choking sob. He looked olde Could a boy grow that much in just months? His skin w bronzed, his hair lightened by the sun. And he looke deliriously happy. Kit could almost feel her heart breakin She glared at the woman, then asked, "Who are you?"

"I'm Savannah's mother."

Kit stared at the woman as if she were crazy. All patienc was gone now. Whatever game this was, she hated it. "Wh the fuck is Savannah?"

"You should know, bitch. You filled her head with sh about me."

A sense of fear overwhelmed Kit as she searched th woman's eyes. There was something vaguely familiar abou them. Ransacking her brain for the connection, all of sudden it hit her. Katie Driver. This was her biologica mother.

Before Kit could speak, she saw an arm slice throug the air. At the end of it a flash of metal gleamed. A torren of pain seized her. Almost instantly she felt a gushin warmth. More calmly than the moment called for, sh touched her neck. When she looked at her hand, it wa covered in blood. The pictures of Cameron fell to th carpet. After the third stab wound, so did Kit Jamison.

Chapter Forty

Everybody was talking about Katie's father. One stupid girl had actually rushed up to her in the hall to say, "Did your dad really kill that movie star? That's so cool!"

Now Katie sat in Mrs. Boozer's class, trying to focus, counting down the minutes to meet Angel for the secret distribution of *Grrl Talk*. A political fireball was about to be unleashed on the student body and administration. Feeling like some kind of activist, she shifted in her desk, ready for the rumble. She couldn't wait to see Derek Johnson's face when he read the headline NASTY BOY, screaming over his photograph.

Katie had gone back to visit the nurse who diagnosed her with chlamydia to get essential facts and quotes for the story. Not only did her article warn girls that Derek was a carrier, it also cautioned them about the seriousness of the disease, like how it can lead to infertility, difficult pregnancies, birth defects, and HIV infection. Then she wrapped up the piece by telling her readers to either abstain from sex altogether or to always insist that the partner wear a condom.

The other big story blasted Thomas Prewitt for sexu harassment. Not stopping there, Katie also slammed Mr Boozer for being aware of his behavior and doing nothin about it. Then she explained the difference between single goofball incident like a guy snapping a bra stra and the kind of severe and persistent harassment th Thomas was guilty of. At the end, she informed her publi about LaShonda Davis, the Georgia girl who successfull sued her school for failing to heed complaints about he abuse from a sex-crazed student. Katie knew this piec would scare the shit out of Riverside Central's administration, which is exactly what she wanted to do.

Yes! Katie had finally found her voice. *Grrl Talk* was powerful tool for education and advocacy. Coming to tha realization had opened up a whole new world, and sh owed a debt of gratitude to Kit Jamison for helping he to the other side.

Katie checked her watch. It was time. She slid her backpack onto her shoulder and approached the teacher's des to request a hall pass.

Less than an hour later, the mood in the cafeteria wa imminent chaos. Proud, giddy, and nervous as hell, Kati watched the scene unfold. She'd left the pink pages to th past and produced the new issue of *Grrl Talk* on solar yello paper. Almost every table was littered with the colorful zine Some students were racing to their lockers, hoping to fin a copy of their own.

Katie felt strong and proactive and competent. This wa her way of taking back her life, and she knew it was th right thing to do. No matter what happened.

"Where is that fucking slut?" Derek Johnson's boomin voice shook the rafters. He erupted from his table in th enter of the packed room, standing on his stool to seek ıer out.

Thomas Prewitt elbowed him and pointed in Katie's lirection.

Angel took hold of her wrist. "Don't let them scare you."

Katie felt remarkable calm. "I'm through being scared, ıngel." She stood up. "It's time for these motherfuckers o fear me."

Derek and his crew stalked toward her, an angry mob ıungry for a symbolic kill. She stood bravely in their path, ike a rebel student in Tiananmen Square before a tank. ı dart of excitement pierced her heart. *Bring it on,* she hought.

A teacher on monitoring duty sensed trouble and moved riskly through the swinging doors, no doubt to round up nore assistance.

Students were suddenly up and out of their seats, crowdng fast, circling the scene ravenously.

"You stupid lying bitch!" Derek shouted. "The only hing you got from me was what you wanted—a hard dick ıll night long!"

Guys whooped and whistled—a testosterone chorus.

"*All night long?* More like two minutes! It takes me longer o brush my teeth."

Her cunning comeback earned bigger laughs—from ooth sexes.

Mamiko pushed through the crowd and took her place ıext to Katie.

"I don't care what that paper says. You didn't get shit rom me. I'm clean," Derek said.

"You're the only person I've ever been with," Katie hallenged.

"Yeah, that's what all the bitches say."

Mamiko raised her voice to address the large gathering. 'Any girl who's made the unfortunate mistake of sleeping vith this loser needs to get tested right away. And don't be shy about coming forward. This guy has already trashe your reputations."

"That's right!" Angel cut in. "Whenever he hooks u with somebody, he shares the private details with his bon head friends and anyone else who will listen. Now it's you turn to get him back."

There was a low hum of conversation.

And then one girl stepped forward, a senior name Trina. "I got chlamydia from that asshole, too."

Katie smiled at Mamiko, then Angel. At the end of th day, her friends had come through for her. Now it was he turn to do the same for the only family she knew . . . Heath Sharon, and Liam Driver.

She prayed it wasn't too late.

When the telephone rang, she expected it to be Jac Newcomb, or maybe another media parasite requestin an interview. But it was Tara Daye, the private investigato At the sound of her voice, something happened at th nape of Sharon's neck.

Tara launched into her report without preamble. "You gut instinct to find out more about Georgette Tucker wa spot on. There are some disturbing findings."

Nervously, Sharon chewed on her lower lip as she too the news.

"Georgette's husband, Ed Tucker, died a short whil ago. The story is that he fell down the stairs after a nigh of heavy drinking." Tara's tone was openly skeptical.

"You don't believe that."

"I don't doubt that he fell down the stairs, but wheneve a spouse inherits a small fortune from an unhappy mar riage, I find the idea of an accident hard to swallow. Gues how Ed Tucker made his money?"

Sharon's heart was on hold. "How?"

"Producing independent films. As it happens, *Score* wa

n preproduction before he died. Georgette kept the movie ;oing. Just before principal photography began, she orought in Holly Ryan to replace another actress in the ole of the coach's mistress."

Sharon just stood there frozen, attempting to wrap her orain around this. The telephone line hummed in the ilence. Finally, she found her voice. "Heath has been harged—"

"I know," Tara cut in. "I've already got a call into Jack Newcomb. That son of a bitch hired another P.I. to look nto Holly's past. But her story's not the interesting one. Peyton Drake and Dr. Ridgeway were murdered about a veek after Ed Tucker died. The lawyer was shot in the face outside a bar, and the doctor got his head bashed in with is own golf club while he was sleeping."

Sharon tried to reconcile the nightmarish events of the oresent with Georgette's so recent past. The worst case cenario chilled her to the bone. The possibility was diabol-cal. It was psychotic. She spoke tentatively, as if she were valking a tightrope. "Do you think . . ."

"There's nothing in her past to suggest that she's capa-ble of all this. Until she married Ed Tucker, Georgette was ust a young girl in Hollywood working one slutty job after another. That doesn't make her a murderer. That makes her a cliché. But bodies are piling up. And this woman is ust a few degrees away from every victim. I'll have more n a few days. Until then, live your life on red alert. She eft the Hamptons weeks ago and hasn't been seen since. 've tried to trace her through credit card records, but I haven't turned up anything. She must be using cash."

A premonition of danger cocooned itself around her. Already Sharon felt the paranoia building.

"Those are the broad strokes. I'll send the full report and a recent photo by e-mail."

"Fine," Sharon agreed.

"Oh, here's another disturbing coincidence that could

be a lead in explaining the vandalization of Bliss. What do you know about java.com at Phipps Plaza?"

"Why do you ask?" Her voice nearly broke. She felt the fear. It was scrambling her mind.

"That business is owned by Georgette Tucker."

"What you're doing is sick. I don't want any part of this anymore. I'm out."

Georgette stared back in disgust. Goddammit! Right now she was so fucking close. The last thing she needed was noise about quitting from one of the bit players.

"I've got feelings for her," Antonio said. *"Real feelings.* Do you even know what those are?"

She glared at him. Since when did actor-model-compulsive gambler types wax lyrical on authentic emotions? Still, the question prompted Georgette to think about Savannah. Every bit of love inside her heart, mind, and soul was bundled up in that little girl. "I have an idea, believe it or not."

"Glad to hear it. But you'll have to find yourself another puppet. I'm through lying to Sharon."

Georgette shook her head in disbelief. Antonio Miguel was a simpleton. Even Holly Ryan had displayed a higher intellect. "That seems to imply that you plan on telling her the truth," she observed silkily.

"Maybe I do. This isn't right. It's gone too far."

"You're right, Antonio. It has. Far enough for Sharon to have shared some of her deepest intimacies with you. How do you think she'll react when she finds out that you were *paid* to befriend her? If you really care about this bitch, then your best bet is to keep on lying to her. What's the old saying? Oh, yes . . . ignorance is bliss."

The stud for hire looked guilt-soaked.

"Just finish the job, pretty boy. Then you can go back to Las Vegas, resume your role in that dreadful show, and start gambling again. Those debts are almost paid off. And don't forget about your wife. I'm sure she misses you."

The urge to run, like a sprinter to the tape, was in his eyes. But Antonio just stood there. It was obvious. He had nowhere to go. "What do you want me to do?"

"Let her catch you with another woman. I'll take care of the rest."

Antonio's pain was palpable, as if his balls were tied up in barbed conscience wire.

Georgette gave him a mirthless smile. "Don't look so sad. At least the pay is good."

In the back pocket of the tight faded Levi's that fit him like a dream, his cell phone jingled.

She raised an eyebrow. "Maybe it's our love-starved friend."

He glanced at the screen and closed his eyes.

"You can start clean, Antonio. No debts. No loan sharks breathing down your neck. The casinos will treat you like a champ again. Those tables are waiting."

He was rigid with ambivalence. She could feel it pulsing from his body. But his weakness for risk, for the thrill of high rolling, won out. Like she knew that it would.

And then he answered the call. "Hi, Sharon . . ."

Chapter Forty-one

Under the cloak of suspicion, Antonio looked different
o her. There was a sense that he had lived twice as long
ıs she. His shirt was off, and his jeans were unbuttoned at
he waist to reveal CALVIN KLEIN on the elastic waistband
of his underwear. A cigarette dangled between his thumb
ınd forefinger. The worst part of all—he could barely look
ıer in the eye. This from a man who had stared into her
soul.

Sharon eyeballed his apartment. It was nothing like she
ıad imagined. If she had to guess, she would say that a
cheap transient lived here. She gave Antonio another stud-
ed glance. Maybe one did.

"I was under the impression that you owned java.com,"
she said. The expression on her face told him that she
knew the truth.

He took a deep drag and blew smoke up to the ceiling
n curls. "Surprise. I'm just a working stiff." His aura
reeked of might-have-beens, missed chances, and nerve-
racking what-ifs. There was a real sadness in his eyes.

Sharon should have known that Antonio was too goo
to be true. The men she knew were not as perfect as th
fantasy she had allowed herself to believe in. They didn'
say and do all the right things. Instead, they were deepl
flawed and built to disappoint. Like this guy. Like Heath
"Georgette Tucker paid you to con me." She had to pu
the words out there, to hear them out loud.

He met her gaze. For a moment, he was the old Antonio
the one she thought she loved. "Yes, she paid me. But i
wasn't a con. Not to me." The longing in his eyes reminde
her of their special times, their shared secrets.

Sharon gave him a blinding slap across the face. "You'r
good. And that kiss was brilliant. Nice touch. On the hustle
scale, I give you a nine point nine." The words were bruta
spitballs of scarcely suppressed rage. Then she was silen
and miserable. Never had she felt like such a fool.

She turned away, unable to look at this fraud for on
more second. Georgette's vicious plot turned over in he
mind. The pieces of the puzzle were there, but she couldn'
put them all together. It was numbing to consider th
unbelievable scope of this woman's deception.

On a wobbly card table Sharon spotted a Macintosh
iBook next to a newspaper and a carton of Marlboros
Then she remembered that Tara Daye had promised to e
mail a recent photograph of Georgette with her report
Suddenly she had a helter-skelter drive to put a face to th
evil name. She walked over to the laptop and turned it on

"I don't know what Georgette wants," Antonio said
"She doesn't tell me much." His voice was subdued.

Sharon ignored the hired hand, activating the Americ
Online icon and typing in her screen name and passwor
to connect.

"She wanted me to set it up so that you found me with
another woman. But I couldn't do that to you. I'd neve
hurt you that way."

Sharon didn't even turn around when she said, "How heartfelt. You're making me swoon."

Her mind was on fire with the idea of Georgette laughing at her for being so gullible to believe that a man as young and good-looking as Antonio would express interest in her without the incentive of an under-the-table cash deal.

"I know what you're thinking. You're thinking I made up all the things I said. I didn't. I meant every word."

Tara Daye had sent two e-mail documents.

Sharon double clicked the photograph file and watched the image download onto the screen. Quite suddenly her world turned. Antonio was still talking. But none of his words registered. Shock squeezed at her neck. The revelation blew her away. And everything became clear.

Horribly, frighteningly clear.

Chapter Forty-two

She waited for Katie in the school's main office. What the hell was taking so long? The secretary had issued the announcement several minutes ago. A thousand fears went through her mind.

"Mom? What's going on?"

Sharon turned to see her beautiful, smart, incredibly resilient daughter. "Oh, darling!" she cried, running to embrace her. "Thank God you're here."

Katie accepted her loving arms and hugged her back tightly. "I'm okay, Mom," she murmured.

"I'm so sorry, honey. For everything. I know that you had nothing to do with the incident at Bliss or all those photographs that were destroyed. Someone's been playing a terrible game."

Katie drew back. "What are you talking about?"

"There's no time to explain. We have to go. I need your help."

"Does this have anything to do with Linda?"

Terror stalked in the undergrowth of Sharon's fearful

thoughts. She gripped Katie's arms. "Why do you ask that
What has she said to you?"

"It's not me. It's Liam. I think she's abusing him. Thi
morning she was making him eat oatmeal with raisins, an
when you were at the benefit the other night I heard hir
crying. She'd taken away his night-light and put him t
bed in the dark. I don't like her. She's weird."

Sharon looked away. There was no explaining this. Ho
would Katie ever deal with the fact that her biologic
mother was a vengeful psychotic? It was an absolute trag
edy. But if Sharon didn't stop her, it could only get wors
She tried to keep her voice from shaking as she spoke
"Let's go, honey. We have to pick up your brother."

She ignored all speed limits, bulldozed through re
lights, and generally violated every traffic law in her despe
ation to see and touch her darling Liam. Hot tears burne
at her eyes. To think that her innocent little boy ha
endured even a moment's cruelty at the hands of tha
monster . . . it felt like a deep and fatal stab.

Everything was her fault. Oh, God, she'd been so fuckin
careless! Not a single reference had been checked. Wher
had her mind been? She'd allowed that woman—with he
twisted bloodlust and raging venom—access to their home
It all seemed like a terrible dream.

She peeled into the parking lot of Liam's preschool an
braked hard. The Range Rover lurched forward. "Sta
here." Leaving the engine running, she swung out an
crashed through the door like the riot police. Her craz
eyes tracked the room. There were lots of kids. But non
of them were Liam. "Where's my son?" Her voice wa
hoarse, her mind spinning round and round.

Three teachers gazed back, startled. The one she kne
as Stacey stepped forward, her apron splattered with fir
gerpaints. "Your nanny picked him up early."

Sharon's heart stopped beating.

Chapter Forty-three

The keys jangled in Sharon's trembling hand. She opened the door to the home that she didn't feel safe in anymore. Electric fingers probed her spine as she entered quietly through the kitchen, listening, searching.

Her mind was a spillover of guilt, regret, and thoughts on the destructive power of family secrets. If she had only done the good thing, the right thing, the decent thing all those years ago, perhaps the evil of one woman might not have been put into motion.

But that was then. And this was now.

She had no plan. Just a goal. To get Liam away from Georgette Tucker.

The gun barrel arrived from out of nowhere into Sharon's back, instantly burrowing between her shoulder blades. She stopped cold, frozen in place, her eyes wide.

"I want my son." There was a coolness in her voice that amazed her. It belied the stark white fear inside.

"Liam is upstairs," Georgette rasped, throwing something onto the floor. A small pill bottle clattered this way and that. Finally, it rolled to a stop.

Sharon recognized the brand. Tylenol PM. *Oh, God, please no.* Her body went cold.

"He's sleeping, and he's not going to wake up."

The tears burst forth immediately. She tried to work out what to do in the minutes Liam had left. Every second counted. But her mind refused to cooperate. All she could do was imagine herself picking out his tiny casket, kneeling at his grave. "He's just a baby." The plea came out as less than a whimper.

"At least you had your baby for two years. That's more than I got." Georgette pushed her into a chair at the kitchen table and hovered the gun inches from her eyes.

On Georgette's face, Sharon saw it with a moment of hyper clarity—total madness. There was no reasoning with the insane. She would just have to try something crazy and hope for the best. It was Liam's only chance.

"I stopped in on your boyfriend just after you left today. He took his bullet straight between the eyes. How do you want yours?"

Sharon's lips parted in horror.

Georgette's smile conveyed such viciousness, such emptiness, such capability for anything. "My original plan was to force you to write your suicide note the day after you found Liam's dead body." She thrust a pen into Sharon's face and slapped a sheet of paper onto the table. "But when I read your e-mails on Antonio's computer, I knew it was time to take things up a notch."

Liam was fading fast upstairs. The minutes ticked by. Helplessness closed in on her. She had to seize the moment. Better to die trying to save him, then to just die. . . .

* * *

Katie sat in one of the living rooms of Angel's massive home, listening to the housekeeper prattle on about the story line of whatever soap opera was on television.

"He's a bad man," Rebecca said, scowling and pointing to a silver-haired actor.

Katie glanced at the screen. The camera angle and lighting were menacing. And so contrived. She hated soaps.

"He's hurt a lot of good people on the show. You see the pretty lady in the yellow? She used to be married to . . ."

Oh, God! No way could she listen to this nonsense all afternoon. She checked her watch. Angel wouldn't be here for at least another hour, assuming she came straight home from school.

Katie couldn't stop looking at the phone. She even tried willing it to make a sound, staring at it like those psychics who move objects with their minds. Her nerves wouldn't rest until she heard her mother say that Liam was safe and that Linda was never coming back.

"Oh, crap," Rebecca whined. "I don't like it when they interrupt my story."

Katie focused on the screen. It was a special news report.

"One of Atlanta's favorite daughters is dead, the victim of a brutal stabbing," the anchor said.

A photograph of Kit Jamison filled the screen.

Katie watched transfixed. She listened in shock.

"Local radio personality Kit Jamison, the daughter of Georgia Tech football great Hub Jamison and grandchild of country music legend Tex Jamison, was found dead earlier today in a suite at the Hilton Towers in downtown Atlanta. Police have officially declared it a homicide. A full investigation is underway. We'll have more on this tragic story during our six o'clock report. We now return to our regularly scheduled programming."

The bad man was back on screen, delivering his equally bad lines.

Katie felt poleaxed by the news. It couldn't be. Not

Kit. Not her miracle worker. Not her friend. She swayed forward and backward, then from side to side, as if somehow it would shake the reality from her mind. Already she missed her. There was a void now where Kit had been, and it would never be filled again.

A strange feeling came over her. An ominous feeling. A dreadful feeling. The voice of Linda Moore played inside her head. *This Kit Jamison has been a strong influence on you. I'll have to make a point to meet her one day.* Why would Linda want to meet her friend? After all, she was Liam's nanny. And there were other odd incidents, too, little comments, probing questions. Her voice always changed on the subject of Kit. It grew suddenly cold . . . hostile.

Katie had nothing to go on but a terrible instinct. From her toes to her temples she felt it. Her father was in jail. Her mother and brother were in danger. It was up to her now.

Rebecca's small mind was fixated on the big screen, and she barely noticed her leave the room.

Katie eyed the key rack in the kitchen. The Fishers were so rich that they bought cars like most people buy detergent. Hanging there were shiny brass hooks for key sets to new BMW, Jaguar, Lexus, and Mercedes models. Only the Jag's remained. Snatching it, she ducked into the garage.

The car weaved along the streets uncertainly. With no license and few lessons, driving wasn't her finest skill. But all she had to do was fucking get there. Her foot slammed down on the pedal that made the motor car go, and the purring European machine took off. She set a new speed record on Columns Drive. Rollerbladers dipped delicately into yards. Bikers and power walkers followed in-line.

The house was just up ahead. She braked gradually, not wanting to screech, coasting to a stop. Usually she used the kitchen entrance. But today something told her to enter through the front door.

At first it was quiet. But after several silent beats, she heard the voices.

"Please, Georgette, he's just an innocent little boy. Why does he have to die?"

Katie had never heard her mother sound so anguished. Who was Georgette? But then it dawned on her. The name rang like a bell. *Georgette is my birth mother.*

"Because it's going to be just the two of us. Me and Savannah!" It was Linda's voice this time.

Savannah. That name again. And then she slotted the puzzle together. Gooseflesh sprang up on her arms, tickling the cuts still in healing mode. Her heart bolted in her chest. The identity of her birth mother was no longer a mystery.

"No fake mother, no fake father, and no fake baby brother. Just me. I'm her real family. I want her all to myself, the way it should have been a long time ago. That's why I killed the dyke, too. She was putting crazy ideas in Savannah's head. I couldn't let that go on."

Like a zombie Katie walked, in the direction of the voices, toward the horrible truth, not thinking, not feeling. She rounded the corner and peered inside.

Her mother saw her first.

But Georgette followed the gaze and saw her next. "Savannah, you're not supposed to be home yet." She was genuinely startled.

Katie's face screwed up with a childlike fear, and she couldn't take her eyes off the gun pointed at her mother. Finally, she looked back at Georgette. "Let my mother go." There was absolute authority in her voice, even though her world was upside down.

"She's not your mother, Savannah. I am."

"Stop calling me Savannah!" Her voice was a mighty roar. "You're not my mother! You're a murderer!" Each declaration got louder, as if the sheer volume would blast this woman from her madness. She looked at her as she might a street whore.

"No, Savannah, you don't understand." The voice seemed to come from light-years away.

Her mother lunged for the gun, seizing the moment of opportunity, catching Georgette off guard.

Katie opened her mouth wide and screamed at the top of her lungs.

Georgette held strong and pushed hard. The two women fell back, hit the table, and crashed onto the floor. Arms and legs flailed about, the gun still in contest.

"Katie . . . 911," her mother managed to scream. "Liam . . dying . . . pills . . . hurry."

For the first time in recent memory, she acted on her mother's wishes without argument. She was running. Fast. She was on the stairs. Faster. She was in Liam's room. "Oh my God!"

Her younger brother lay on his back, limp, lifeless, maybe dead.

Katie was sure he was gone. She cursed herself for every time she'd been mean to him and knelt down. After shaking him violently, she put her ear to his mouth. "Yes!" The relief was total. He was breathing. But only barely.

Oh, God, what should she do? At first she tried to wake him up again, shaking him, even slapping his cheek. Liam remained motionless. *He should throw up,* Katie thought. But then it occurred to her that he could choke on his vomit. She couldn't stay with him every moment, and time was running out. *No,* she decided, *the paramedics are his best chance.*

Katie raced across the hall into her mother and father's master bedroom to call 911. No dial tone. Shit! Jamming down on the receiver several times, she tried again. Nothing.

"You don't need to call anybody, Savannah." The voice was close. Too close. She heard footsteps on the stairs.

Think! Katie put her razor brain to work. Liam was dying. He needed an ambulance. There was only one phone line. She didn't have a cellular. Her heart picked up speed. Through the chaos a brilliant light began to shine. The image flashed. In her mind the scene rolled. Just like a movie. Because it was one. She'd seen it only days ago. *Scream.* Neve Campbell uses her computer modem to dial 911. Well, goddammit, Katie had a computer, too! One with a dedicated line.

She returned to Liam's room, scooped him into her arms like a rag doll, and sprinted toward her own near the stairs. Just meters away. Suddenly two shadows hit the sun gold wall. No! They were near the top. A mother she loved. A mother she hated. But the gun was pointed at the wrong head.

Katie ran flat out. She reached her room, slamming and locking the door in the nick of time. Tenderly, she placed Liam onto her bed. Now she flicked on her computer. "Come on!" It deserved her impatience. Why did it take so fucking long to boot up?

"Aaaaaaaaaaaaah!"

Katie stood paralyzed. It was her mother's shriek. Boom! A thud rocked against the door. The wood buckled. Crash! No doubt the family portrait going down. Glass shattered. But the grappling thundered on.

The computer glowed with readiness. She punched at the keyboard and clicked the mouse madly, highlighting FAX MODEM. The program came up. She typed 911 and clicked SEND. The wait seemed endless. Now a prompt instructed her to continue. Her fingers attacked the keys.

KILLER IN THE HOUSE. TWO YEAR-OLD GIVEN PILLS. 601 COLUMNS DRIVE.

She clicked SEND once more. Suddenly everything was quiet.

The words she longed for hit the screen:

POLICE EN ROUTE.

But they failed to comfort.

The silence dragged on, filling her up with a crazy fear. She stopped breathing. Katie closed her eyes. A hot tear rolled down her cheek. She sensed movement outside the door.

Only one word was spoken. "Savannah?"

Katie sank to her knees in despair.

"Open the door, Savannah."

She was truly frightened, her throat dry and parched. "The police are on their way!" she screamed.

"Don't lie to me, Savannah. I took the phone off the hook downstairs."

"I used my computer modem!" Katie yelled back triumphantly.

There was a dark silence.

"The bitch who stole you from me is knocked out, but she's still alive. Are you going to open this door, or do you want me to pump her full of bullets?"

Katie's heart nearly stopped beating. She knew this psycho would do it.

There was only one way out. For her. For her mother. For Liam. Slowly, she approached the door and disengaged the lock, finally, fearfully, easing it open.

Georgette stood there, the gun at her side, a disturbing mad love in her eyes.

For a fleeting moment, Katie saw herself. There were similarities in the eyes, the shape of the nose and mouth, the dark hair. But that's where it ended. Inside, where it counted, they were worlds apart.

"Don't hurt me, Mommy." It took every cell of strength

within her to murmur the last word, but Katie somehow managed to force it past her lips.

The moment that acknowledgment hit the air, Georgette seemed to soften before her eyes. She exhaled deeply. "Oh, Savannah, I would never hurt you. I just want us to be together." And then she moved to embrace her.

Katie accepted those arms of sick, twisted love . . . at first stiffly, but then she willed her body to relax. "We will be," she promised, her voice cracking.

Georgette held her tight.

The feeling was grotesque, and Katie shut her eyes. When the courage arrived, she rode the wave, allowing her right arm to ease down toward the firearm in Georgette's right hand. In her peripheral vision, she saw her mother gaining consciousness.

"They'll never find us," the insane woman was saying. "I'll buy you anything you want. Anything in the world. We'll be so happy."

Go for it, Katie told herself. *Make one fast move.* And she did.

But Georgette was too quick for her, and in a blink her eyes changed. From sweet mother . . . to bitter killer. "I did it all for you!" she spat.

Katie's body turned to ice. Still, she had a hand on the gun and yanked it toward her with all her might. Locked between them, the battle for the wedged weapon raged on and on.

Until the sound and force of the gunshot shook Katie's body.

Epilogue

Atlanta, Georgia, One Year Later

Nava was a beautiful restaurant, Taos-flavored in decor, piping hot with Southwestern cuisine, and teeming with trend worshipers in its Buckhead location. The perfect celebration spot.

As far as large cities go, only Denver exceeded Atlanta in terms of elevation. They lived in a city way up high. And tonight more than ever, it felt that way.

"I want a pear margarita," Katie announced.

Sharon broke off a piece of bread, slathered it with butter, and placed it on Liam's plate. "You're sixteen. You can have one in . . ." She pretended to do the math in her head. "Five years."

"Oh, that's so lame! Angel drinks wine with her parents all the time. And Mamiko, her parents hand out the Prozac if she gets anything lower than a B." Katie grinned and tilted her head demurely. "Besides, you promised to make a grand toast. I want a real drink for that."

The waiter, who looked like a college-aged Brad Pit smiled at the teen manipulation and stood ready, penci poised. "That's a pretty good argument. I should've use that one on my parents."

Katie blushed and gave Sharon one of those girl to gi looks that translates, "He's cute!"

The waiter caught Liam's eye and winked.

"Charmander is the best Pokémôn," Liam knowing informed him.

The waiter nodded with upbeat cheer. "Charmander' cool. He's got that fire thing going. Nothing wrong wit that."

"Okay," Sharon caved. "One drink." She turned to now beaming Katie. "And this is a special occasion. I other words, if you get caught indulging at the next my parents-are-out-of-town party, I don't want to hear, 'Bu you let me drink at Nava.' "

"Whatever. Like I'd try that."

Sharon observed Katie as she flipped her hair, surveye the scene, and just sat there, sparkling with radiance. I was hard to believe that a year had passed already. Some times the nightmare seemed like only yesterday. In fact, i still haunted Sharon's dreams.

Katie's struggle for the gun had been a fight to th death. She had punched, clawed, and kicked with a pos sessed frenzy, alive with the single, terrifying fear that al their lives depended on it. When she finally grabbed hold pulling the trigger had been so painful . . . but so necessary Sharon had witnessed that agony in her teenage daughter' eyes.

Even now, the sense memories remained so vivid. Sharo could still hear the blast of that single shot, still feel th sickening wave that rippled through her nervous system Yet Katie had remained standing, immobile, tragicall heroic.

The first words Katie had spoken answered the onl

question that mattered in the whole world. At that moment, every doubt, every insecurity, every uncertainty about Sharon's connection to her daughter had disappeared. This was her child. Not by biological standards, but by natural ones. Katie's voice had been calm, in control, decidedly adult when she said, "He's still breathing."

The quick thinking to call 911 through the computer had saved precious minutes. Sharon had held Liam's hand and stroked his face until they reached the hospital because she knew that once the emergency team went to work, she would be banished to the Siberia of the waiting room. They had pumped his tiny stomach. Her darling Liam had barely escaped death.

She had not realized how powerful Katie's bond with Kit Jamison had been. It seemed as if her daughter had taken that death the hardest of all. But she had slowly come to terms with it. Day by day. Week by week. Month by month. The sense of loss never went away. It just became a little easier to deal with.

Sharon had gone through a similar emotional journey in her acceptance of Antonio's murder. For closure, she had attended the funeral in Las Vegas. His wife, a young, and beautiful showgirl, had wept quietly. Their son, a breathtakingly handsome boy of about four and the spitting image of his father, had gripped his mother's hand and stood strong throughout. As much as she resented Antonio for deceiving her, Sharon had forced herself to believe in their special friendship. Deep down, she knew that most of what they shared had been real.

Suddenly a whiff of Tommy Hilfiger's Freedom hit strong in Sharon's nostrils, taking her away from the past. The waiter was back, holding a tray up high, the coveted pear margaritas balanced in the center. Sharon shut out the past, putting all her focus on the present. This was Katie's night.

Her daughter eyed the waiter like a heartthrob. "What's your name?"

"Chaz," he replied, putting her delicious looking drink down with a crooked smile.

"Cool name," she said.

Liam pointed to Katie. "Her name's pooty head!" he teased.

Chaz laughed in spite of himself.

Katie's cheeks turned as red as her new Anna Sui lipstick. "It is not," she insisted. And then, "He's such a three-year-old," sotto voce, for Chaz's benefit only.

"I'd like to make a toast," Sharon began ceremoniously, "to a young lady I'm very, very proud of."

Katie smiled, a little bashful, obviously touched. She raised her glass.

Liam held up his kiddie-size Sprite, wanting in on the action.

"This is only the beginning of your exciting future," Sharon continued.

Today marked the official launch of grrltalk.com. Katie had hit the Web with an on-line version of her zine, a major smash with the Riverview Central crowd but soon to be a fave of young girls worldwide as well. The content of the zine was smart, funny, and informative—just like its creator.

Sharon's eyes began to water. She touched her throat, feeling a lump there. "I'm so proud of you, sweetheart. And I love you."

Katie's voice shook slightly when she said, "I love you, too."

"I want somebody to love me!" Liam demanded.

Sharon and Katie laughed, and the three of them clinked glasses, smiling as they sipped.

Dinner was divine. They feasted on huge salads, green chili lobster tacos, and Key lime chicken. Conversation was fast and lively, covering everything from grrltalk.com and an upcoming sale at Bliss to Angel's new diet and Pokémôn trading cards.

Sharon left the table for the ladies room. Upon entry, she stopped abruptly, thankful Katie had not fallen upon this scene.

A brittle blonde in a tight red dress was bent over the sink and snorting a thin line of cocaine. "This place is dead. Nobody's here tonight," she complained.

Her glassy-eyed friend faced the mirror, applying another glop of mascara as she sniffled. "Heather told me that Doug Conover and Adonis Waters *lived* at the bar. Obviously, that was, like, a year ago."

They glanced at Sharon, dismissed her, and turned back around. She quietly slipped into one of the stalls.

"It's not a total loss, though. At least Heath Driver is here."

"I partied with him once a few years ago," the blonde boasted. "His best year with the Infernos. Now he's just a *former* coach. An old loser."

"I think he wrote a book or something. I saw him on Larry King one night talking about it."

"Really?" the blonde said with renewed interest. "I didn't know that. Maybe we should go talk to him."

And then the bimbos were gone. Sharon exited the stall, washed her hands, and checked herself in the mirror, searching deep for her feelings. The sting was less painful now. Maybe she had come to terms with it all. Because the last thing she wanted to be was bitter. Heath may have been a lousy husband, but he was still a reasonably good father.

Time-out: My Life in the NFL had been a runaway best-seller. When the Infernos didn't reinstate him after the Holly Ryan murder charge was dropped, Heath had signed the book deal out of anger. The tell-all tome had taken the football world to task—players, agents, owners, sports journalists, and wild women. Everyone had been furious. And sales had soared.

Heath had written the manuscript himself in a refreshing, fast-paced, no-nonsense style. Sharon had actually enjoyed it. Some of the kiss-and-tell parts had been troubling to read, but he actually handled that subject with a degree of restraint. She had to give him that much.

When she left the ladies room, she turned the corner and scanned the bar. There Heath was, holding court with the barely dressed cokeheads who craved proximity to sports fame on any terms. At forty-nine, he had crow's feet and crepey skin. He looked ridiculous flirting with those vapid girls, who sandwiched him with their pliant and willing gazes.

Sharon turned and walked away. She didn't feel angry or sad or sexually inferior. None of the emotions that had plagued her for so many years rose up within. Instead, as she stepped closer and closer to the dessert course of a family dinner with her incredible daughter and her delightful son, she thought of Heath back there with those women who didn't love him and felt perversely sorry for her ex-husband.

Grow up, she wanted to tell him. But what good would it do? She picked up her pace, moving farther away. At least Nick was a card-carrying adult. Sharon had met him at, of all places, one of Katie's soccer games. Like her, he was divorced with school aged kids, a son two years younger than Katie and a daughter in first grade.

Nick was a marketing executive with Coca-Cola, very funny, refreshingly unassuming, and a gentleman to the nth degree. When they were out together, his eyes never left her to check out other women. They had agreed to take things slow, to proceed with no pressure, no expectations. But there was a magical spark between them. She felt it. And she knew that Nick felt it, too.

Sharon returned to her table, suddenly feeling like the richest woman in the world. There were so many blessings o cherish—her children, her business, her health, and er dignity.

She smiled secretly to herself. The phone would ring efore she went to sleep tonight, and it would be Nick, houghtfully calling to find out how the celebration dinner ad gone. It was a nice feeling to know that he was thinking bout her.

Sharon caught Katie watching her from across the table. ometimes she felt like her daughter could see straight nto her thoughts. She was so smart and perceptive.

"You know what I think would be great, Mom?" Katie aid.

"What's that, honey?"

"The next time we go out to dinner, let's ask Nick to oin us."

"I like Nick," Liam chimed in. "He's silly."

Sharon grinned and sipped her margarita. From the ar came a loud burst of boozy laughter and flirtatious quealing. But she pitied Heath and the bimbo squad for heir shallow and empty lives.

Because the real action was right here.

ear Reader:

received so much wonderful feedback about my first ovel, REMEMBER SEPTEMBER, I'm pleased to be back vith another. Allowing my characters to take me on a wild rip is my favorite part of writing, and the cast of this new ffering, THE PERFECT MOTHER, did exactly that. I ope you love my new heroine, Sharon Driver, as much as loved creating her. She's a mature, contemporary woman, ery complex, and full of heart, intelligence, and courage.

If I've done my job here, then you started page one and ontinued reading way into the night. I always promise lenty of heartbreak, obsession, murder, betrayal, passion, eception, and shocking revelations to keep things inter- sting!

Happy Reading,

P.S. I love to hear from readers. Let me know what you hink.

c/o Pinnacle Books
850 Third Avenue
New York, NY 10022
or e-mail jonsalem@aol.com